HER WEREWOLF HERO

MICHELE HAUF

MILLS & BOON

First Published in Great Britain 2016
By Mills & Boon, an imprint of HarperCollins*Publishers*
1 London Bridge Street, London, SE1 9GF

© 2016 Michele Hauf

ISBN: 978-0-263-92168-7

89-0416

Our policy is to use papers that are natural, renewable and recyclable products and made from wood grown in sustainable forests. The logging and manufacturing processes conform to the legal environmental regulations of the country of origin.

Printed and bound in Spain
by CPI, Barcelona

Michele Hauf has been writing romance, action-adventure and fantasy stories for more than twenty years. France, musketeers, vampires and faeries usually populate her stories. And if Michele followed the adage "write what you know," all her stories would have snow in them. Fortunately, she steps beyond her comfort zone and writes about countries and creatures she has never seen. Find her on Facebook, Twitter and at www.michelehauf.com.

This one is for Sam and Dean. Because why not dedicate a book to a couple of fictional hunters? Works for me. And their adventures inspired the cheesy hotels in this story. Fight the faeries! (That has nothing to do with this story, but you *all* know. Right?)

Chapter 1

"Go right in, Mr. Everhart." The pretty secretary with bright blue eyes gestured over her shoulder with a pen while typing on the keyboard with her other hand.

Bron nodded his thanks and stepped toward the scanner portal positioned before the Director of Acquisitions' door. He paused on its springy metal threshold, felt the prick of its supernatural scanning mechanism throughout his nervous system and knew the data that showed on the director's monitor would report he was werewolf, approximately two centuries in age, and did not wear an Acquisitions-issued tracking chip.

He refused to be chipped like a dog. If he ever went missing, then tilt a glass to him at the local pub and warn Beneath he was on his way.

A stream of green light beaming from inside the metal scanner alerted him the scan was complete. Stepping forward activated a sliding steel door, and he entered a dimly lit office. The decor featured dark woods and rusted steel ceiling beams that lent a rustic atmosphere to the room. The director was a vampire, but really? Bron knew they could go out in the sunlight for short periods, and an overcast day generally did not cause them harm.

He wouldn't ask. He never did. He wasn't a curious man. He simply acted. Let the shrapnel fall where it will.

Ethan Pierce had an alarmingly bright smile and a scattering of silver within the short brown hair spiking from his scalp. "Everhart! Just return from Romania?"

Bron took a seat on the ultracomfortable leather chair before the director's desk and propped a combat-booted foot across his opposite knee. "Two days returned and eager to put my hiking boots on again."

"Excellent. I've a new assignment for you."

The director slid a piece of paper toward Bron. As with most Acquisitions' dossiers, it featured a small photograph or drawing of the item that required retrieval, and below that were listed details. This one featured what looked like a woodcut drawing of a human heart with a faintly hand-shaped mark across the muscle.

"The Purgatory Heart," Ethan explained. "The mission is find and seize. I've sent the digital file to your phone, which includes a link to a related article found online. I'm afraid that's all the printed research we've had time to gather, though Archives has provided us further details. We've been gauging activity regarding the object for a few days. There's chatter circulating about it, and while we can't pin the origin of that chatter, someone or *thing* very powerful wants it, judging by the universal vibrations that alerted us to the item."

Universal vibrations. Early in his career as a Retriever for Acquisitions, Bron had learned everything put out a sort of pulse or tone, whether it was animal, vegetable, mineral or man. And thanks to magic, those vibrations could be read, sometimes even tracked.

"Since we don't have a location or ID on the thing," Ethan continued, "it seemed right up your alley. You do like a good adventure."

Always.

Bron had already opened the file on his phone and tapped the link. He scanned over an article detailing a small museum in Prague. It displayed items that had been touched by souls from Purgatory. An open book featured a blackened handprint burned onto the pages. A rusted tin bucket showed a few fingerprints burned into the metal. A tattered hemp skirt again brandished a burnt handprint. Nothing about a heart, though.

Of course, had the heart been at the museum, the mission would not have been assigned to him. Simply stopping by and stealing an item displayed to the public was generally assigned to newer Retrievers. Not to those who viewed risk as their very lifeblood.

"Purgatory exists?" Bron wondered as he leaned back against the chair. It wasn't often he sat—he craved movement, always—but the cushy leather chairs in the director's office enticed him to relax and exhale. It was a rare feeling, and it sometimes made him uncomfortable.

Just thinking about relaxing made him sit up straight.

"Yes, it's closely related to Daemonia, the Place of All Demons," the director explained. "Purgatory is the midpoint between good and evil. A balance, if you will. And there is a portal from Daemonia to Purgatory, but not vice versa. Though, I understand there's not a demon that would purposely make such a trip to Purgatory."

"No demons eager to torture mortal souls? Sounds surprising."

"There is torture, but it is a permanent and endless job. The demons you'll find there are prisoners themselves. They are called Toll Gatherers; they test the purgatants." The director tapped the paper. "The heart we want to secure and keep from nefarious hands has been gripped by a purgatorial soul and scarred with a handprint. You should recognize that when you find it."

"Most certainly. What does this purgatorial heart do?"

Most objects Bron—any Retriever—was sent to obtain were usually of a highly volatile and magical nature. If put into the wrong hands? Devastation could occur. Not to mention things like mortal deaths, plagues, zombies and even a Cereberus, if he recalled that bungled snatch correctly.

"Unlike the passage from Daemonia, the heart opens a gateway into Purgatory—that goes both ways. Should Purgatory be breached by an unknown, there is the probability of souls breaking free. The balance between good and evil will be severely tilted toward evil. It's on the same lines as all hell breaking lose. We've deemed the mission Necessary."

Necessary, but not Critical, as were the top-secret missions. And a *find and seize*, which was the usual Retriever assignment. Rarely was a mission labeled *find and finish*.

"No known location?" Bron asked. "Where do I start?"

The director opened his top drawer and pulled out a thin square piece of crystal and set it on top of the dossier. Compelled by the promise of new and interesting technology, Bron leaned forward.

"A tracker," Ethan provided. "It's the latest tech addition to our arsenal. Had Crafts and Hexes bespell it. Press it between your thumb and forefinger and say 'begin.' Once it's activated it'll lead you right to the heart."

"Siri will be jealous," Bron said as he took the small but surprisingly hefty piece of crystal. It was about the size of a one-euro piece, and he couldn't see through it despite its clear composition. He tucked it into his shirt pocket. That's all he needed to get going. "Just activate and follow, got it." He stood and nodded. "Appreciate the work, Director."

"You're our top Retriever, Everhart. I always go to you first. You've never let me down."

"I don't intend to start."

"One thing about the tracker. The witch who bespelled it said the heart was something different than our usual nabs. Picks up soul vibrations or some such. Once you activate the tracker? It'll lead you to the prize. But it'll also send out vibrations that communicate with the heart. Anything or anyone who is interested—even those who are not and just want to cause trouble—will also feel the signal."

"So it'll be a race," Bron said, tapping his shirt pocket.

"Yes. Go fully armed. Can't imagine what creatures would like to get their hands on the key to Purgatory."

Bron nodded. "Always ready for some action. Thanks, boss."

* * *

Kizzy Lewis stepped through the dried grass that crunched underfoot along the ditch hugging Highway 2. To her right a faded plastic red ribbon fluttered in the breeze, and a bouquet of plastic geraniums that had been secured to a makeshift wooden cross offered a bright red spot along the stretch of summer-scorched country roadway.

Bright colors. Sad and terrifying memories.

This is where she and Keith had veered off the road on an icy January night. The yellow VW Bug Keith had been driving had soared over the concrete culvert and landed thirty feet below in the shallow stream that bisected two farmers' potato fields. A mass of field stones and boulders had been piled up over the years, dug from the ground to prevent damage to farm equipment. The VW had hit the boulders grill first. Keith had flown over the steering wheel and through the windshield. Kizzy, wearing her seat belt, had been pinned inside the small vehicle.

Lifting her camera, which she wore around her neck on a leather strap, she exhaled and sniffed back the tears that had started the moment she'd stepped onto the roadside. Aiming, she clicked snapshots of the boulders. Not a trace of the car remained, yet yellow paint scrapes still marked some of the rocks.

This return to the scene of the accident had felt necessary. A means to finally push that horrible night into the past and lock the door? More like revisit it to confirm her nightmares were real. Eight months had passed since that devastating evening when her emotions had gotten the better of her and she'd spoken what she had been feeling for weeks. That their relationship was over. And she'd wanted out.

Keith had taken it hard, as he always took any criticism or suggestion that went against his designs on the world. She hadn't realized how controlling he was until four months into their six-month relationship. He'd insisted she move in with him, so he would always know where she was.

The roads had been glare ice that January evening, following a rainstorm that had begun halfway home from a trip to the casino. She'd asked Keith to drive slower, to even pull over and wait it out. But he was not a man she could tell what to do.

"He didn't deserve death," she whispered. But she couldn't quite bring herself to say something like "because he was a good man."

Keith Munson had never raised a hand to her, though he had wielded his words cruelly. He hadn't known how to treat her the way she expected to be treated. So she forgave him for that. And she would not think ill of the dead.

Now the terror of that moment when the car had taken flight and soared off the road returned to her with thunderous, thumping heartbeats. The sound of her screams, muffled in her memory, resounded much louder now. She clutched her camera against those crazy heartbeats. Hopes to stand back and observe the scene as a bystander, to take pictures, perhaps even go over the photos in detail after she'd processed them, had led her here.

And, yes, she sought closure. To take one final look, then walk away. And maybe the nightmares would stop.

She checked the view screen. In the past half hour,

she'd taken well over a hundred photos. She'd return to the apartment in Thief River Falls and look them over.

In the past few months, Kizzy had grown accustomed to living on the road. Her soul demanded the movement and the unsure yet wondrous discovery of the new and even the familiar. Her Minnesota hometown, Thief River Falls—tucked close to the North Dakota border and a couple hours south of Canada—had felt like a place to stay and relax a bit before returning overseas to Romania for her next photography adventure. Europe had been her home since the accident. Her parents had been living there for nearly a decade, and the extra bedroom had been waiting for her as soon as the doctor had signed off on her feeling well enough to travel.

She'd rented the apartment here for a week. Not because she'd been homesick and had thought to catch up with friends. A week had simply been the best deal. And okay, she'd visited a few relatives and friends the first two days she'd been in town.

Kizzy headed back to her rental car, which she'd parked off the road, the wheels hugging the grassy ditch. Another hour would bring twilight, and she wanted to stop by the city park to end the day. She remembered how the setting sun would highlight the gorgeous northern pines in the forest edging the park and wanted to capture that light on film.

And maybe, she might discover a creature or two.

Her photography captured the otherworldly. Or at least, her *idea* of what could be something different, perhaps even paranormal. A creature or monster that had only been imagined on the page or in movies. She liked to play with shadow and light in an attempt to make others question their own reality. That was what art was about to her.

But her quest to capture myth and legend went deeper than that. Because those creatures did exist. She knew it. They just had to.

She'd been a believer since a young age. And her blog, *Other Wonders*, was wildly successful, her fan base being those with paranormal interests, as well as artists and creatives. The blog was five years old, and she boasted half a million subscribers with millions of hits yearly. The money she made by monetizing that blog funded her travel.

She'd snagged a few freelance jobs after a prospective employer had viewed her online galleries, including a photo shoot for *National Geographic* last year. It had been a dark, moody piece, and she'd framed silhouettes of trees and rocky outcrops to suggest dragon heads peering out from their lairs. They'd used it for a medieval piece. It hadn't paid much, but it had been the catalyst to rocket her online stats.

Her next trip was to Romania. She'd managed to win a sponsorship from the Romanian tourism board to cover half her expenses. They'd been impressed by the *Nat Geo* feature. All she had to do was provide the board with scenic photos and grant them all rights to use. The Romanian forests promised to offer unique photography moments. And who knew? Maybe she'd catch a vampire hanging out at a dilapidated castle. Or a ghost? At the very least, she'd try to capture the essence of the otherworldly. It's what she did. It was what she was compelled to do.

She was blessed to be doing something she enjoyed and not stuck behind a desk nine to five.

With a turn of the key in the ignition, the Taurus hummed to life. Kizzy didn't own a car. Never had and couldn't foresee ever needing to. She currently held no permanent address that required a car to get from a home to an office job. But she did appreciate the freedom a rental car granted when it was necessary to travel beyond city limits.

Shifting into gear, she allowed her gaze to linger on the boulders below. Her heart tightened, almost as if someone were squeezing it. She shook her head, thinking it was too early in the day for another nightmare. Why she dreamed about a werewolf grabbing her heart was beyond her. But the recurring dream had haunted her about twice a month since the accident.

"I've spent too much time seeking monsters," she muttered as she turned the car around on the two-lane highway and headed toward Thief River Falls. "Bound to catch up with me in my dreams sooner or later. But a werewolf?"

Such creatures were on her list of most feared paranormals. As a believer, she knew to have a healthy fear of the more dangerous sorts, especially those who sported claws or talons. And there had been that one time when she was six and her dad had taken her camping at Lake Bronson. Had it been a werewolf lurking behind the outhouse on the moonlit summer night? She'd screamed so loudly, her father had thought she'd been attacked by a bear. He'd laughed when she'd told him what she thought it was.

Why did men always make her feel stupid for her beliefs? What was so wrong with having a healthy imagination? With not ruling anything out until it was proven otherwise?

Once back in town, she dropped off the car at the rental site because she didn't plan to drive anywhere else out of city limits. The city was very walkable, and she would take a taxi to the airport at the end of the week. The apartment rental had included a bicycle, but she shook her head as she studied the pink ten-speed. The park was only a half-hour jaunt across the river.

With her trusty DSLR camera on a strap around her neck and the camera bag slung over one shoulder, she headed down the sidewalk and toward the vast city park. Her faded red Vans got her most places comfortably. And her standard slim jeans and a loose but comfy faded pink T-shirt saw her through summer like a pro. The gray linen scarf she'd slipped around her neck this morning hung out of her back jean pocket so it didn't get tangled in the camera strap.

Crossing a street, she held up her hand to the honking car and swished her long brown hair over a shoulder to cast the driver a thankful smile. He waved her off, a disgusted grimace clouding his face. Didn't he notice the gorgeous light on the horizon so swiftly slipping through the sky? Grump.

She quickened her steps. The park was not busy; maybe half a dozen people were scattered about, and a few of those were headed toward their cars. It was the supper hour. As she passed the swing sets, she had to laugh at the little girl getting a push from her dad. She screamed madly, but as soon as the swing made its return—from a mere two-foot lift into the air—she giggled.

Striding beyond the semiformal 4H gardens in which she'd spent her high school summers volunteering— clipping, trimming, getting the hornbeam and roses ready for fall—she leaped over the final box hedge. In her peripheral view, she sighted a man walking to her left. No kids in tow. If he had any appreciation for shadows and light, he should be taking in the glimmer of sun setting just beyond the jagged silhouette of forest. He looked a bit older than her, but beyond that she didn't linger on his appearance.

Though she was twenty-nine, having kids was not on Kizzy's radar. She'd not once heard her biological clock tick and wasn't worried about that, either. A husband might add a new angle to this adventure called life but wasn't necessary to her happiness. As long as he didn't mind her wanderlust and constant need to move, a man would fit into her life nicely. As a partner in adventure, but never as someone she needed to take care of and expect the same from in return.

And he should never laugh at her beliefs.

Kizzy had been off the market, as her mother liked to call it, for eight months. Call it a bad relationship. Call it dying on the operating-room table and having to have her heart massaged back to life. She hadn't been in the mood for dating. Sex? Always. But she wasn't sure she could trust a man beyond a one-night bootie call.

Unless of course they happened to look like Jared Padalecki or Jensen Ackles.

She'd once thought a man could complete her. Probably all women had that thought at some point in their lives. But thankfully her mother, merely by example, had proven to Kizzy that the best relationships are not needy or demanding but rather a shared experience that thrives thanks to the independence of one another. And never balks at the partner's need to explore anything meaningful.

In Kizzy's case, what felt meaningful to her was to travel. This trip to Minnesota had been a gift from her parents. Really, though, she much preferred traveling Europe. And who knew? Maybe she'd grow richer in a few more years and could afford a trek to China or Australia.

It didn't matter where she landed on the map. Wanderlust had officially settled into Kizzy's soul.

"Ma'am?"

She was pulled from her musings fifty feet from the forest's edge by the man walking toward her. He wore one of those panama hats tilted jauntily over one eye. Canvas pants tucked into high-laced combat boots, and a plain short-sleeved T-shirt stretched over remarkable pecs. Though he'd called out to her, his attention was riveted to something he held in his hand.

He looked mid-thirties. Dark hair swished to his shoulders. A beard and mustache framed his jaw and mouth. Whatever held his attention, he seemed to be using a guide for which direction to walk in. Perhaps doing a geocache, as her father loved to do. The city had a geocaching club.

He was probably harmless. Yet she wielded her camera as a shield before her chest. "Can I help you?" she asked.

"I'm not sure." He stopped ten feet from her and looked around, stretching his searching gaze for a long time across the playground area. Whatever he held in hand glinted with a beam of sunlight. She had probably guessed right about the geocaching. Could be tracking it with GPS on his phone.

Overhead, a dark shadow skimmed the sky, and she glanced above him. Those were some big birds.

"Ah, shit," the man said. He tucked what he was holding into his pants pocket and turned to her. Panic brightened his blue eyes.

And Kizzy squinted to better sight the birds. They were bigger than vultures, which she rarely saw here in Minnesota. They looked…the size of dogs. Big dogs.

Seriously? "What the hell are those?"

"Harpies," he said quickly and grabbed her by the arm. "Into the woods. We can lose them there."

"What?" She struggled against his grasp, but he'd managed to seize her wrist and tugged her across the mown lawn toward the line of pine trees. "I'm not going with you!"

"And how will you get away from them?"

"Away from them?" She glanced up to the sky. Harpies? No way. Those were…mythical beings. And much as she believed—

One of them dove toward her.

Suddenly lifted from the ground, Kizzy was tossed over the man's shoulder as he ran toward the woods.

She couldn't scream. She should but did not. A curious fascination overwhelmed fear. She reached for her camera, banging against the man's back, and tried to get a shot even as she was carried off by a stranger into the dark forest.

Chapter 2

"What are they, really?" Kizzy asked as the man set her down but wouldn't let go of her wrist. He tugged her into the thick brush and trees. Cockleburs brushed her ankles, and she wished she wore longer pants than the capri jeans. She put up a hand to block her face from stray branches that whipped into her face.

"Harpies," he said. "Come on!"

Yes, that's what she thought he'd said.

A harpie was a mythological creature. Half bird, half man or woman, or some such. She had read about them. Had even written a blog post about them, accompanied by a photo she had taken of a blurred raven high in the sky. Gray cloud streaks had remarkably thickened its body, granting her a photograph with just enough about which to speculate.

A half man, half bird? It didn't get much cooler than that.

Yet behind her, something screeched like her worst movie nightmare. So Kizzy forced herself to follow as her mysterious rescuer tugged her farther into the woods. The camera hung around her neck. Taking pictures could wait. Right now she needed to steer her guide out of the sticky, thorned stuff.

Dodging the bramble and brush the best she could, she called, "There is a path to the left!"

"I see that. They are taking it."

"Oh. Then go right!"

"Doesn't that lead back toward the park?"

It did. And it would give her an opportunity to break from this guy and run for freedom. Because if it was a choice between harpies and some weirdo intent on luring her deeper into the forest, she wasn't sure which was better. She wasn't stupid. Nor would she allow fear to cloud her judgment. He looked safe enough, but what defined safe?

On the other hand. If they lured the creatures back toward the park, the children and their parents could be in danger. Had they seen the harpies? Had someone called the police? What could the police do but stare in wonder as she had?

The whisk of wings brushing overhead tree leaves set her heart to a thunderous pace. Her breaths gasped, not so much because she was exerting herself—picking through the brush did slow their escape—but, okay, she was a little scared. The flying creatures were bigger than dogs. And there were three of them.

Their pace had slowed. She needed to pause and get a picture. Never before had she an opportunity like this. Those creatures were exactly what she'd hoped to capture on film! And the light in the forest was perfect.

The red/orange sun crisping around the edges of the tree canopy would define the wings for sure.

Having released her wrist, the man stalked five paces ahead of her, forging a path as he stomped fallen branches. Kizzy stopped and lifted the camera to her eye. Trying to focus through the tree trunks and thankful the zoom lens was still attached because she generally used a prime lens. She tracked one creature, snapping repeatedly. If she took a hundred shots she might end up with a handful of good ones.

"What are you doing? They are after *you*!" He tried to grab her wrist again, but she kicked toward his shin. He dodged swiftly, and she missed. "Don't you understand?"

"What makes you think they are after me? I was doing fine, enjoying a nice stroll in the park, until you showed up!"

"Is that the way of it?" He gestured with a splay of hands. "Fend for yourself!" He turned and loped off, tracking through the brush to the right.

And Kizzy saw the dark shadows trace the ground and felt the chilling sweep of wings overhead. She may be brave, but she wasn't stupid. "I changed my mind!"

Her day had morphed into an Alfred Hitchcock movie on testosterone. And she wasn't about to become bird food.

She stuffed the camera into the bag at her hip. Tramping over the loamy, leaf-covered forest floor, she stumbled on a fallen log and caught her hands against a wide tree trunk frosted with moss. While normally she'd inhale the scents of nature, all she could smell was her anxiety.

One of the birds lunged toward the man in front of

her, and he shot it with some kind of arrow. From a small device that looked like a pistol yet it hadn't made a sound when it had fired.

Like a small crossbow? Who was that guy? And what fairy-tale chase had she fallen into? Robin Hood had always been her favorite, even the Disney cartoon fox version of the hero held an appeal.

Carefully, she crept closer to him and witnessed him take out another of the harpies with the arrow-shooting pistol. When the final harpie swooped over her head, she ducked and loosed a necessary scream.

"Stay there! Low!"

Clasping her hands over her head, she followed directions, cowering against the base of an oak tree's gnarly roots. Heartbeats racing, she was suddenly thankful that if attack by crazy birds was her fate, at least she had some kind of rescuing hero who wielded a worthy weapon on her side.

So she would trust him. Because right now he offered her best hope.

She observed him watching the circling bird. Lean and tall, his biceps and pecs flexed beneath the gray T-shirt as he tracked the remaining creature with the hand-sized crossbow. His footing sure, he turned at the hips, a graceful predator. Aiming, one eye closed, a twitch of his finger released the trigger. The bird screeched and dropped out of the sky, its wings snagging the leaves and landing…right beside Kizzy.

She swore and scrambled over a tree root and toward the man. But then she stopped. She had no reason to be afraid of a dead creature. And, holy Hannah, it was a creature!

She pulled the camera out of the bag, and—

"Oh, no." He slipped his hand into one of hers. "No time. More could be coming. I made clean shots, straight through the hearts. They'll dissipate to feathers in minutes. No worry of cleanup, thank the gods. My truck is this way."

She followed him, regretting only that she hadn't time to snap a photo, but thinking that she had tons of questions that he would answer before she let him get away. Maybe. The urge to flee from him was also strong.

At the forest's edge, which was about two city blocks away from town, he paused and searched the sky. But a few streaks of pink and gold lingered from the setting sun.

"All clear. Come on!" With her hand still in his, he raced across the grassy lawn toward the curb where a black Ford truck was parked.

"I can get home on my own," she said, her voice wobbling as his pace did not let up until he'd reached the vehicle. But really? She'd head back into the forest first with hope of getting a picture before the creatures turned to a heap of feathers.

"Absolutely not."

Controlling much? So she'd forego the questions. A sudden nervousness urged her to run from him. Forget about the awesome creatures lying dead in the forest. This man might be the one she should fear the most.

When he opened the passenger door and waited for her to get in, Kizzy took a moment to really gaze at his face. Wide-set blue eyes didn't look at her so much as keep her in peripheral view as he scanned the sky. A thick beard hugged his square jaw, and an equally dark mustache stretched down to the beard. He still wore the hat. How he'd not lost it while racing through the forest was beyond her. The whole outfit gave him an Indiana Jones vibe.

With a paranormal bent? He knew about those harpies. Had come armed to take them out. She'd be a fool to run off without questioning him.

"Who are you?" she asked. "Or maybe the better question should be *what* are you?"

"Bron Everhart," he said, his attention averting to the sky. "There's more!"

She looked over her shoulder in the direction he pointed. Holy Hannah, there were more. Flying toward them. She gripped the camera. "Why are they after us?"

"I was tracking…" He shoved her at the shoulder. "Get in. I'll explain as we drive. I want to lure them away from the town. And if they continue to follow the truck, then I'll know it's you they're after."

She hadn't a chance to protest that maybe it was *him* they wanted. But Kizzy didn't need a shove to get inside the truck. Stand her ground and refuse the crazy man's assistance? Or get inside the vehicle where she had a metal frame and glass to protect her from the weird flying things?

She climbed up and pulled the door shut. The driver's door slammed a second later, and the ignition fired up.

"I don't understand why harpies would come after me," she said as the truck pulled away from the curb. "I'm not anyone. I'm just a photographer. Yet, how cool were they?" she said with an incredulous tone. "I mean, I believe in faeries and vampires and have always dreamed of seeing some kind of creature some day."

"Vampires, eh?" He shifted into Drive and cast her

a head-shaking smirk as he turned the vehicle away from town.

"Just take me home," she said quickly. Then she could hop on her bike and return to the forest. "I'm staying in an apartment in the middle of town. It's a couple miles that way."

"And lure them into the city? *And* give them the location of where you're staying?"

Put like that it didn't sound like a smart thing to do. Her eagerness to get a good photograph of the myth was making her foolish. She had to think of others. Would the harpies risk flying into the town? She didn't have any weapons. And while she took risks to get the perfect shot, she wasn't a danger seeker who would stand at a cliff's edge peering over.

"Bron? Is that what you said your name was?"

"Has been all my life. Buckle up."

She did so, unstrapping the camera bag and setting it on the floor. She pulled the camera off from around her neck and turned to track the harpies through the back window.

"Put the camera away," he insisted. "The last thing the world needs is evidence of those bastards' existence. I'm surprised they are so blatantly out in this realm."

"Yet you know about them? You're familiar with birdmen?"

"Harpies. They can be male or female. And, yes, they are real, if that's what you're asking."

"I know they're real. I narrowly dodged one!"

She sighed and tilted her head against the back of the seat. A self-awareness assessment checked her heartbeats had slowed. And her skin felt cool when she thought she should be sweating from the jaunt through the woods. Perhaps she was in shock.

"I've searched for proof of the paranormal all my life," she said. "For some reason I thought my first encounter would be less…"

"Harrowing?"

"Yeah," she said on a nervous sigh. Though why should she have expected a friendly "how do you do" instead of an attack? The creatures she believed in were deadly and dangerous, and, hell, yes, they flew and had claws and went after people.

But still, the surprise of suddenly *knowing* was exciting. Things she'd always wanted to believe in *did* exist. How cool was that?

Suddenly the truck swerved, and they turned right. Toward town.

"Wait? What are you doing?"

"They're veering toward town. I can't let them out of my sight."

There were two of them. They soared toward the small town and circled back like vultures eyeing the kill. Harpies had minds like birds yet also like men. The human side of them was calculating; the animal side ruthless. Bron knew they had identified his truck. But were they aware the woman was still with him? Why had they gone after her? Because it hadn't been him they were after. Harpies generally avoided his sort.

He turned the vehicle sharply into an alley. It was strange to find himself back in this town. He knew this area. Had been here about fifty years earlier on a mission. He'd met a witch… Lots of memories—both good and bad—he didn't have time to resurrect now.

Here in the tight confines of the town, night darkened the narrow tarmac; there were no streetlights, so he pulled over to park and turned off the vehicle's headlights. Leaning across the seat, he opened the glove compartment. Half a dozen arrows tumbled forward, and he grasped them all. The hand-sized crossbow he utilized was a sweet little weapon designed by the Acquisition's Armoury. It had biothermal-GPS tracking to lock in a target and pinpoint accuracy. Also, the fletchless arrows were tipped with silver, and the hollow core was filled with rowan wood. Useful against werewolves, vampires and, fortunately, harpies.

He got out of the truck and the woman followed. Standing in the narrow alleyway, he didn't worry for her safety. He'd have her back if the creatures swooped down toward her. The trouble was, she was fascinated. Not scared enough to look out for herself.

No matter where his journeys took him or what creatures he encountered while on a mission, Bron always strove to keep that which shouldn't be known from humans. Having the "it's real" talk with them never went over well. And if it did feel necessary, it was always easier to walk away and pretend they were the crazy ones. A vampire? Eh, you're nuts.

But this woman? In the heat of the moment when she should have been cowering and screaming, instead she'd taken pictures. And one of the Retrievers' unwritten rules was to never provide proof. He had to get those digital files. Or destroy her camera.

As well, he had a moral obligation to make sure she was safe before bringing her home. He couldn't drop her off in the middle of this small town. She'd be a target. Why the harpies had pursued her was beyond him.

Perhaps they'd been following the tracker's vibrations, and when he'd gotten too close to her they had picked up her scent and gone with it. Harpies were flesh eaters. Though, if hungry, why hadn't they simply gone for the children on the swings?

Why were they even in the mortal realm? Their habitat was Faery.

A bone-twanging screech alerted his attention to the left. Crossbow at the ready, he tracked the creature soaring overhead. The other was out of sight. Until he heard the screech behind him.

And the woman's scream.

Releasing the trigger, the arrow caught the first bird in the heart. It faltered into a death spin and dropped out of sight behind a wood fence. Bron quickly reloaded. A *whoosh* of wings moved his hair. He ducked, landing on one knee, and twisted to see the harpie's claw extend toward the woman's head. She plunged to the tarmac. His arrow found its target.

He lunged to grab her arm and pull her forward to avoid the heavy drop of the creature's body. She clung to him, her body heaving, breaths gasping. Moonlight caught in a glint on the tiny gold cross she wore on a delicate chain about her neck. But before he could begin to consider the sensual curves hugging his torso and the warm, fresh scent of her, she pushed away and shuffled backward.

Her shoulders hugged the brick building. "So not a cool first date," she said.

"Date?"

Ah. She was joking. More points for bravery on her part.

The harpie's body glowed and burned without flame.

The embers quickly dissipated, leaving behind a scatter of black feathers.

"But that was cool," she said. She patted her chest, then snapped her fingers. She'd left the camera in the truck.

And Bron had veered madly off course.

"Get in," he said. "More could follow."

She quickly got into the vehicle.

He tugged the crystal tracker out of his pocket and turned it over. Around the edges it glowed a soft blue.

"What is that?" she asked. "Is that what you were looking at when I first saw you in the park?"

"This?" He leaned back and flipped it between his fingers, but then it suddenly shot out of his hand.

And landed right on the woman's chest.

"What the hell?" He reached for it, but she slapped his hand away. "Sorry."

"What is it?" She didn't try to touch it but was clearly afraid of whatever it was attached to her T-shirt. It had landed right above her breast, which Bron couldn't help but notice was nicely shaped and—ah hell, no, it stuck to *her*.

"Are you wearing metal? Something magnetic under your shirt? Maybe a bra with a metal ring in the strap?"

"I, uh… No bra today."

Yep, he noticed that now. Her nipples were pert and erect.

"What is it? Why is it stuck to me?" She pried gently at it, and the tracker came away briefly but then snapped back to nestle on top of her breast. "Get it off me!"

Why did it stick to her? Made from crystal and infused with Light magic, it wasn't even magnetic. It shouldn't be reacting this way. On the other hand, he had no idea what its properties were.

Bron reached for the tracker, more than willing to pry it from her breast, but then he paused. A realization hit him hard. "Blessed Herne. Really?"

The director hadn't specified the heart he sought would be live and beating inside someone's chest.

Chapter 3

Kizzy peeled the weird little piece of glass from her shirt and handed it to Bron. He clasped his fingers over it, closed his eyes and shook his head. As if regretfully? She didn't know what the thing was, but everything associated with the man was out there and strange. And if he was up on all things paranormal, then the glass piece could be magical.

That didn't mean she wanted it stuck to her chest.

All of a sudden he shifted the truck into gear and drove onward. "We need to fill up with gas. I saw a station at the edge of town."

"Fill? Where are you going? Because I'm not going along. I'm staying in town. That way." She pointed out the back window. "Just drop me off anywhere, and I can walk. Really. It's not that far. Pull over here, and I can make it on my own."

"They are after you—what is your name?"

"Kizzy. *Who* are after me? Harpies?"

"What kind of name is Kizzy?"

"It's short for Kisanthra. Kisanthra Lewis." She offered her hand to shake, which he ignored as he swerved toward the gas station. "Photographer. Blogger. World traveler. Soon to be getting the hell out of your life."

"Blogger?"

"Yes, I've a blog called *Other Wonders*. All about— oy." She sighed heavily. "Is this for real? I mean, really? Am I being punked?" She peered out the side window. "Where's Ashton Kutcher?"

Bron pulled up before a gas tank and shut off the engine. When he turned, he held the piece of glass before him. "Kisanthra, I'm a Retriever. I work for an organization that retrieves lost artifacts, items of magical nature and various other things that I'm sure you'd understand if I took the time to explain, because your acceptance of the harpie was easy enough."

"I believe in a lot of things. But this is the first time I've ever been given tangible proof. I sure hope those photos turn out." She snapped the small, square piece of glass with a fingernail. "You retrieve things? Does it have to do with harpies?"

"It shouldn't. It's to do with this."

She took the piece of glass when he offered it, and again, it slipped out of her grip and affixed to the front of her shirt.

"Hell," he muttered. "This mission was supposed to be find and seize. There's no way—" He beat the steering wheel with a fist.

His anger had come on so suddenly and felt palpable to Kizzy. The thought to flee resurfaced. But it was already dark outside. Not as easy to spy a raven-winged bird man flying overhead.

"I don't get it." She tore away the square piece from her chest, which looked innocuous enough. Maybe it wasn't glass? It wasn't clear but was smooth and had a good weight to it like some kind of stone. "What is this thing?"

"It's a tracking device. Sometimes the items I'm sent to retrieve are in an unknown location. Acquisitions had a tracker bespelled, and, apparently, it led me straight to the item."

"Acquisitions?"

He nodded. "That's the name of the organization I work for."

"Generically nonspecific. And you are a Retriever. That's kind of cool. You get more points for the Indiana Jones vibe you're putting off. And you had me right up until you said bespelled."

"Right." He snatched the tracking device from her and opened the truck door. "The item I'm looking for is the Purgatory Heart. And—" he stepped out and leaned his head in "—apparently it's inside you."

Door closing behind him, he turned and shoved the gas nozzle into the tank at the back of the truck.

Kizzy sat frozen, her jaws agape as she watched him stride inside the station. Long sure strides. Peripherally aware as he glanced side to side. His hands flexed at his sides, where she noted a holster strapped to one thigh, but she couldn't determine what was in it. He was some kind of Indiana Jones Wild West gunslinger. No one would mess with that man. He knew how to take down harpies.

"Purgatory heart? What the…? He's not making

sense. That tracking device landed *on* me. Right over my heart."

And if she gave it any amount of thought, putting the words *retriever* and *find and seize* together...

"Oh, hell, no. No one is seizing my heart. I think we've shared enough adventure for one day, Mr. Jones."

Checking through the gas station windows, she couldn't see his tall, dark-haired figure. Must have wandered toward the back of the store.

Grabbing her camera bag, Kizzy slid out of the truck, and, with careful glances toward the red-brick-walled station's front doors, she ran around beside the building and down an alley hedged on both sides by glossy-leaved forsythia that had long ago shed its bright yellow flowers.

She wasn't afraid of walking through the town so late. It wasn't people she had to worry about. She had to hope there had only been five harpies. Of which, Bron had slain them all. She was no longer in the mood to take pictures of vicious flying bird men.

A stretch of garage bays where the gas station mechanics worked on vehicles grew up behind the hedges to her right. The sounds of tools clanking and a hydraulic lift disguised her stumble over a mess of tangled plastic shopping bags and weeds.

Her rental was at the city center. It was a small town, population around eight thousand. When she'd resided here before the accident, she'd lived in a quaint neighborhood, but a handful of blocks' walk from her elementary and middle schools; it had been her home since birth. Small town. Small, safe upbringing.

Wildly expansive imagination.

Oh, yeah, she had always been the weird girl.

Striding quickly, she guessed it was a couple miles' walk to her rental apartment. She dodged left and let out a yelp when a growl alerted her to a dark, man-shaped shadow looming beneath a willow tree.

"Bron?"

"Sorry, sweetie, your dog of a boyfriend isn't here to save you."

"My dog…?" She didn't understand that. Bron was actually very handsome.

A man stepped from the shadows. Thin, blond and clad in enough black to give a goth a run for his money. Goths had never been big in Thief River Falls. But they did have a few token outliers that represented all sorts. He grinned at her, revealing fangs that jutted downward from his upper row of teeth.

"Seriously?" Kizzy knew to her bones those were not the fake dental acrylic fangs some goths sported. She clutched her camera bag, then thought better of taking advantage of a photographic moment at a time like this. "Vampires exist, too?"

"Surprise," he offered with a splay of hands and no humor whatsoever. "You want a bite?"

"Uh…" Did she?

Was she considering the offer? No, she was not. He'd taken her by surprise and… It was just so cool to learn about yet another paranormal creature.

And then her brain did the right thing and switched to survival mode. "Thanks, but no thanks."

She took a few cautious steps backward and gripped the gold cross on the chain around her neck. She wasn't deeply religious, but when faced with a vampire—oh, yeah, she believed.

"Not going to help," the vampire said and laughed. "Not baptized, bitch!"

She didn't know what that meant—the man lunged for her and managed to grip her wrist. Kizzy shrieked. She was three blocks away from the gas station and didn't think Bron would hear her over the sounds echoing out from the garage. For all those times she had mused over whether or not carrying a wooden stake would be a wise decision, she now regretted not going with her instincts.

The vampire was strong. Even as she struggled and planted her feet, he managed to drag her under the long, spindly branches of the willow tree. It was darker under there, and they weren't in a residential area. Most businesses had closed for the evening. Would anyone hear her scream?

He twisted her wrist, yanking her closer. Kizzy went for the scream again.

"Quiet! Just a quick bite, and then I'll take that heart of yours."

"My heart? H-how do you know about that?"

"Followed the vibes, baby." He grinned a bloody smile. One of his fangs must have cut into his lower lip.

Vibes? What was he talking about? He sounded more like a stoned sixties hippie than a bloodthirsty creature of the night.

This was not happening.

But, yes, it was. And if she wanted to escape unbitten—and, apparently, with her heart intact—Kizzy needed to get smart. Fast.

She grabbed at the willow branches with her free hand. The long, slender branches were remarkably strong. Pulling up with that hand, and using the elastic-like give of the branches for propulsion, she was able to kick up toward the vampire and landed him on the chest. He released her with a grunt—but then a vicious growl preceded his lunge for her. Arms opening to clutch, he wasn't able to grab her again because something slammed him against the tree trunk.

Some*one*, that was.

"Bron." She gasped and stumbled backward, then answered the call of the adrenaline rush and fell to her knees, clutching her chest and, in the process, her camera bag.

Beneath the concealing umbrella of the willow's slender fall of branches, the vampire howled. Bron stepped back, a wooden stake clutched in hand. He replaced the stake in the holster strapped to his thigh.

"Crap," Kizzy muttered in awe.

She crawled to the side to get a better view. The creature who had threatened her diffused into a cloud of ash, which then settled in a heavy heap before Bron's feet.

"Ohmygosh." She leaned forward, clutching her stomach. She could get sick, but she hadn't eaten since breakfast, and just… "Ohmygosh."

"Come with me," Bron said as he strolled past her. "Unless you want to take your chances on your own again?"

Against bloodthirsty vampires? She shook her head and forced herself up to her feet. "I'm right behind you. Could you walk a little slower? On second thought, I'd like to be beside you just in case something comes for me from behind."

He thrust back his hand, and she grasped it. It was a sure, warm clutch. Making a fast pace toward the gas station, she couldn't for the life of her figure why she'd so stupidly fled from him in the first place. With her hand in his, everything felt right. Like he would protect her.

Until he tried to seize her heart.

"Wait." Kizzy tugged him to a stop in the middle of the hedge-lined alleyway. "Are you going to protect me?"

He bowed his head and propped his hands at his hips, looking up at her with a rueful sort of admonishing stare. She'd had enough of dominant males who liked to tell a woman what to do. And her relationship with Keith had ended horribly. And left her scarred. So she wasn't about to give this guy the benefit of his alpha take-charge attitude.

"Answer me!"

"I don't know." He splayed out his hands. "I honestly don't know what the hell is going on right now. I will protect you from whatever comes after you, but—"

"But what about when *you* come after me? You said you were here to retrieve my heart. That's just…so not cool." Her fingers shook, and she shivered as if the wicked Minnesota winter had suddenly swept in on an icy wind. "I don't know what's going on. You're freaking me out. Creatures are coming after me. I can't trust you, but I think I need to because I'm not prepared to stake vampires or dodge harpies. But you apparently are."

He exhaled and took a step toward her. Just when she thought he might embrace her, he stopped, his hands extending before her as if to warn himself away from such intimate contact. Wise move. She didn't need the physical empathy. She needed real answers. Right now.

"As long as the tracker is homed on to you, it will

send out vibrations to any creature nearby and alert them to you. And, as I understand it, they will know about your heart."

"Vibrations? The vampire said something about the vibes leading him to me."

Bron scrubbed a hand over the back of his head. "I suspect the harpies were lured by the same vibrations. It's to do with universal vibrations. No time to explain it. Right now I've got to get you to a safe place. Away from…here."

Kizzy planted her feet and gripped the camera-bag straps at her chest. "How am I going to protect myself from you?"

"I won't harm you. Promise."

"I don't know if your word is good."

"No, you don't. You've a choice, Kisanthra."

"Please, it's Kizzy." She shook now, nerves making her wish she wore a jacket to stave off the shivers. And it was a warm September evening!

"You've got two choices, and you'd better be quick about your decision." He held out his hand for her to grasp. "Come with me. Or take your chances with the four vampires heading our way right now."

She twisted at the hip to look over her shoulder. Down the alleyway the silhouettes of four men raced toward her. Mercy. She'd always been a fan of Buffy and Spike. (Nope, not an Angel girl.) None of the creeps barreling toward her looked like the sexy British vampire who had stolen the slayer's heart.

Yikes. One of those things wanted to rip out her heart? Kizzy turned and slapped her hand into Bron's. "Let's get out of here."

Chapter 4

"I'm sorry," Bron offered as he headed down the highway away from the vampires, who could run fast but not faster than the seventy miles per hour he currently drove. He was surprised to find so many vamps in a town of this size. On the other hand, they could be a tribe. "I haven't had the opportunity to handle this correctly."

"This?" Kizzy asked with as much disbelief as he would expect after everything she'd experienced in the past few crazy hours. "What is *this* exactly? Show me that tracker thing again."

He dug the tracker from his pocket, and before he could hand it to her, it flew from his grip and landed on her chest.

"Seriously? This is getting ridiculous." She peeled it off and studied it. "What's it made of?"

"Crystal."

"And you said it was bespelled? Does that mean a witch did something to it?"

"Yes," he answered, because he wasn't good at lying. And some humans could handle the truth. And he trusted those who could. But that didn't mean he was going to spill every explicit detail. Need to know. And she didn't need to know much.

"And this thing is supposed to lead you to the Purgatory Heart," she said, working it out as she turned the tracker over in her hands. "And since it's landed over my chest, I assume that means it's *my* heart?"

"The spells from the Crafts and Hexes department have never led me wrong before."

"Crafts and Hexes? What is this place you work for?"

He navigated the truck around a tight country curve. His jaw remained as tight as the curve.

"All right, no answer for that one," she said. "Will you at least tell me what's a Purgatory Heart?"

"Can I explain when we stop?"

"When are we going to stop? Where are you taking me?" She scanned the darkness that swept by the vehicle. The ditches had been freshly mowed, and the scent of grass carried in over the gasoline fumes and her distractingly alluring perfume. "I need some answers, and I think you've got time now. The vampires are no longer on our tails. So spill."

He noticed her holding the tracker with one hand and positioning her camera to snap a shot.

"Do you have to take a picture of everything?"

"Yes. It's my job. I have a blog that yields millions of hits a year, and I publish pictures of—"

"Vampires?"

"No. Yes. Well. My pictures capture the *idea* of the paranormal."

He shot her a raised brow.

"They are convincing, but I've never actually met a real vampire. Until tonight. Do you know how I've longed to capture the paranormal on film? I think I got the harpies, but I didn't have a chance to get the vampire. Vampires!" She chuckled. "I actually just said that. What a crazy night. I think I need vodka. There's a dive bar in the next town. We should stop there."

"It would be wise if you could retain all of your senses. At least until I can be assured no one else is after you."

"Spoilsport. Just as well. I'm a teetotaler. My drinking is like my photography—it's more of an idea than the real thing." She tapped the crystal with a fingernail, and it produced a crisp *ting*. "You said this tracker thing sends out vibrations?"

"Yes. I've been told it somehow communicates with the item—that being the Purgatory Heart—and sends out vibrations. Or maybe it's the heart that sends the vibrations. Not positive on that one. Unfortunately, any paranormal within range of those otherworldly vibrations will also feel them. If they've an interest in obtaining the heart, or even not—they may simply be curious—it will bring them round."

"What is it about my heart?" She clutched her T-shirt, then shook her head. "No, wait. Let's do it your way for now. Let's put some distance between whatever is after us and find a place to rest. I'm so tired. And hungry. There's a town about ten miles ahead. Basically a truck stop with a diner."

"And a dive bar?"

"I was kidding about the drink. Unless you want one?"

He shook his head.

"Can we stop at the truck stop?"

Her eyes pleaded, and Bron felt a twinge in his chest that he'd not felt in a long time. Compassion? Or perhaps just hunger. He hadn't eaten and was hungry. Had to be hunger.

A human woman sat beside him. She was not a part of the mission. The heart wasn't supposed to be beating. Nor was it supposed to be inside the chest of a pretty woman who had an insatiable curiosity for the paranormal realm and—that damned camera. She couldn't be allowed to have such damning photographs of anything from the paranormal realm. Would she post them online? A million hits? That was something he must not risk.

"Yes, something to eat," he muttered. "And a room for the night."

"You honestly don't think it's safe for me to return to Thief River Falls?"

"Do you?"

She considered it a few seconds, drawing her legs up to her chest and wrapping her arms about them as she shook her head. "No."

He'd rent a room. She could sleep. And he could make sure all the photos she had taken were erased.

The truck stop sat before a small motel featuring fewer than ten rooms in the back lot near a sunflower field. The decor sported dark wood paneling and pine furniture with rough-cut carvings of grizzly bears on the headboards and the chair arms. Red-and-yellow plaid curtains matched the bedspreads. Kitschy country. Bron had seen the inside of enough motel rooms and hotels not to care anymore. As long as the bed was halfway comfortable and there was running water, he was satisfied.

Kisanthra had made a beeline to the bathroom as they entered the room, calling out that she wanted to freshen up and that might take a while so not to worry about her.

He wouldn't worry about her. Unfortunately, their paths had crossed, and now he did have to deal with the situation. Find and seize? Unlikely.

He pulled out his cell phone and dialed Acquisitions. It was late, and the office was overseas, which put their time early in the morning, but dispatch, a 24/7 position, answered. He asked her to patch him through to the director's messages and left a short one.

"The Purgatory Heart is in someone's chest. Unable to seize. I await further instructions."

If that didn't get the point across he didn't know what else would be required. The director would probably pull him from the mission. Bron had never taken an innocent life to gain an object he'd been assigned to retrieve. Not unless that life threatened him or others, that is. And in that case, it generally was not an innocent.

But could he leave the heart—and the woman—just like that?

Sitting on one of the two twin-size beds that had seen better days—probably better decades—and facing the bathroom door, he listened to the water splash in the sink. A vampire had almost sunk his fangs into her neck. Kisanthra Lewis was—and would be—pursued by every degenerate that could pick up on the universal vibrations. She was not safe. And while it wasn't his job to play babysitter, he had inadvertently been the one to lead those aggressors to her.

He couldn't walk away. He had to ensure she was safe. Yet how to do that? So long as her heart beat in her chest, he felt sure she'd be a target.

The director had said the heart had been grasped by a soul from Purgatory. How was that possible?

There were a lot of times he didn't completely understand the nature or power of the items he had been ordered to retrieve. Didn't matter. He had a job; he carried it out. He looked forward to the next mission and the next. He enjoyed the adventure, the quest and, oftentimes, the race for the prize. The satisfaction in completing a task that very few could. He did not require accolades, only another assignment. The next fix.

But never before in his nearly one hundred fifty years of working for Acquisitions had such a race to the prize involved ensuring the safety of a human woman. This was a twist he wasn't sure how to handle. And even if he did, he didn't want to.

He didn't get involved with human women romantically. That way lay heartbreak. And unfathomable grief. He would never be forgiven for one moment of indiscretion with a human woman and the results that had followed. Nor did he deserve such forgiveness.

He hadn't thought about that time for ages. Had been so involved in his work that he hadn't afforded a moment for regret. And now, in the midst of a strange connection to this human woman, memory had chosen to bombard him with images of a sweet blond child, alone and...beyond hope. So precious and fragile.

That horrible, horrible day. It had been his fault! All because he'd chosen to dally with a human woman.

Pressing his hands to his temples and shaking his head, Bron shook away the image. The best thing he could do now was get Kizzy out of his life as quickly as possible. Because he didn't need the grief of memory or the tease of her sexy scent. She was pretty and tough and independent. All things that attracted him to a woman.

But she had no fangs or wings or the ability to shift, so that made her dangerous to his very soul.

"I'll take her home. Maybe Acquisitions can assign a watch to her for a few days."

He couldn't be responsible for her safety. Because he wasn't capable or, rather, didn't want to remain in such close proximity to her.

The bathroom door opened, and Kizzy wandered out, twisting her hair into a ponytail as she did. He hadn't noticed if she'd worn makeup earlier, but now her face was clean and fresh. A sweet, fruity tease clung to her skin. More of that seductive perfume?

He quickly looked away, finding the remote on the nightstand to look busy.

"That felt good to wash my face and take a few minutes to regroup." She wandered to the bed, where she'd dropped her camera bag.

Damn, he'd forgotten to go through the camera. Distracted by morbid memories. He'd wait until she fell asleep. Her focus was fixed on the LCD screen on the back of the camera.

"Wish I had a toothbrush, but a hand towel worked well enough. You want to use the bathroom? It's all yours."

"I will. I'm just going to, uh…"

She eyed him up and down, setting aside the camera. "Stand guard?"

He nodded.

She plopped onto the bed and toed off her red shoes. Reclining, she pushed back the coverlet and shoved down the sheets with her feet. Propping up the pillow, she sat back against it. "So, tell me about this Purgatory Heart."

Bron exhaled and pulled the curtain back before the window. He didn't want to do this. But she had a right to know. Maybe if he answered her questions now, that would put an end to them, and he could focus. And be done with her.

"I was commanded to retrieve the heart and return it to Acquisitions," he offered. "That's how my assignments work. I get an electronic dossier on the object, a location if available and off I go. I had no idea the Purgatory Heart would be inside someone's chest. Nor do I believe the Director of Acquisitions knew that."

At least, he hoped Ethan Pierce had not known such information. What kind of duplicity would that be if he'd been sent on such a task? No, Pierce had been the director for two centuries. He was solid and trustworthy.

She pressed her fingers over her breast. Feeling her heartbeats? "So I've got to keep one eye out for you and a big butcher knife? Not like I haven't been through that before."

He gaped at her.

"Not like that." She swept a dismissive hand before her and yawned. "I mean, no man has ever come after me with a knife before. Without my permission. You know." She shrugged and splayed out a hand. "I had open-heart surgery eight months ago. Got a nasty scar down my chest." She lifted her shirt just enough so he could see a thick red scar vertically climbing her chest wall. "So I suppose, if when the time comes and you do intend to take out my heart, you can just use the 'cut here' line."

"That's…" He didn't know what to say to that. She was too blasé about the possibility of such a hazard. Truly, her fear manifested strangely. "I won't do that, Kisanthra."

"You don't sound very sure of yourself. I'm too tired to care right now. And hungry. But I think I'll fall asleep before I can look up the diner's number for takeout. So why were you tasked with finding my heart? Is it important? You said you retrieve objects of magical nature. I know this heart isn't magical."

"It's a portal to Purgatory."

She lifted her head from the pillow and gave him a wide-eyed assessment. Deep brown eyes that held such curiosity while at the same time managed to disturb him. Because her gaze compelled him to wonder about her. What made her tick? What did she see through those eyes when she held the camera before them?

Bron nodded in confirmation. How fucked was it to learn your heart could allow others access to Purgatory?

"That is so crazy. You're saying someone can get to Purgatory from my heart? By…using it? How? I didn't think Purgatory was a real place. I'm not even Catholic!"

"It exists. And in the wrong hands, your heart could provide an entrance to the place. Should that occur… things could get out."

"What kind of things?" Her wide eyes beamed fascination.

"Souls. Bad things. I'm aware that Purgatory is populated with Toll Gatherers and the souls of the dead. But that's not important, because no one is going there by means of the heart."

"You mean *my* heart. It's not *the* heart. It's mine. Right here." She thumped her chest. "Still beating. And I'm not willing to give it up anytime soon."

He nodded. "As you should not. But as I've said, I had expected to find…an artifact. A preserved heart or some such. Not one still beating. The photographs show the objects bear a burned handprint on them."

"Photographs?"

Bron sighed and tugged out his cell phone. As he scrolled to the dossier files, he considered whether or not he should show her classified Acquisitions information. But then he clicked on the link to the museum, which was on the internet for anyone to access, and handed her his phone.

She scrolled for a while and read the website. "That stuff looks fake. Anyone could have burned a handprint into a book or bucket and called it that. Or Photoshop! You actually believe this stuff?" She handed him back the phone.

"I thought you said you believed in the unbelievable?"

"I do, but I'm not stupid. Check the Snopes website. I'm sure it debunks that museum."

"All files are fact-checked and verified as genuine before they become an assignment. I have no reason to doubt the validity of the object's value or use." He tucked the phone away in a pocket. "The tracker led me to you. I've never doubted witch magic before, and I'm not about to begin now."

She placed a palm over her chest and closed her eyes. With a nod, she seemed to accept his statement. "This is so out of my pay grade. And I don't even have a salary. But I'm willing to listen and learn. To believe."

"A willingness is more than most can manage." He hooked a hand over the end of the stake holstered at his hip.

"Do you always carry that stake?"

"Always."

"I've seen the crossbow you carry. That was cool. What other kinds of weapons do you have? A knife?"

"In the truck I've a bowie knife and a garrote. The crossbow and some other weapons. Why do you ask?"

"I suppose a bowie knife would do nicely to cut out my heart. Just needed to know what I'm dealing with."

"Kisanthra, I've promised you that I will not cut out your heart." He cast his gaze toward the window but couldn't see beyond the curtains. How to make her believe him? And why did he care? "My word is always good."

Except when he had been younger, and ego had ruled his life, and he'd done whatever he'd pleased whenever he'd pleased with whomever he'd pleased.

Hell, this trip down memory lane could prove brutal if he did not strike it from his thoughts right now.

"What makes it a portal?" she asked.

Her curiosity was a good sign. He hoped. While he sensed her fear, it was also balanced with a tremendous dose of curiosity. She should not fear him. And if she were to keep her head about her if any other paranormals came after her, then she would be much easier to protect than a screaming madwoman.

"I've been told such a heart—your heart," he said, "bears the handprint from a purgatorial soul. Such as is shown in those artifacts from that museum. Someone gripped it and, well, I'm not sure how that can have happened. That's where I lose all sense of rationality with this situation."

"So you have as much trouble believing as I do?"

The best he could offer was a noncommittal shrug. Because, really? It was pretty far out there. But again, he did not question his missions. Sometimes it was simply better not having all the facts.

She suddenly clasped both hands to her chest. Eyes tracing the bed covers, she winced and shook her head.

He could sense her increased breaths and smell the worry on her. "Kisanthra? What is it?"

She shook her head frantically. "Nothing. I…nothing. I think I just need to sleep this off." She snuggled down into the sheets. "Right. That's it. Maybe a good night's sleep will see me waking up from this crazy dream. You going to sleep?"

"In a bit. I'm going to stand watch for a while."

"Fine. Me and my Purgatory Heart will just catch some shut-eye."

He turned to face her bed, and just when he almost reached to smooth a reassuring hand down her shoulder, he cautioned himself. Not necessary to protect her in that manner. "You're taking this very well."

"How else should I take it?"

"Not sure. Are you sure you're okay?"

"I'm tired, Bron. I appreciate you looking after me today. And I just want to not talk to anyone right now if that's okay with you."

"Fine. We'll talk in the morning and decide what next to do."

"Sure thing." She pulled the sheet over her head.

Chapter 5

Kizzy pressed her shoulders to the brick wall. A hint of orange on the horizon teased at daylight. Standing in the shadows, she clutched the camera bag to her gut. The T-shirt she wore could have been warmer. She shivered, but not so much from the touch of chill in the air.

A heart that has been grasped by a soul in Purgatory.

It made too much sense to her. And that is what freaked her out.

And as if the universe wanted to cram that insane punch line into her psyche she'd woken in the dream again this morning. The recurring dream she'd been having since the accident. The one where a werewolf pulled her heart out of her chest. It was vivid and bloody, and she screamed loudly. Just when she thought the beast was going to eat the pulsing organ, she'd startle herself awake, and the dream would never finish.

Thank God for that. She didn't want to know why she'd envisioned a werewolf going after her heart. Could be because of all the creatures she believed in, werewolves scared the crap out of her. It all went back to that camping trip with her father when she'd thought the bear was a werewolf. And she could guess at a few reasons why it was her heart, in particular, that was always at the fore of her dream. Open-heart surgery is not something a person goes through without scars. And she had them. Inside and out.

Wakened by the dream, panting from fright, she'd glanced to Bron, fully clothed and with combat boots still on, sleeping on the bed beside her, and had decided to sneak out. Because the dream of some big, furry paw clutching her heart had never made any sense.

Until now.

Kizzy had woken two days following the open-heart surgery, a result of the car accident. After being rushed to the hospital by the ambulance, she had died on the operating-room table. Dead for six minutes the doctor had reported. They'd had to crack open her chest to massage her heart back to life. He'd also reported, almost as an afterthought, there had been odd scarring on her heart that he'd noticed while inside her chest cavity trying to bring her back to life.

But seriously? Keith, who had died instantly following the impact of car to boulders, would have never gone to Purgatory. That man had been destined for Hell. And she knew Keith had not been a werewolf, so that part of the dream must be a crazy manifestation of her beliefs. What better way to illustrate the horrors she'd survived than by inserting a wild creature into it?

"Or maybe I'm going crazy?" Guilt clung to her,

because she had survived while Keith had not. She'd never wished that for him. Not even when he'd berated her into tears.

She wanted to run. To her left stood the truck stop. To her right, a stretch of highway that led to the North Dakota border. Running wouldn't get her far. And it could perhaps even land her in a vampire's toothy embrace.

Could a bloodthirsty bite be considered an embrace? Why did everyone always romanticize the vampire? She'd looked into that creature's eyes last night and had seen the hunger for her blood. And he'd smelled like rotting blood. There had been nothing whatsoever romantic about the lustful craving in his eyes, either.

Of course, she wasn't stupid and knew it was the *idea* of immortality that attracted those who romanticized the creature. Because, really? Edward was just too damn old for Bella, and Dracula had been a sadist.

Kizzy had almost lost her life at the beginning of the year, and she said blessings for every morning she woke. But to live forever? She imagined it would get tiresome. Yet she couldn't help a small thrill at now knowing her beliefs were real. Verified. Vampires really existed! And so did harpies.

And what other sorts of creatures would sense the weird vibrations she apparently gave out as a beacon and come to rip out her heart? Why was Purgatory such a seemingly popular vacation spot for the lifestyles of the weird and otherworldly?

Bending forward and gripping the backs of her calves to stretch out her back muscles—the motel bed had been lumpy—she vacillated over whether it would be wise to come clean to Bron with what she knew about her heart or to just cut her losses and run.

Could she trust the man? She wanted to. But she didn't know much about him. He'd suddenly *appeared* in her life. And sure, he was handsome and stirred up thoughts of romance and heroes. She was a woman. She'd have to be dead not to be attracted to him. But he worked for some weird organization that—well, for as strange as it sounded, it also fascinated her. Acquisitions? A Retriever who searched for magical artifacts? How cool was that?

But she'd never claim any talent at picking the right guy, the one who was trustworthy and normal. Someone who wouldn't laugh at her beliefs. Would she ever find the right one? She wasn't in a hurry, but she didn't like to waste her time on the less-than hopefuls.

After Kizzy's first dramatic breakup as a teenager with the guy who had given her her first kiss and her first third-base feel, her mother had hugged her teary daughter to her chest and said something about finding the right man. One day when she least expected it, she'd turn around, and there he would stand.

"No," she muttered, shaking her head. "Don't be seduced by the strange and wondrous, Kizzy. You don't need a man. Take care of yourself. You're the only one who can do that."

Bron woke on the bed, coming instantly alert and looking about the room. He'd heard something. Or was it the odd scent he noted? Smelled like…stale mattress. This place was nowhere near worth the forty-nine dollars he'd laid out for it. A tile above the toilet had fallen off when he'd been in there earlier. And the sink's rust stains… It should be condemned.

He rubbed his temple, easing away the lingering

remnants of sleep. He must have been more tired than he'd thought. He hadn't expected to fall asleep. Of course, a flight across the ocean from Berlin, topped by an evening chasing harpies and vampires, could be the reason for exhaustion.

A beam of morning sun teased behind the faded curtains, and he glanced to the bed next to his. It was empty.

She had fled him once again. "Damn!"

Grabbing the truck keys on the nightstand, he mustered a small blessing she hadn't the forethought to steal his vehicle. He hooked a hand in the canvas duffel in which he carried all his life's possessions and rushed through the door.

Two steps out onto the tarmac, and he sniffed the air to determine which way she had gone. To the right.

And there she stood, not ten feet away. Against the brick wall. Offering him a small smile and a shrug. "I didn't run off."

Dropping the duffel bag where he stood, he then stalked up and gripped her by the shoulders. Relief surprised him, but he didn't question it. "I thought you had. Kisanthra, I can't protect you if you keep running away from me."

And then he did something he would have never done had he taken a moment to think it through.

Bron pulled her into his embrace and wrapped his arms across her back. She sighed against his chest, tucking her head against him, and he remembered how easy it could be to hug a woman and simply let her warmth melt against his own. To recognize the shape of her and welcome her curves and softness. And to brace his arms about her a bit more tightly than a friendly hug allowed.

Because he'd thought he'd lost her. And he wasn't done protecting her. Bad things were after her. She needed him.

That was his story, and he was sticking to it.

"I wasn't running away," she said against his shoulder. "I was just thinking about heading into the truck stop to buy us candy bars for breakfast. Bron?"

He still held her. Inhaled the sweetness of her skin. And what was that about? He didn't hold women like this. Did he still have to fear what involvement with a human could mean to him? He shouldn't. It *had* been a long time ago. And she smelled so good. Like candied peaches. But his dislike for human women had become an ingrained belief. And besides, it was easier hooking up with paranormals. He got a lot less questions from them.

Bron abruptly pulled out of the hug and ran his fingers back through his hair, then scruffed his beard. "Right. Breakfast. There's got to be some place that'll sell us eggs and bacon instead a candy bar. Doesn't the truck stop have a diner?"

"Yes. And I love bacon. I just don't have any more than a couple dollars on me, so a candy bar was all I could hope for." She tapped the front of his shirt, and her smile beamed at him. "You don't have to worry about me running off. I thought about it but changed my mind. I know I'm safe with you until we get this all figured out."

"You're a smart woman."

"I am. But allow me some fumbling in this new world I've just been tossed into. Vampires and harpies? Much as I've always believed in mythical creatures, I'm going to have to fire up a new set of brain neurons to accept it all."

"Good enough. Let's go eat. My treat."

Kisanthra secured a table for them inside the diner that, on the front door in big white vinyl-cling letters, had advertised the Man Plate, featuring two kinds of sausage, bacon, ham and steak. Bron's stomach was ready for the challenge. He told her he'd meet her inside after a quick phone call.

This time the director took his call.

"What do you mean the heart isn't attainable?" Ethan Pierce asked.

"It's in a person," Bron said. "A young human woman who is staying in a small Minnesota town."

"I see. You're in the States? Tough luck."

"You had no idea the heart was intact?"

"Of course not, Everhart. I wouldn't have sent you off on the mission knowing such a detail."

"So, the mission is off?" he asked.

"I'll have to look into it," the director said. "Stand by until I can get back to you. Affirmative?"

"Yes." Bron hung up before his disappointment would register with an argument.

Wasn't as if he could walk away from Kisanthra now anyway. She needed a guard. An armed guard. And he'd have to do it without falling into a nonsense hug again.

Standing so close to her, feeling her body relax against his had felt damned good. But he didn't like the hope that brief contact had stirred in his gut. Because it had been a lie. It was simply good to hold a woman, of any kind or species. He and his monkish lifestyle tended to go too long without satisfying his physical needs.

And then things happened.

He looked to the sky. The sun was high. The moon last night had been waxing. More than half full.

He spoke to the phone, "Siri, when's the next full moon?"

She replied with the date, which was four days away.

He couldn't remain on this mission much longer without risking a shit-storm of questions from the insatiably curious Kisanthra Lewis.

Kizzy popped a straw into the orange juice she'd ordered for Bron when he sat across from her in the cherry-vinyl booth. "I ordered you the Man Plate. Same for me. I can seriously put down any and all breakfast meat."

"Coffee?"

"It's coming. I'm going to guess you're a no-cream kind of guy. Am I right?"

"Black as the devil's ass is how I prefer it."

"Okay, now I have that image in my mind." She sipped her juice. "Was that call business?"

"It was."

"About me?"

He conceded with a nod. He wasn't going to give her too much information, but she'd angle for as much as she could manage from him. Because she was a woman in peril. Figuratively, of course. Because while she appreciated him wanting to protect her, she sensed rescue would only come by standing up for herself and being smart. And that meant learning as much as she could about the situation.

"Have you been given instructions on how to obtain the heart?" she asked.

"Kisanthra."

"Please, Bron, I'm curious, and I have a right to know. Me, being the owner of the sought-after object."

He exhaled, and, pulling the straw from the juice and setting it aside, he then swallowed half of it before speaking. "We had no idea the heart was intact. I've alerted the Director of Acquisitions, and now I'm waiting for further instructions. No doubt the mission will be canceled."

"I certainly hope so. I mean, I may have avoided the vampire's bite last night, because, you know, immortality? Not interested. But I do have a long life ahead of me. Plan to live to one hundred. I'm expecting that birthday card from the president. And I sure hope she's a cool president."

Bron chuckled. "So do I. We could use a woman POTUS. But vampires can't give you immortality from a quick bite."

"Really? But I thought—well, of course, movies and books are fiction. So how does it happen?"

He rubbed his temple and winced.

"Face it, Bron, you're stuck with someone who is open to the paranormal and whose middle name may very well have been Curious instead of Ginelle. I have questions. Lots of questions."

"Yes, but I don't think it's the best conversation for a public place."

She glanced around. They were the only couple in the diner, sitting at the end of a line of booths that paralleled the front windows. At the counter sat an old man gobbling up his eggs with Tabasco sauce, earphones stuffed into his ears. If he could hear them she'd be surprised.

"Right. Wouldn't want to tell this big empty place about vampires."

The coffee arrived, along with their breakfast. Kizzy made quick work of the over easy eggs and followed with bacon, sausage and ham—she gave her steak to Bron—while he seemed to inhale his plate of meat but in a way that seemed elegant and mannered. He was interesting to watch, and she did it casually, over her juice or while glancing out the window. His eyes were so blue she felt certain they were not real. Like something enhanced by Photoshop for a romance-novel cover. And his tousled hair seemed styled that way, purposely bed rumpled. It gave her ideas. And, man, those ideas were sexy.

She'd slept next to this gorgeous man last night. And she wasn't going to tell anyone it had been in separate beds. Sometimes all the details weren't necessary. And then this morning he had hugged her as if she had been the last woman on earth. And she'd wanted to kiss him because she'd been in a weird mental place, struggling with the facts about her heart and wanting it to not be real. And because, well, she'd never kissed a man with a beard before. Curiosity strikes! And when a handsome man pulled her close, well—bam. Need had kicked in. She wasn't beyond sex for the sake of placating her emotions or because she just needed to connect with another person for a few blissful moments.

"You have a girlfriend, Bron?" Sitting back, she poured another cup of coffee, then tinted the dark brew with three creamers.

"The job I have doesn't allow time for relationships."

"Really? Lots of people travel and are able to maintain relationships."

He delivered her a castigating flash of blue eye from behind a fork load of eggs.

All right, so the man had also mastered the dirty look. She'd try a different tack. "You must travel a lot."

"Always. I'm never in one place for long. Women tend to want to see a man more than once every six months or so, wouldn't you say?"

"Yes, I suppose. But you must have a home base?"

He shrugged. "Paris is one of my bases. I own a loft in the sixth. I've been there twice this year for less than a week total. This is the first time I've been in the States in over a dec—uh, a long time. I also own a tiny apartment in New York but don't anticipate stopping there unless my return flight has a layover. My missions usually run back-to-back."

"Sounds wonderful."

He raised a brow as he buttered the last piece of rye toast on his plate.

"I travel, too," she offered. "Or I'm just getting into the traveler's mode. Have been traveling for a couple months and hope to make it a permanent career. My blog has become so popular I need to expand my horizons and take in new places for my photo shoots. It feels right to me. I can't imagine settling to live in one place for too long now. I've been in Thief River Falls a few days, and it already seems like forever. It's my hometown, but I've found I prefer Europe."

"You have family here?"

"Not anymore. My parents moved to Brussels eight years ago, and I had always meant to follow them and then explore the world. But, well…" She sighed and sipped the coffee. "Sometimes relationships get in the way, as well as the lack of money. But no more! Everything changed eight months ago. I've prioritized what means the most to me. And that is seeing the world. Now I'm a free soul blowing about on the breeze."

"Breezes sometimes turn into hurricanes," he remarked drily.

"Really? Because I've always thought they were pretty gentle. I wouldn't mind a stronger wind. I like going to new places. When I'm finished here in Minnesota, I'm on to Romania. I've already put in for an apartment. I'll be shooting pictures for their department of tourism."

"Romania is beautiful country. But for a woman alone? You don't go wandering about in the woods all by yourself, do you? You do take along a friend or guide?"

She shrugged. "Haven't had the need or the desire." Though it was something to consider. She wasn't worldly-wise yet. And if vampires were real, she should definitely bring along a guide or a protector. Or a vampire slayer. Did they hire out? "I'm careful. Besides, now I know how to fight off a vampire. That should count for something."

He smirked, and she wanted to reach across the table and trace her finger over the crinkled lines at the corner of his eye. And stroke his beard. It was thick along the jaw, dark and—now the idea of testing out a kiss from a bearded man popped into her brain. And then she wanted to stand in his arms again and release her worries into his strong hold and fall into him. That hug had been awesome. And much needed.

"That hit the spot," he said and pushed his plate to the table's edge.

Kizzy startled out of her daydream. Her father had always said her biggest problem was that she was a daydreamer. She had never considered daydreaming a detriment. It had gotten her this far. She hoped to follow the reverie all the way to the end.

So long as that end didn't come about because of a missing heart. Plucked out by a werewolf.

The waitress appeared to retrieve their plates and leave them a fresh pot of coffee.

"Thanks," Bron said. "Have you pie?"

"Cherry, apple and boysenberry," the waitress supplied cheerfully.

"How about a thin slice of each?"

The waitress bristled gleefully and headed off to the kitchen.

"You must really like pie," Kizzy said.

"I do intend to share."

"Thanks. That must not come easily to you."

"What? Sharing?"

She nodded.

"Just because I'm a lone man making my way through the world doesn't mean I've not the capacity to empathize with others. Besides, I have a theory. Pie is a universal means to friendship. And, I'm hoping, an olive branch necessary to make up for the past twelve hours. I didn't mean to bring all this into your life."

"I think that tracking thing was the culprit."

"Yes." He patted his jeans pocket and then pulled the device from his pocket. With a crisp snap, it broke in two in his hand. "Should have done that as soon as I figured out you were the target. Still might have some residual magic attached to it. I'll ditch it in the garbage bin out back when we leave. Another cup of coffee and then I'll be fueled up."

"Where to next?"

"Perhaps keep driving. With the tracker destroyed, it shouldn't take long to notice if it's effective. If we don't run into anything wanting to rip out your heart today, I'd say you could be safe to return to Thief River Falls."

A day didn't seem like a good bet, but Kizzy wouldn't argue. Besides, spending the day with this guy would give her time to learn about him. And he about her. Which reminded her…

"I need to tell you something, Bron. It could be important to your mission. It's about my heart."

The waitress delivered three pie plates and two forks and offered extra ice cream. All they had to do was call for Alice. Bron said they'd be fine and thanked her.

Kizzy pulled the apple pie toward her, and, sitting up on one folded leg, she leaned over the table and teased at the warm apple slices swimming in cinnamon beneath a crispy crust. "I think I can verify my heart is what you're seeking. At least, my dreams do."

"Dreams?"

She sighed and set down the fork. "I've been having a recurring dream since the surgery. I wake up feeling a pressure in my chest and remember the feel of a hand clutching my heart."

Did she need to tell him it was a werewolf clutching her heart? It didn't matter, did it?

Bron paused before taking a bite of the cherry pie.

"The open-heart surgery I had? I was in a car accident eight months ago. It was my boyfriend's fault. Keith. He uh… No, it was my fault, really. We were arguing."

She bowed her head and swallowed. If they hadn't been arguing, Keith may have never felt compelled to drive them off the road. And he would still be alive. Much as she had wanted to get away from him at the time, she had never wished for his death. For that she would always have regrets. And guilt.

"I wanted to break it off with him," she said, swallowing down the lump in her throat, "and had been biding my time for the right moment. We'd dated for six months. He was very possessive. And obsessed with me to the point that I'd find him going through the messages on my cell phone and telling my friends when they were allowed to call me. He didn't beat me, but he had begun to be verbally abusive. Always saying he'd never let me go, no matter what."

"Doesn't sound very loving."

"I think it was his way of expressing love. Loud and in my face. He grew up with an alcoholic father and no mother. I always wondered if that was why he was so possessive."

She forked in a slice of pie. It was warm and sweet. But she couldn't enjoy it, because she had to put it all out there before she chickened out.

"But anyway, for the last four to six weeks of our relationship, as Keith's verbal abuse increased, I could only think about how to break it off. I let it go on too long. I should have walked away sooner. I have a tendency to either put things off forever or to just dive in without thought. So I sort of did both.

"I told him one night when he was driving us home from the casino. Bad idea. It was January and raining, which instantly froze to ice. He got so angry. Accused me of being a whacko. I had shared with him my belief in the paranormal, and he'd always thought it was cute. And he knew about the blog. But he accused me of being a tinfoil-wearing maniac. Then he shouted that if he couldn't have me, no one could, and he swerved the car off the road while driving eighty miles an hour."

Bron blew out a breath and set down his fork. In that moment their eyes met, and she saw something in the blue depths. Compassion? Understanding? It felt tangible and almost as needed as that warm hug had been. He didn't say anything, and she was thankful that he didn't feel the need to reassure her or offer her condolences.

"I was told he died instantly," she said, finding her voice didn't tremble, but it had softened to a whisper. "When I came to in the ditch, I felt as though my chest had deflated, and I couldn't get out of the car. An ambulance rushed me into the Grand Forks ER, and my heart stopped on the operating-room table. The doctors had to crack open my chest and massage my heart. Brought me back to life after six minutes without a heartbeat."

She spread her fingers over her chest, feeling the long scar beneath the thin T-shirt. It would forever remind her of a bad decision. Of how a life had been lost because of her poor timing.

"A few days after I'd been lying in the hospital I finally got to talk to the operating surgeon. He was nice. Cute. He said he'd almost thought he'd lost me. And then he made a weird comment how my heart had been scarred. Almost as if someone had grasped it with their fingers and left behind the impression. Then he jokingly said it hadn't been him."

"Really?"

She nodded. Her heart beat rapidly now. She didn't like to retell that night. Because she'd been stupid to have actually stayed with Keith that long. Hadn't found a better means to break it off with him. Had almost died because of her rash, ill-timed announcement.

"So you think your boyfriend…?" Bron asked.

She shrugged. "Maybe? All this just came to me earlier when I was standing outside the motel. I mean, I never thought Purgatory would be open to Keith. He's not very deserving of anything but Hell."

"Has he ever killed, maimed, committed a mortal sin?"

"I don't think so. Oh, I'm sure not. His bark was always worse than his bite."

"Then who are you to judge where his soul was capable of going upon death?"

"I'm not judging, I'm—" Angry that Bron seemed to be accusing her of something. Kizzy stared out the window, no longer interested in the crinkles at the corners of his eyes. Hadn't he the capacity to sympathize with her?

"The ways of the soul are something we can never know," he offered peacefully. "And I didn't mean to sound as if I was judging you, Kisanthra. I do think it a possibility that man's soul clutched your heart in death. You said he'd told you he'd never let you go?"

She nodded. How creepy to think that her boyfriend had been so obsessed with her that even in death he had tried to possess her?

"You think it could be Keith's handprint on my heart? Does that mean we're still connected somehow? How long does a soul stay in Purgatory? This is even weirder than vampires. It's freaking me out, Bron."

He clasped her hand, and she met his soulful blue eyes. Hero eyes. Eyes that showed more compassion than he was probably comfortable physically showing. And why all of a sudden did she crave that physical connection from him? If she could have leaned across the table and pulled him into a hug, she would have.

"I don't think he can cause you any more grief," he said. "It's the living creatures who might like to get their hands on an entrance to Purgatory of which you have to be cautious."

"That's so not reassuring." He smiled and that lightened her heavy heart, and she laughed terribly. "Promise you won't leave me alone until it's clear I'm not in danger?"

He nodded. "I give you my word."

"Yes, you've said that. But how can I know if your word is good?"

He pushed the untouched plate of boysenberry pie toward her. "I'll offer you the last piece as a sign of good will."

She chuckled and dug into the rich purple dessert. "Pie does cover a world of aches and pains."

"Thanks for telling me about your accident and the relationship with your former lover, Kisanthra. It may indeed provide some help with this mission, though at the moment I'm not sure how."

Now she laid her hand over his. "I prefer Kizzy."

He winced. "It sounds so…"

"You're a little old-fashioned, aren't you?"

He shrugged. "Guilty. These young, strange names are too modern for my tastes."

"Seriously? You're not that old."

"Yes, but— It's beautiful. I will give Kizzy a try."

"It's easy. Like fizzy or tizzy or dizzy. Should we

see if they have to-go cups, so we can take more coffee with us for the drive?"

"Sounds like a plan."

"Off to adventure," she said. "Do you have an extra stake?"

His raised his eyebrow and waited for the punch line.

"I should probably practice my thrust and stab while we're driving."

"I'd expect nothing less from you. I'll see what I have."

Chapter 6

Bron tossed the broken tracking device into the garbage can outside the gas station. He'd forgotten to throw it at the truck stop, and twenty miles later Kisanthra—Kizzy—had him pull over to use the restroom, so it was a good thing he'd remembered it now.

An antiques store across the highway beckoned with red flags fluttering at the four corners of the old barn building. Kizzy had said she'd like to check it out. And he'd agreed. He didn't mind sorting through antiques. It was a kick to recognize the things he'd once used in daily life. And they weren't in a rush. Unfortunately, they had time to waste as he waited to see what might come after Kizzy.

His eyes tracked the sky, seeking any sort of flying creature that may have had a bead on the tracker, broken or otherwise. He didn't know how witch magic worked, but the fact it had led him to her meant it was so powerful that it probably could still function even after the crystal device had been broken.

Could he take her home and walk away? He didn't think it was going to be that easy. And that wasn't any kind of emotional thing. He just had no way of knowing she could be safe.

Her dead boyfriend had actually clutched her heart from Purgatory while she lay dead on the operating-room table. How bizarre was that? But he believed her. She'd had dreams. Had said the doctor had remarked on the weird scarring he'd noticed on her heart.

No doubt about it, Kisanthra Lewis owned the Purgatory Heart.

He checked his cell phone. No calls from the director. He wasn't sure he wanted to talk to him again so soon. Good, bad or ugly.

Much as an afternoon of antiquing sounded like a ridiculous detour, it would keep him close to Kizzy and perhaps take her mind off the situation.

He checked to see if his phone could access the internet—he could do more research on the Purgatory Heart while wasting time here—but no luck. He shoved the phone in a cargo pocket on his pants leg.

From behind, Bron felt a woman's hands embrace him about the stomach, and she leaned in to give him a generous hug. He squeezed her forearms in reply, simply reacting.

But when she bounced around in front of him and put her arms around his neck, he knew what was coming. And he didn't have time to stop it.

Kizzy tilted up on to her toes and kissed him. Her fingers spread along his jaw, brushing his beard—yet she faltered and their lips lost connection. A giggle, and she returned for more.

An awkward first kiss, but Bron didn't push her away. Some crazy part of him wanted her to find her footing. To stay at his mouth. So he wrapped an arm across her back and spread the fingers of his other hand through her long, thick hair that felt clean and soft and like something he could get lost in and anchor himself to.

The second attempt at a kiss was sweeter and longer. She moaned into his mouth, and the vibrations hummed against his teeth. She tasted like coffee and boysenberries. Her chest hugged his, and the subtle weight of her unbound breasts felt good against him.

He had the sudden thought that beneath the shirt and flesh and bone beat a heart that had been touched by something other. Something that had once been cruel to her and hadn't the desire to let her go even in death. No man should ever be cruel to a woman, whether such treatment be manifested with bruises or words.

And yet, Bron had once been cruel to a woman. Had committed an unforgivable act against her.

He stopped the kiss, their lips close and his eyes opening to seek hers.

"What's wrong?" she asked.

He shook his head, unwilling to detail the thoughts that threatened to crush the good feeling coursing through his system. A visceral sort of sensual adventure. Instead he asked, "Why did you do that?"

She shrugged and stepped back, shoving her hands in her jeans' back pockets, which lifted her breasts as she teasingly swayed side to side. "I wanted to know what it was like to kiss a man with a beard."

Really? So she came out with it just like that? That was a new one to him. But he sensed her total honesty. "Glad to have obliged. I'll drive across the highway and park at the antique shop."

She followed his path to the truck and grabbed him by the sleeve. "Are you really glad?"

"Sure."

"Or do you think I stepped over the line?"

"No. I like a kiss from a beautiful woman any day."

"I could kiss you again, if you're interested."

He stopped at the passenger door and opened it for her. Her eyes twinkled in the sunlight, and she must have put on some ChapStick because her lips were so soft. Sure, he'd take another kiss. But then again, what was he thinking? This was a mission, not a date. And she and her crazy heart could never be compatible with his closed heart.

"There's something going on in there," she said as she twirled a finger near his temple. "Deep thoughts?"

"Possibly too deep. Get in, Kizzy."

He closed the door behind her and walked around the front of the truck. Inside the cab, she played with her camera, and when she aimed the lens at him, he put up a palm to block the shot. "I'll want to know you've erased the shots of the harpies. And the vampire, if you got pics of that."

"I will. I just…want to study them a bit first. I promise you can look at my camera before we part ways. That's what we're doing, right? Tonight you're going to drop me off at my doorstep and run away?"

He did not run away. But he never stayed beyond need or his welcome.

"I promised you I would protect you."

"How do we know I'm safe?"

"We'll play it by ear. But I'll want to recon the place where you're staying first. When we arrive, I'll get a room for the night. Then, once I've determined all is clear, you can move back in."

He navigated the truck across the highway and into the antique store's gravel parking lot.

"You don't need to get a room," she said. "You can stay on my couch. It's comfortable. And you don't actually want to leave me alone for some big bad creature to come after me, do you? I mean, even if the coast is clear, it might be a good idea to hang around awhile to ensure that. Yes?"

"All right then. Your place it is. But I don't mind wasting some time this afternoon."

"Yes! Let's get to the antiquing. I like to look for old cameras, so let me know if you spot any."

He followed her into the dank and dark shop, and they spent the afternoon going through the dusty treasures on two levels in the barn. No cameras to be found, but they did have a soft-serve ice cream machine. Kizzy bought a vanilla and shared it with Bron.

They sat on the truck bed gate, Kizzy finishing the ice cream cone. She'd eaten most of it. Bron wasn't much for cold treats, but he wasn't going to refuse when she offered.

"You should have bought that branding iron," she said of the iron that had fascinated him. It had a wolf's head with a bar across the neck. Some kind of cattle brand? Didn't make sense. But the other option, using it to brand wolves, had made him feel sick. No, it must have been used for decorative purposes. Either way, he wasn't a collector of things.

"I thought you said you understood the concept of traveling and living light?" he commented as he jumped down and offered his hand to help her down.

"That's why I didn't buy the iron rooster doorstop. My mom would have loved it. But you're right. Traveling with stuff? Not cool. We spent a long time in there. The sun is setting."

"It's a few hours' drive back to Thief River Falls. Let's get going." They hopped in the truck cab, and Bron steered them out on to the highway. "With luck, whatever is out there can no longer track the vibrations. I'll stick around through the night to make sure you're good to go. I'd like to see your work, actually."

"Really?"

"You said you try for a paranormal atmosphere?"

"Yes. I've managed werewolves out of tree shadows and mermaid tails out of sun shimmering on waves. I'm always drawn toward the scene, and it either happens or it doesn't. I guess you could say the picture chooses me."

"I enjoy playing with all the new devices, though I never find much time to snap a shot of the picturesque places I pass through."

"New devices? Are you talking about my camera? Because that so makes you sound like a man from a long-past century. Are you sure you're not a time traveler?"

"I know for sure I am not. But I do know some witches are capable of time travel."

"Really?" Attention captured, she turned on her seat to face him.

"I'm going to have to tell you about witches now, aren't I?" he guessed. It was a better diversion from revealing his knowledge of the centuries. "Here goes everything."

They chattered on the drive that took them through small towns that boasted populations of less than three hundred and others that were merely a few businesses along the highway that offered antiques, beer or gas. Bron didn't speed. He wasn't in a hurry to return Kizzy to her home.

"When did you start believing?" he felt compelled to ask. "In the paranormal?"

"It all started with an outhouse."

"Do tell."

"I was on a camping trip with my dad. He'd take me out every summer. Gave Mom a little vacation from us. We owned a cabin on Lake Bronson, but it didn't have an indoor toilet. The path to the outhouse was lighted, so I was never scared to make the trip alone right before I had to go to bed. But one night I heard the howl just as I was stepping out of the outhouse. And I saw eyes. Big, gold eyes. I know it was a werewolf."

"Did you now?"

She nodded, her eyes as wide as he imagined they had been when she'd been little and had heard—most likely—a bear.

"I never ran so fast in my entire life. I was shaking and screaming when my dad got hold of me. I explained to him the werewolf might be out there. He just laughed and said it was probably a bear."

"But you believed otherwise?"

"I did. I've heard bears growl. This was different. It put the hairs up all over my body. Anyway, after that I started my education in all things paranormal. I read every book I could get my hands on. Watched all the late-night movies I could manage without my parents finding out."

"How old were you?"

"Eight."

Bron nodded. And then he fell dead serious. Eight. The same age as Isabelle. Had his long-lost Isabelle ever been so afraid? Of course she had. And he had not been there to protect her or even to laugh and tell her the scaries were just something else.

"But the real catalyst to believing in all things dark and creepy?" Kizzy eyed him and waited for his nod. "I took a picture of a ghost when I was twelve."

"I didn't think ghosts were photogenic."

"Oh, it showed on film. I used my mother's old Polaroid camera we'd found in the attic. It still had a film packet in it, so I rushed downstairs and took a picture of my dad sleeping on the couch. When it developed, there was this orb near his head, and I know it was a ghost. Grandpa had died just a few months earlier.

"My mother grabbed the photo. And get this, I swear I saw her sniff back a tear, but then she tossed it in the garbage and said I was being ridiculous. Ghosts were nonsense. Later that night, I snuck down to the kitchen and claimed the photo from the garbage can. I stuck it in my copy of *Rebecca of Sunnybrook Farm*. I think that book got sold at the rummage sale before my parents moved to Brussels. I should have saved it."

"You know those odd orbs of light are a common occurrence on photographs," Bron said.

"I know that. Could be dust or the play of sunlight. But this was different. And I simply *knew* it was a ghost. You know, like when you get a visceral feeling of what is real or right?"

"Intuition."

"Exactly! And ever since, I've been fascinated with the paranormal. I was actually convinced one of the boys in my twelfth-grade English class was a werewolf. Not one of my finer moments. I sat behind him. He was so hairy and always scratching the back of his neck. Yuck."

"You don't like a man with hair?"

"Not all over his hands and arms and neck. It was thick and black. I knew he was a werewolf. The most evil of them all. I actually followed him on the night of a full moon during a kegger out in the woods. It was a bust. He was just another stoner looking to score some drugs beneath the bridge."

Bron rubbed his beard. "So no on the hair, eh?"

"I like beards. I learned that when I kissed you." She winked at him. "But werewolves? They freak me out."

"Huh." Not great. And all because of a hairy boy and an outhouse adventure in the dark?

"So I know you believe in the paranormal, Bron. I mean, holy Hannah, you're armed and prepared to take out all sorts of creatures. How did you get involved with all things woo-woo and become a Retriever?"

"It's a long story. I was in a weird place with my life. Drifting. Met a guy in a tavern—er, bar—who needed assistance finding an Egyptian lycanthropy totem."

"More werewolves," she chimed in.

"Right. It started with that mission, and I've been doing it ever since. It feeds my desire for constant movement and exploring new places."

"We're a lot alike in those matters. I can't stay in one place too long now. I'm always searching."

"For vampires?"

"Been there, done that. I think I'll try something a bit tamer next time, like faeries."

"Faeries are the nastiest of the nasty. I'd steer clear of them."

"Really? But they seem so…"

"Fluttery and magical?"

She nodded.

"The realm of Faery is dangerous and mysterious, and—I don't know a lot about the sidhe, but what I do is that I'd rather take on a whole tribe of vampires than one angry faery."

"Wow. That's fascinating. I wish I could bombard you with questions, but—can you pull over?"

"There's nothing out here." Darkness had fallen during the drive. Bron took in the nearly full moon in the sky to his right. It glowed like a warning beacon that demanded his attention. When she hooked the camera around her neck, he asked, "You're going to take some pictures?"

"No, I need to pee. I shouldn't have had all the free water from that vintage water carafe back at the antique store. Seriously. Pull over now."

He did so and shifted into Park. Kizzy stepped out and, before walking off, turned to Bron and said, "Thanks."

"For what?"

"For not laughing when I told you about the werewolf I heard when I was a kid."

He shrugged. "Kids know things."

"They do." Her smile beamed, and she turned and took off.

With the camera swinging about her neck, she hopped through the long grasses edging the road. The ditch was low and the land was dry, so he didn't suspect she'd have to splash through water. Darkness thickened the air, and while he could still see her shadow, he turned his head to scan the moonlit horizon, giving her privacy.

He'd told her about time traveling witches and that he knew witches divided themselves into the Dark and the Light. They'd spent hours talking about all things witchy, so he hadn't needed to venture on to any other creatures like vampires or demons. Or werewolves. No, he'd not laughed. But it might have been wiser if he had.

He itched his neck and glanced at the moon. Four days out for the full moon. He normally had an innate sense of the lunar calendar, but his focus had been altered. He was off his game due to the surprise of finding the heart in the least expected place. No way could it be classified find-and-seize now.

The other option, a find-and-finish mission, was not something he had ever balked at accepting. He had no compunctions regarding pulling the trigger or dragging a blade across a pulsing carotid if it meant protecting mankind from evil.

Once, he'd had to gut a vicious berserker and pull out an ancient chakra power totem it had swallowed to keep it from changing into an undefeatable killing machine. He hadn't blinked an eye to end the berserker's life. It would have murdered so many with such power at its command.

Kizzy wouldn't harm a bug. She was an innocent in possession of a powerful talisman. And she had no intention of using it to harm others. She did not deserve death simply to offer up the prize.

But would someone else reach in and grab her heart?

The thought made him shiver. He squeezed the steering wheel in an attempt to stave off memories of the innocent eight-year-old. A child harmed by the ignorance of others.

A scream raised the hairs on the back of his neck, and he reacted. Jumping out of the driver's side, Bron raced down the ditch, through the knee-high grasses and into the darkness. He smelled the intruder now and cursed himself for not paying attention while sitting in the truck. As he raced through the night, the scent of sulfur bled into his being.

Demon.

Kizzy's breaths homed him on to her position. She ran toward the dark line of a nearby forest. Not an easy place to escape the creature that pursued her.

Shit. He didn't have any weapons on him, save the wooden stake at his hip. That wouldn't kill a demon. And he rarely packed salt, a sure means to slow a demon down, even kill it. And while he'd often thought he should learn some demonic expulsion spells, he'd never taken the time. Hand-to-hand combat was out of the question—not in his human form.

There was only one way to defeat this creature. It was unavoidable. An option he rarely utilized unless he knew he'd need the strength and endurance to defeat a powerful opponent. He just prayed the darkness would conceal his secret from the woman who was far too curious about paranormal breeds for his well-being.

Chapter 7

Whatever was chasing her was ugly. And it smelled like rotten eggs. Daring a glance over her shoulder, Kizzy got a look at its face in the brief second it dashed through a beam of moonlight. What the—? It was missing its lower jaw.

She screamed again and tripped on a clod of dirt, going down hard and landing on her forearms. Thank goodness her camera was secure on the strap about her neck.

Something scratched her shoulder. Hot blood oozed from her skin. She felt the thing hovering over her, its sulfurous breath wilting the air. And just when she had Bron's name on her tongue to scream, the growling and drooling creature above her was lifted away and tossed through the air.

And in its place stood something bigger, hairier and

wilder. It had a face like a wolf, and its furred body resembled a man who ate steroids like candy. At its hands were long claws. And she caught a glimpse of a tail whipping wildly behind the thing.

With a chest-expanding inhale, the wolf creature let out a long and wicked howl.

"Shit, a werewolf." Kizzy crawled across the ground, her hands finding purchase in the long ribbony grass. The forest she'd fled toward was close. But on second thought… "Nope. Never lose a werewolf in there."

But the expected attack did not happen. Instead the wolf stomped away and into a run, meeting the approaching creature missing half its face in a body slam. They battled, growling and clawing and snarling. The clash of their claws sounded like swords meeting in battle.

And Kizzy realized that maybe the werewolf was trying to protect her. Or was it fighting off the other thing so it could have her all to itself? Where had it come from? Since when was the upper Midwest so fraught with paranormal creatures? All her life she'd hoped to capture one on film, with no luck, and now…

Now!

Where was Bron? Still waiting for her in the truck? He must have heard her scream. If not, by now he should be worried that her dash into the ditch to pee was taking an inordinately long time. She could see the distant headlights from the truck up on the road and hadn't realized she'd run so far from it. When one was being pursued by the otherworldly, apparently they grew wings themselves.

Remarkably, the camera still hung around her neck. In a moment of clarity, she pulled off the lens cap and adjusted the flash and shutter speed by feeling the buttons along the left side of the camera. The creatures battled one another not forty feet away from her. They were silhouetted by moonlight that crept through the forest's latticework of branches. She snapped shot after shot. Likely nothing would appear on film with the terrible light and the frenetic action, but she couldn't let this opportunity pass.

Pushing up to stand, she noticed the tweak at her shoulder and only then remembered she'd been injured. It didn't hurt, but she felt blood soak her torn shirt to her skin.

No time to bother with assessing her life-or-death status. She hadn't fainted. And she'd already cheated death once. What was more important was getting as many shots of the werewolf and that thing. She lifted the camera, took aim…

With one grand sweep of its deadly paw the hulking werewolf took off the creature's head. The sky about the headless body darkened as a black mist curdled the air. It was smoking out or turning to dust or ash, much like a vampire.

The monstrous werewolf swayed its head toward Kizzy. Predatory gold eyes narrowed, targeting her face. It was probably scenting her with its black, leathery nose, placed at the end of a stretch of jaw. Its maw opened to reveal dangerous, sharp teeth she would not like to feel sink into her flesh.

"Shit." She dropped the camera to let it dangle from the strap.

If she ran, the werewolf would run faster. But if she stayed put, she became a blinking sign advertising a free meal. The beast would snatch her with those wicked claws. And tear her to bits. Her bones tossed aside. Her heart likely kept for the prize it apparently was.

She clutched her throat, her muscles stiffening with fright. What to do? Either way, she wasn't going to survive long.

The decision was made for her. The werewolf suddenly took off toward the forest. Whew! Kizzy's breath chugged in her throat. And not sure if the other creature could function without a head or in its current smoky/ash state, she decided to get the hell out of there herself.

She raced toward the truck, and finally her shoes landed on the loose gravel that edged the tarmac highway. Slamming her palms against the warm metal hood, only then did she dare let out a shout. It was a cry of relief, of letting out the fear tightly coiled in her veins. Of triumph, as well. She had gotten away. All in one piece. Heart still intact.

Heartbeats thundering, she said blessings for the fact her heart did still beat. She'd come back to life on the operating room table. She'd not died tonight. She was more resilient than she'd ever thought possible.

Then she remembered she had not been alone.

"Bron?" She peered inside the truck cab. No one inside. Maybe he had gone in search of her. Certainly he would have after hearing the two creatures battling. "Oh, no."

She turned and scanned the darkness that was too black to make out any more than the jagged line of trees edging the horizon. "The werewolf is still out there." And who knew if the missing-jaw creature had been alone or had friends close behind?

"Bron?" Her voice shivered.

She was brave, but her legs wouldn't allow her to

rush into the darkness in search of him. Common sense told her to climb into the truck and lock the doors. Pray he had left the keys behind. So she did. And, yes, the keys were in the ignition, which was why the lights were on.

She pressed a palm to the closed passenger window and peered into the blackness that loomed beyond the reach of the headlights. "I can't just sit here. What if he's…"

Attacked. Mauled. Or worse.

"Eaten," she choked out, clutching her throat.

Despite her fascination for the otherworldy, she'd always hated horror movies. Anything that involved a creepy creature attacking innocents. The chainsaw-wielding maniacs didn't scare her. But Kizzy was enough of a believer to know that things that went bump in the night did exist and would go after people.

Like werewolves.

She clutched the door handle, prepared to rush out and call for him, when something loomed closer from out in the ditch. Heartbeats rocketing to her throat, Kizzy slammed her fist on top of the door lock button.

"Like that's going to help. It took the head off the thing chasing me. It can certainly break into a flimsy truck and—ohmyGod."

Bron wandered up from the ditch, clutching his tattered pants to his hips. They were split down the seam of one leg. He wore no shirt or shoes. His hair was tousled. And he had red scratches that bled on his arms and chest. He must have battled the werewolf. But really? To have lost his shoes? Though the cuts were indicative of a fight. Maybe? Had to be. How else could he have—

And for all the times Kizzy had hoped to capture

the paranormal on film, to be validated that her beliefs were indeed real, in that moment, she knew exactly what Bron was.

"Holy Hannah." Her heart actually stopped beating. "No. Way."

But it made sense. Especially with the job he had, traveling the world and collecting magical artifacts. Things that normal people—humans—couldn't conceive existed. Why hadn't he told her? Was he really? Yes, she knew it as she knew her own heart had been scarred by the touch from a purgatorial soul.

Bron climbed the ditch, wobbling as he reached the roadside. She didn't see claws at his hands. His face was normal shaped. No vicious teeth jutting from a stretched wolflike maw. And his bare chest and abs were shadowed with dark hair but nothing resembling fur. Was he—could he be—dangerous?

Immediately on the tail of her apprehension rose an intense anger. That he hadn't the courage to tell her he was a werewolf, had even thought to keep it a secret, pissed her off.

She opened the door and hopped out. "What the hell?"

He put up a palm to dismiss her demanding query and wandered around the front of the hood. Kizzy followed, no longer fearful of what else might lurk out in the darkness. It stood right before her.

"Did you forget to tell me something about yourself?" she asked as he leaned a palm onto the hood and bowed his head. "Bron?"

He winced. Exhaled. Then gasped out, "Are you okay?"

"Me? Yes. Er, I think so. Just a scratch on my shoulder."

Maybe. She couldn't be bothered with her own problems now. "What is this? You look like you've been through a shredder. You didn't fight that creature. Because…" The next words came out on a nervous shiver. "Are you what I think you are?"

"I didn't want you to see that. But I didn't have another option. Wraith demons are tough to take out. I needed more strength than wielding a knife or crossbow would have offered."

"So…" She reached to touch his arm but retracted when he flinched. "You're a werewolf?"

He nodded. "I have extra clothes in my duffel bag. Let me change on the other side of the truck and then…"

"Right." She stepped back, giving him the space he obviously wanted. But so stunned. Unbelieving even while she believed. "Werewolf," she whispered as he opened the door on his side and got some things out of the cab.

Turning, she leaned against the front grill of the truck. The headlights framed her on each side, so she closed her eyes against the brightness and bent forward, catching her palms on her knees. The past few days had been insane. Unreal.

Exciting.

Weird.

Beyond comprehension.

Her dead boyfriend had grabbed her heart from Purgatory. Vampires and other monsters wanted to rip said heart out of her chest. The man who claimed to want to protect her also wanted her heart and…he was a creature who shifted from man shape into a big, hulking, furry, dangerous howling beast.

Kizzy shook her head. A dizzy wave wobbled the world. She reached out for stability. A feeling of dread overwhelmed. Her body suddenly swayed, and she went down.

Chapter 8

Bron set Kizzy inside the truck cab on the passenger seat. Her body, limp and loose, sagged, so he carefully propped her head on the headrest. Just as he had walked around the front of the truck, knowing he'd have to face her questions, she had passed out. Fortunately, he'd been able to catch her before she'd hit the ground.

He took the quiet moment to pull on a T-shirt and stuff his feet into the extra pair of hiking boots he always carried with him. The first thing he did after landing in a new town or country was to rent a vehicle and then buy extra clothes. Generally, he did not need the emergency clothing change until the night of the full moon. And even then, when the urge to shift came upon him, he had the forethought—and time—to undress before shifting, thus saving a big clothing bill.

But he'd known he'd had to act fast if he were to

save Kizzy from the wraith demon. He'd almost been too late. That thing had been crouched over her as if she had been prey; the predator had been hungry for the kill. There was a lot of blood on her shoulder and shirt. He'd inspected the wounds after setting her down. Three long scratches on her shoulder that stretched to her bicep but, fortunately, not deep. The blood had already coagulated, which led him to believe she would be fine. He was sure that breed of demon did not have poison in its bite or claws.

And now. The fallout of such a rash decision to perform heroics. She knew what he was. He had to explain things. It would be a mess. He'd probably regret it. She'd probably flee. Either that or she'd want to take pictures. That was the worse option to him.

That damned camera. It rested on the cab floor right now, ever there, a virtual extra limb that completed her. With pictures of harpies, vampires and maybe even the demon that had attacked her.

Why *were* they still after her? He'd destroyed the tracking device. Had some weird kind of latent magic attached itself to Kizzy's heart? It was possible. Anything was possible when witches were involved.

But a wraith demon? They kept more to the underground and Daemonia. Bron could only suspect that someone or something must have commanded the demon, because wraiths didn't have much brain—about as much as they had jaws. They were stupid but instinctually predatory. Yet to journey to the mortal realm to hunt Kizzy didn't make sense to him. Why would a wraith demon seek the entrance to Purgatory?

As he slid in behind the wheel he reached over for Kizzy's camera bag. Just as he touched the strap, she stirred on the passenger seat. He retreated, not wanting her to think he was snooping. The ignition was on and the engine running, but he kept the truck in Park. They had to come to terms. Like it or not.

"Whoa. Did I…faint?" She shoved a hand through her hair and pressed it against her temple. She looked a tangled mess. But a beautiful tangle. Had the demon killed her Bron might never get beyond his regret at putting her in such a dangerous situation. "Bron?"

"Here. And, yes, you fainted. You've been through a lot. If you hadn't fainted I would have been surprised."

"A lot? Oh. Right. Yes." She pushed up on the seat and finally looked at him. She made such a start she cringed back against the seat from him.

To be expected. He was the monster. The werewolf who had spooked her when she was a child. The one creature she most feared.

"Oooo…kaaaay," she said. "Uh, right. I, uh… I saw you. All wolfie and fur everywhere. Your head was like a wolf. And your body… You howled like an animal. And you were big. And you took that thing's head off. OhmyGod."

She clasped her hands over her mouth. Even in the darkness the moon managed to land in her eyes and blink at him. Teasing. Defying him to face this truth.

"It was a wraith demon. Not common in the mortal realm and stupid as bricks."

"The mortal realm," she whispered nervously.

Those moon-drenched eyes implored him. Her beliefs would have been easier to swallow had she perhaps learned about *one* paranormal being. Say, the vampire. And leave it at that. But unfortunately the universe had plans to inundate her with myriad knowledge of the otherworldly. And that could mess with anyone's sanity, open-minded or not.

"I suspect someone must have been commanding the demon," Bron offered softly. He always felt invigorated after a shift, but the simple act of facing Kizzy's innocent stare challenged him and even forced him down from what might turn into an aggressive denial.

"Commanding it? To go after me?"

He shrugged. It was a ridiculous response, and he hated knowing next to nothing. "I knew the only way to defeat it was to wolf out. So—" he squeezed the steering wheel with both hands and offered her a sheepish smirk "—I did what I had to do."

"Wolf. Out." She tugged up her legs and pulled her knees to her chest, making herself small against the door. A wince reminded her of her wound, and she touched her shoulder.

"I checked it when you were passed out," he offered. "Surface cuts. They'll heal."

"Am I going to turn into one of those things now?"

"Why would you think that?"

"It clawed me. I might have its venom or essence or whatever inside me. Maybe it was poisonous?"

He couldn't help a chuckle, but she did not share his levity, so Bron turned to her, and when he almost touched her shoe, he kept his hand but inches from doing so.

"That's not how demons are made," he said. "Same with werewolves. You don't create werewolves with a bite or claw wound. We're born this way, and that's the only way we come into existence."

"You've been like this all your life? Ohmygosh, I told

you about the guy in high school who I thought was a werewolf. And you didn't say anything."

He sensed a tendril of her usual fascination in that tone, and that gave him some hope this conversation wouldn't result in tears or screams or her running from him. Much as she had every right to do so.

"Would you have really believed me if I'd said, over a plate of sausage and eggs, oh, hey, that guy you sat behind in school might not have been a howler, but I am?"

She bit her lower lip. Those big brown eyes. They were wondering and yet condemning at the same time!

"Kizzy, it's something I thought I could keep to myself. It is my usual mien. The last thing I ever want to do—any werewolf or paranormal species, for that matter, wants to do—is just come out with what we are and invite the worst."

"Right. I suppose. But you knew I was a believer."

"I figured a vampire *and* harpies in one day was enough for you to handle."

"Good call. Maybe. I don't know. I might have been okay with it. I mean, learning about you being a Retriever was cool. So, all your life? That's... Wow."

"Yes, but we don't come into our first shift until puberty."

She clasped her arms about her bent legs and rested her chin on her knee. He could sense her heartbeats slowing and her fear shifting to allow her fascination. "That's interesting. Is it the same with other...uh...creatures?"

"It varies. Vampires can be born or made. Witches are born into the craft, though some humans can study and reach a certain level of magic comparable to a natural witch. Demons come from Beneath. Angels come from Above."

"Beneath and Above?"

"You call them Heaven and Hell. And somewhere in between all that is Purgatory."

She pressed her fingers over her heart.

"I'm sorry," he offered. "I didn't want you to find out about me in such a manner. I didn't think it would come to this. I was to retrieve a heart and be gone. Kizzy, this mission is everything I never expected. It's become a tactical nightmare, and I must constantly be on the defense. I usually go into such missions fully armed and prepared to fight all the random creatures that might come at me. But I'm fresh out of salt bullets. A blade would have proven ineffectual, as would have my stake. So the shift was necessary."

"Salt bullets. That's so Sam and Dean."

"Sam and—? Should I ask?"

"They're characters on a TV show about demon hunters."

"I am nothing like the fiction you read or watch. This is real life, Kisanthra. What I do is dangerous, and it kills me that you've been dragged into the middle of such a violent situation."

She nodded, and her fingers crept forward to touch his. She slid them into his grasp, and they held a loose clutch. "This adds a whole new dimension to our friendship forged by pie," she said.

"That it does."

"And I don't know if that's good, bad or ugly."

"You haven't run screaming yet."

"I may still be a little out of it from fainting. Let me get my bearings and—where's my camera?"

He pointed to the floor before her seat. "Please, tell me you didn't snap any pictures of me or the wraith?"

She closed her eyes and squinted.

"Kisanth—"

"Kizzy. Please?"

"Kizzy. You have to erase them."

"I'm sure none will turn out. It was pitch-black. My shutter speed was not adjusted for night photos. I saw only silhouettes battling it out like King Kong versus Godzilla. Except I don't think you're as hairy as King Kong. And really, you're not overly hairy now. Not like the guy in school—uh, that's stupid. Sorry."

Bron rubbed his brow, sensing a headache. But it wasn't a physical feeling, more the regret he would endure in attempting to break the damned camera. Her livelihood. Which could very well contain his secret.

"So it's not a full moon thing?" she asked.

"I can shift whenever I choose. But on the eve of the full moon it is a necessary call to shift to my werewolf shape. And the night before and after the full moon things are, well…my werewolf wants out, but I can control it with specific, uh…actions."

"Like what kind of actions?"

"I think I've said enough for now. I want to get you home and have a better look at your wounds, if you'll allow."

"I don't want to go home. Bron, if they are still following me, I don't want to lead any creature to my front door. The apartment I'm renting is smack-dab in the middle of town. Businesses line the street below. Can we go to another motel? Just for tonight?"

"You're right. I had thought to test things, but now I know you're still being followed. Why they are still following you is beyond me. For what reason? I destroyed the tracking device."

"Here's an idea. Maybe, instead of killing whatever next comes at me, you asked it why?"

He met her hopeful gaze. She had a way of stating the obvious without making him feel like a fool for not thinking of it in the first place. Of course, questioning the attacker made sense. But wraiths hadn't speech. So he hoped the next one was a vampire. Those bastards he could handle. That was, if there was to be a next one. By all the gods, he prayed there would not be.

He shifted into Drive, then rolled down the road.

"I think we were about five miles away from Thief River Falls," she offered. "Let's get two rooms."

Right. So she wouldn't have to stay in the same room as the monster. She might think she was open to all things new and curious to her, but she was like all other humans. They feared those things unfamiliar to them. Even the things that piqued their curiosity and which were only best viewed from afar or caged behind steel bars.

The very few who could accept? Oftentimes they were in it for the monetary rewards that pictures or stories could bring. And Kizzy did wield her camera for profit. He'd have to play things carefully now.

The soul bringer felt the disconnection to the wraith demon as a jerk to his system that twinged up and down his spine. He sat up in the chair, gripped the arms tightly and opened his eyes. The darkness meant little to him. He could see all things in all lights or even lack of it.

He'd been shirking his soul-ferrying duties of late and had found solace in a quiet home long abandoned by its residents through natural death. The brick walls were solid, but the shelter was unnecessary for his welfare. He could withstand the elements, and he lived. Ever after.

As she had not.

Catching the dismal thought before it could blossom into a full-blown melancholy—how he hated such emotion—he stood, paced to the broken glass window and looked out across a field of drooping sunflowers. He'd thought summoning the wraith demon would prove more powerful than the ineffectual harpies. Apparently not. But how had the owner of the Purgatory Heart managed to defeat such a vicious predator?

He couldn't get a fix on the surroundings of the death because he was only capable of a sort of mind meld with the creature he had commanded. And that was now vanquished.

He did not like to rely on Nightcat, but it seemed his only recourse at the moment.

Squeezing a fist at his side, he gritted his teeth.

"I must have that heart."

Chapter 9

Kizzy stepped out of the shower and dried off with the thin towel the motel provided. At least it was steamy and warm in here. She'd been shivering when she'd bid Bron good-night and had entered the room right next door to his. She'd needed a room to herself tonight. Not because she feared now having to share a room with a werewolf, but because she required some space to think. And maybe cry. And definitely scream into her pillow.

She brushed her teeth with the corner of a hand towel and wondered if it would be safe to go back to the rental apartment. Where her toothbrush and comb were. Where her clothes were.

Where all the strange creatures in the world might convene if she were still somehow attracting them to her.

What was that about? She had watched Bron destroy

that freaky crystal tracker. Could it work when broken? But he didn't need it anymore. He'd already found the object it had been bespelled to lead him to: her.

"This is all your fault, Keith," she muttered as she wandered into the room and pulled on the pink T-shirt and her comfy Rock & Republic jeans. The jeans had grass stains on the knees. She craved a change of clothing.

As well, sleeping in clothes sucked. She could keep her jeans off, but she wasn't willing to risk the sudden need to escape half naked. She hadn't washed her hair, so she flopped back on the bed, spreading her arms, and closed her eyes to the blinking red neon from the motel sign positioned outside her window.

She was alone, and her world had been upturned. Even more so than it had been following the accident that freezing January night. For then she had been able to cry for reasons that had been tangible and necessary. Reasons she could blame on herself, like guilt and regret. And on Keith. He had swerved into the ditch purposefully. So she had hated him while lying in the hospital recovering from open-heart surgery.

And she had not hated him. Because she hadn't hated him enough to want him to die. Besides, she didn't hate people. And she had cared for Keith. Though she'd never really loved him. Not as a possible rest-of-her-life partner. Perhaps in those initial weeks of their relationship their lust had felt like love to her. But that mattered little now because Keith was gone.

And he'd tried to take her with him.

Had her going to the crash site something to do with the things coming after her now? Had she somehow activated the weird vibrations that drew crazy creatures to her? Was her heart giving off those vibrations? Maybe she shouldn't have returned to the scene of the accident for closure?

She hadn't gotten the closure she'd sought. But what did that feel like? Would she even know it if it came to her?

Tears streamed from her eyes. But it felt right to let them flow. She wasn't afraid to cry. Crying released the anxiety and made her feel better. A good cry allowed her to then step beyond and look at the situation from a stronger, braver perspective.

But the situation she now had to face harbored demons and vampires and werewolves. Did she want that?

She had *always* wanted that before. Photographic proof of the supernatural. Verification that her beliefs were not ridiculous. Something to *really* write about on her blog that would increase its traffic and her income.

But now? *He's a* real *werewolf.* What had she wished for?

She felt for the camera lying on the bed beside her and, sniffing back the tears, turned it on and scrolled through the shots she'd taken earlier while out in the dark field. There were over a hundred, and 95 percent were black. A few showed dark silhouettes against a blurred gray background with pixilated white blobs of blurred moonlight. One startlingly clear picture featured the werewolf's head, its maw opened in a howl and a clawed hand slashing through the sky.

Kizzy sat up on the bed. It was a stunning shot. Something she could only dream of creating on her usual shoots by capturing the rare moment with shadows and lighting.

"This is real," she whispered with fascination.

And the photograph looked genuine. No one who studied this picture could come to the conclusion it was anything but a werewolf. She could make a fortune if she published this shot.

Maybe?

There were more skeptics than believers. Just because she knew the truth didn't mean photographic evidence would convince the majority of the population. People had become jaded. Most would assume it was an actor in costume. Photoshop. Or both. Although, there were plenty of magazines and online speculation sites that would post the pic, real or not.

Those sites weren't her style. She'd been published by the *National Geographic*, for heaven's sake. A speculative site like Paranormal Possibilities that published pics of the bat boy and squid man would certainly bring her reputation down. A reputation that she was only beginning to build.

But was it so wrong to sidetrack once in a while to a few speculation venues? Her own blog speculated with the use of clever camera angles and her own designs on interpreting mythology.

With a sigh, she turned off the camera and set it aside. Now that her fascination for the otherworldly had been proven real, she wasn't sure she was so fascinated by the topic anymore. Sitting in the passenger seat earlier, listening to Bron's explanation had intrigued her. And it had frightened her.

I was born this way.

How amazing to imagine growing up as Bron had, as a werewolf, and not knowing anything else. Humans must seem the creatures to him. He hadn't elaborated on the full-moon situation, but she was curious. What means did he employ to not shift to werewolf on the night preceding and following the full moon? Would she see him in werewolf form again? She wasn't sure she wanted to. Because it was a short trip from fascination to horror.

And while she'd initially marked him as closed and protective, she now knew why. Certainly he would continue to protect his identity and not give her any more information than necessary.

Because he was only here to grab the heart and report back to Acquisitions on a job well done. And he could fulfill that task. He need only shift into that monstrous werewolf form and shove his claws into her chest and be done with the mission. What had he called it? Find and seize.

Kizzy curled up on her side, protectively pressing her fists against her breasts. She had no means to fight off a werewolf. *How* to fight a werewolf? Was the thing about silver true? She should do an online search for werewolf-killing techniques.

She shook her head and squeezed her eyes tight. "No." She didn't want to kill anyone or anything. Not even a werewolf.

But could she continue to trust Bron?

More tears fell onto the threadbare polyester bedspread. She'd never been so lucky in love to find a man who had wanted to treat her with respect and to protect her. To truly care about her. Yet Bron had shown signs of just such intent. In a moment of silliness and curiosity, she had kissed him. And he had kissed her back as if it was the only thing in the world to him and that it was what he'd wanted to do.

She'd kissed a werewolf.

Kizzy didn't know whether to be thrilled or to puke. That kiss had been a weird, surprise checkmark in the "things to do in life" column. And the really disturbing thing? Not only had she photographed a paranormal creature, but she just might lose her heart to one.

In a manner other than having it ripped from her chest.

Bron paced the floor before the bed. He wasn't tired. He wouldn't sleep tonight. He couldn't. She was in the next room. He'd heard the shower running. And now he could hear her crying softly. His hearing and other senses were turned up to twelve. He could turn them down when in crowds, but right now he didn't want to miss a thing about her.

Her weeping tugged at his insides. She'd been through a lot. Monsters were after her. And he'd handled the whole werewolf-reveal thing incorrectly. Poor woman.

Finally, he had to sit on the bed and bow his head, covering his ears with his hands. He'd known getting involved with a human woman was a mistake.

Why? Because she's human or because she's simply a woman who appeals to you?

And that was it, wasn't it? She appealed to him. Human or otherwise. When she'd kissed him, he'd pulled her closer and had deepened the kiss. It had felt great. And at the time he hadn't been thinking "back off, human woman." Only that she'd smelled awesome. And he wanted to stand close to her. And as well, she possessed amazing emotional strength. That quality right there attracted in ways he couldn't even fathom.

When the knock sounded not thirty feet away, he

knew it had been at Kizzy's door. He stood up, tilting his head to home in on a conversation. But all he heard was the door slam and Kizzy's muffled cry of his name.

He dashed outside and kicked in her door. She struggled with a man he immediately scented as vampire. The thing smelled strongly of blood, and when the asshole turned to see who had come in, Bron saw blood drooling down his chin.

What the hell? Was he too late?

"Did he bite you?"

"Not yet!" Kizzy yelled. She slapped at the creature's face as he tried to wrangle her wrist. "Get him off me!"

Bron grabbed the disgusting thing by the back of its leather jacket and flung it against the wall. Skinny, its eyes were hidden behind a slash of greasy brown hair. The vampire grinned. The blood on its chin was dried. The front of his ripped T-shirt was bloodied, as well. Did the idiot have no sense of personal hygiene? What an awful thing for Kizzy to have to see.

He slapped a hand to the stake in the holster—but, no, he recalled what she had suggested earlier. Talk before slaying.

"Come here," he said, motioning Kizzy to approach as he kept the vamp in eyesight. She came over cautiously. He grabbed the gold chain about her neck, tearing the cross off. "Get back!"

She obeyed. And the vampire lunged. Bron caught it across the chest with a forearm and slammed it against the wall. Wielding the tiny gold cross before it, he was pleased when the creature flinched.

"That's right, this one is baptized," Bron said.

"What does that mean?" Kizzy asked.

"Holy objects will give it a nasty burn." He taunted

the vamp with the cross. The gold symbol was no more than an inch high, but the creature pressed its head against the wall and shook it in fear. "A burn that will never heal. If I press this to its forehead it'll eat all the way through skull and brain. Slowly."

"Dude! Get that thing away from me."

"Who the hell are you, and what are you doing entering a lady's room looking like some kind of horror-show freak? Ever hear of a napkin?"

"I was snacking down the street on a nice plump number, and I felt the vibrations. She puts out a powerful draw. Just like I read online."

"Online?" Losing her fear, Kizzy walked up behind Bron. "What does he mean by that?"

The vampire slid left along the wall. Bron punched a fist into the Sheetrock, denting it in next to the vamp's ear. "Going somewhere?"

"What do you want, man? You want her heart? Take it. I probably wouldn't be able to sell it for much anyway. Just let me out of here, okay?"

Bron was so close to pressing the cross to the idiot's skin, but he had to keep his cool until he could get information from the longtooth. "How do you know about her heart? What's happening online?"

"We all know about it. Least, you do if you follow the Nightcat. He's been Tweeting about it since you found her in the park the other day."

"Tweeting?" Bron asked.

"Dude, seriously? Come into the twenty-first century."

Bron pressed the cross to the vampire's forehead, and it screamed, so he slammed his other hand over its mouth. It tried to bite his fingers, but he pressed hard. A little more force and he'd break off fangs.

"Twitter is a social media," Kizzy said over his shoulder.

"I know that," Bron snapped. "I just think it sounds like an excuse. Something he's making up."

"Let him talk. Is Nightcat the person's Twitter handle?" Kizzy asked.

The vampire nodded from behind Bron's hand.

"How does he know about me?"

"Tweets," the vamp mumbled, so Bron moved his hand to smash his cheek and hold him firmly against the wall while allowing him to talk. "Those that see you pass through their town Tweet about it. We know you're driving a black Ford F150 with rental plates. Some have posted pics. That's how we know what you look like. We've been following you through Nightcat's Tweets for two days."

"This is insanity." Bron pressed his fist hard into the vamp's face. "Where is this Nightcat?"

The vampire shrugged. "Don't know. Don't care."

"What was the initial Tweet?" Kizzy asked. "He must have seen something at the park here in town to know to Tweet about it."

"Maybe he did, maybe he didn't. You got a phone. Check it out yourself."

Bron punched the vampire in the jaw. It howled and grasped its bleeding mouth. He was too loud. And the cross wound on his forehead reeked of burnt flesh. He slapped his hand to his thigh holster and pulled out the heavy wooden weapon. Bron staked the vamp, and it ashed in a pile at his feet. He turned to find Kizzy standing there with her camera and a hopeful look on her face. Really?

Yes, she was that kind of strange but wondrous woman.

He sighed and shook his head. "Fine, take the pic. But you know I'm going to destroy that camera when all is said and done."

"Then you'll owe me a couple thousand dollars to replace it."

"I'm good with that."

While she snapped away at the pile of ash, Bron closed the door and paced along the side of the bed. He knew about Twitter and Facebook. Much as he had to have the latest in technology and could never pass up the newest iPhone, he'd never had a use for social media.

He tugged out his cell phone and asked Siri to open up Twitter. A few seconds later, the screen brought him to a sign-up page. He didn't have time for this!

Tossing the phone to the bed, he turned and punched the wall beside the door.

"What's wrong?"

He gaped at Kizzy. "You have to ask?"

"We got information from him. The vampire."

"Yes, but someone is out there broadcasting to others your every move. How is that possible?"

"The vampire may have Tweeted my location, or not." She glanced over the ashes. "If he had a cell phone on him, it's too late to check now. So everything goes up in ash? Even my cross?"

"Sorry about that. I hope it wasn't a personal keepsake."

"It was from my grandmother. But after you got vampire gunk on it? I'm good with it being destroyed. That's weird. Takes a lot of heat to burn metal and stuff like cell phones." She grabbed his phone from the bed. "I have a Twitter account. Let's see if we can find this Nightcat."

She sat on the bed and started doing that rapid typing, zoning out on the world thing that Bron found so annoying when he went into public places. People had become literal slaves to their electronic devices. He couldn't count the times a person had walked right into him because they'd been enraptured by their tiny screen.

"Come here," she said, patting the bed beside her. "I found a few Nightcats listed. Two are eggs, but this one is a black cat."

"Eggs?" He sat next to her and leaned in to look at the screen. She smelled of fear and salted tears and steamy skin.

"If you don't put up a profile picture, then the app gives you an egg," she explained. "Those are usually people just checking it out and who never get too involved. Yep. Both eggs show no Tweets and no followers. But the black cat has six hundred followers and just as many Tweets. His Tweets are protected, so if I want to follow him he has to approve me. That's probably not wise."

She looked at him. He noticed the constellation of pale freckles on the tip of her nose. And there, just a smattering of the sweet dots on the bloom of her cheeks.

"Uh…" Bron refocused. "Why isn't it wise?"

"Then he'll know Kizzy Lewis is following him."

"Right. We want to remain anonymous. Does it list his address?"

"No. Though, let me look through all the Tweets and

find the initial one about me. That might give us a clue. If he had witnessed that first time you found me and the harpies coming after me… Do you recall any people in the park that day who seemed out of place? I thought it was just a few mothers and their kids."

"If someone was following you they would have been stealthy."

"But not if this was the first time he or she had seen me and the harpies. I mean, they couldn't have known what was to come. Right? And have any of the others been stealthy? I mean, really?"

She had a point. Unless that person had somehow alerted the harpies? No, didn't make sense. Whoever Nightcat was, he or she must have also been following the tracker's vibrations.

"Nightcat?" Bron worked the notion about in his head. "What about a familiar?"

"You mean like an actual cat?"

"Yes, that shifts to human form."

"Seriously? They exist, too?"

"You should be to the point where you have no doubts about any creature I mention."

"You're right." Her sigh indicated she was having more trouble with this than her earlier admission of belief suggested.

"So, a cat-shifting familiar," she said. "If it had been out—as a cat—it could have witnessed the harpie attack. Here is the orignal post." She tapped the phone. "'Creatures of the Night,'" she read the Tweet, "'find the Purgatory Heart. Werewolf protecting the human who bears it. Caution. Post your positions. First one to the prize wins!'—Oh, that's terrible. But he apparently knew you were a werewolf right from the start."

"Cats have a thing for recognizing our species. And vice versa."

"Cats and dogs, eh?"

"We are not dogs," Bron insisted firmly. "It is a slang term to use that word to describe us."

"Oh. Sorry. I suppose you're not. It was dogs who descended from wolves, right?"

"Yes, and we werewolves have always been pure wolf."

Kizzy lay back on the bed, cell phone still in hand as she typed in something. "I've always been afraid of dogs."

"Why is that?"

"One bit me once. I was eight. It was a Chihuahua."

He lifted a brow.

"Don't laugh. It scarred me. Not physically, but mentally. I can't be around dogs now. I go to great lengths to walk a wide circle around them. It's not that I hate them. I just don't trust them. I never know if they will snap at me or try to attack."

"Well, you've survived an attack by a wraith demon and a few vamps. I'd say if something smaller, such as a Chihuahua, comes at you now, you've got that covered."

"Maybe." She smiled, but it quickly dropped. "I just don't want to get too close to anything with snapping teeth and four legs. Oh. Sorry." She sat up and set the phone aside. "I didn't mean…"

"I know what you meant. And again I'm not a dog."

"No, you're not." She clasped his hand. "Thank you for saving me, Bron. Again. From yet another vampire. Maybe I should start carrying a stake?"

"Wouldn't hurt. I can make one for you using that coffee table below the window. It's seen better days.

Might be a mercy to borrow the legs. Why don't you stay in my room tonight, and I'll stand guard outside? We'll have to pay for this door. I broke the lock mechanism when I kicked it in."

"I'll grab my stuff and be right over."

"I'll wait," he said. "Outside."

She nodded, and he heard her intake of breath. A nervous inhale.

Yeah? So he wasn't so pleased to be guarding someone who wouldn't admit she placed him in the same category as dogs.

Before leaving, he turned the table upside down and broke off all four legs. They were cheap pine and about a foot long. He'd have points carved into them in no time.

Chapter 10

Kizzy woke and yawned, then realized she'd crawled onto the bed last night without pulling the sheets over her. She remembered Bron standing by the door, looking out the window, keeping guard as he'd whittled away at the table legs with a bowie knife. His profile had been tall and fierce, a warrior.

A werewolf. Whom, remarkably, she trusted and was thankful to have on her side.

Now he lay next to her, his arms across his chest, eyes closed and breathing imperceptible. Must have decided the night watch could be done while lying down. He probably had supersensitive hearing and a sharp sense of smell. If anyone had approached the motel door last night, he would have been up and on them before they'd even had a chance to touch the knob.

Carefully, she moved up onto her elbow and stretched

her hand closer to his face. Slowly. She didn't want to wake him. But she couldn't resist the curiosity that had shaped her very being since a young age.

Landing her fingers on his beard, she stroked it. It was short and well-groomed for someone who claimed to constantly travel the world. A few shades lighter than the dark hair on his head. Perhaps from sun or even a long life? She wondered how old he was. Were werewolves immortal? She couldn't imagine what immortality would actually be like, but she wanted to know everything about him.

A heavy exhale through his nose, and without opening his eyes, Bron asked, "What are you doing?"

She wasn't surprised he'd been awake. And she didn't flinch away from the touch. "Your beard is soft. I like touching it. I couldn't not touch it."

He smirked but didn't open his eyes and didn't move, so she stroked along his jaw and up where the hairs were shorter. She avoided his mustache, though her fascination lured her gaze to mark a few hairs that curled over his upper lip, escaping from the neat trim that emphasized his mouth. She really wanted to touch his mouth. Not with her fingers, but instead with her lips.

"Kizzy?"

"What?" she sighed out.

"Are you going to kiss me?"

A sweet burn blushed up her cheeks. She leaned closer, and now she did dare a soft tap to his lower lip. "Can I?"

He turned his gaze on to her. Clear and true blue. Had he loved others who had fallen into wonder over his eyes in the brightness of morning?

"Knowing what you now know about me, do you still want to?"

That he was a werewolf. That he'd kept that a secret because he hadn't thought she'd need to know—she could excuse him for that. That he wanted her heart, literally, in his hand.

Damn her, but she'd always chosen the wrong man. She didn't seem to have the instinctual radar that would lure her toward Mr. Right. Something about Bron agitated her compass arrow, though. It neither swung toward the wrong nor toward the right, it simply coaxed her to move forward.

Kizzy leaned closer. Inches away from contact, the heat of their breaths mingled. "Yes, I do want to."

He closed his eyes and smiled.

She lowered her mouth to his and tested his heat against hers. The tickle of his mustache tempted her to dash her tongue over his top lip. Tiny hairs pricked teasingly at her skin. Warmth suffused her senses as the tender contact thrilled through her system. Shiver bumps coursed her arms.

The pressure of his hand finding her hip urged her to make the kiss firmer. She closed her eyes and sank into him. His solid, broad chest was the perfect place to land. The world fell away. Gone were the vicious creatures that wanted to rip out her heart. Only this man remained, who also wanted to put his hand on her heart. If he succeeded, he would be the second man who had done so. But the first she wanted to see try.

Turning onto his side, he slid his hand up her back and eased her against his body. She hooked a knee over his leg, the rough canvas fabric of one of his pants pockets melding into her inner thigh. His tongue dashed against hers. Sweet taste of playful discovery. His hair glided within her fingers. Thrill tickles shivered across her breasts, tightening her nipples. His heartbeats pulsed a steady dance against hers. A timpani of desire.

She could lose herself in him. Strip away her clothing and inhale his heat into her skin. Melt with him. Because he was powerful and handsome. Protective and commanding. Easy, but not too open. His kisses were not forceful; they were a presence she could not deny. Bron's kiss showed her he would take what he wanted yet return with equal measure.

He was a man. Nothing about him seemed remotely animal-like in form, not his structure, his muscles or his kiss. And she wasn't sure why it mattered, but it did. Because she had seen him adorned with fur and fangs. With a tail and claws and a wolfish head. And she was kissing that very same creature right now.

Kizzy abruptly stopped the kiss. The image of the wild creature taking off the demon's head in the field attacked with such sharpness that she bit her lower lip. Bron's eyes searched hers. Questions. Worries. *Knowing*. His thumb stroked her jaw as he waited for her to show him some sign it was okay to resume their connection. But she didn't react.

And then he closed his eyes and rolled to his back. "I've seen that look before."

"What look?"

He sat and shrugged his hands over his hair and stretched back his shoulders. "Does it matter? We should be on the move. We have to find that Nightcat person."

"Bron, I—"

But he stood and strode toward the bathroom, closing the door behind him in a manner to end the conversation. And Kizzy buried her face against the pillow. She'd screwed up. It had been fleeting, but he'd sensed her sudden aversion. She shouldn't have recalled what he'd looked like in werewolf form. She couldn't imagine being intimate with him in such a shape. So it had disturbed her. Yet that form had also fascinated her.

"Sorry," she whispered, more to herself than him.

Kizzy went online and grabbed herself a new email address: *vampchick71*, and had to smirk that she was likely the seventy-first person with that handle. How many were real vampires? Because would a real vampire use such a handle? Seemed too obvious for a creature whose very survival must rely on living under the radar.

Either way, it was now her online disguise. She filled out the details to open a new Twitter account, and after following a few vampires and werewolves, the TV shows *Supernatural*, *Witches of East End*—canceled far too early—and *Orphan Black*, and some paranormal romance and horror authors, she figured she'd laid ample cover to then follow Nightcat.

Bron took a long shower, and finally, the bathroom door opened and he strode out. He wore a different T-shirt, the same cargo pants, and sat on the end of the bed to put on his boots. "You ready to leave?"

"Yes. Let's get going." She sensed his need for distance. And to not talk. But she wanted to make things right between them. Though, a "sorry" felt wrong and not enough. So, she'd just have to try harder. "You want me to drive?"

"I got a couple hours' sleep. I'm good." Boots on, he

collected the wooden stakes from the windowsill and grabbed his duffel bag. "How about we drive through McDonalds for breakfast?"

He really wanted to get rid of her now. She was surprised he even offered breakfast. Why not just drive her into town and drop her off?

Kizzy sighed as she stepped outside and followed him to the truck. "Whatever you want." But when she climbed into the cab it just came out. "Did I do something wrong? Was the kiss that bad?"

The engine revved, and Bron navigated the truck out of the parking lot and onto the road that led into the retail strip edging the town. "Bad is not a word to describe kissing you," he finally said.

She wiggled on the seat, pleased with that answer.

"But I know you think I'm a monster like all the rest of the things that have been chasing you."

"No, I—"

He caught her hesitation and shook his head as he adjusted the radio volume up higher. She'd have to shout now to hold a conversation, so she kept quiet. She'd almost said something like "Well, what makes you different than the other monsters?" Good call to stop that question from falling out.

Because what defined a monster? Something that killed other things? Hunters killed for food. Murderers killed for sick sport. She'd watched Bron kill in defense to save her ass. But at the time she'd seen it as two monsters battling one another.

A monster had always been anything that didn't look human to her.

She really needed to reconsider that definition.

Leaning back and sinking her spine into the seat, she

put her feet, sans shoes, up on the dashboard. Bron cast her a dirty look. She pulled her feet down and crossed her legs on the seat. He'd stuffed the stakes in the center console, so she plucked one out and managed a decent baton twirl with it. Another side glance from the stoic werewolf.

So, he was going to give her the silent treatment? She was so over that high school idiocy.

Kizzy turned down the radio and twisted to face him, stake propped on her knee. "Tell me what it was like when you met your first human. I mean, it had to have been weird."

He cast her a glance. Back to the road. The big yellow McDonald's sign loomed just ahead. Then another glance. He should know her well enough by now that questions were de rigueur. "It was weird. And I didn't know how to act around one, even though we are exactly alike when I am in *were* form."

"Were form? Were means human, right?"

"Yes."

"I'm sorry," she offered. "Give me some leeway while I'm learning about you. Okay?"

"Why bother? You'll be home soon enough."

"Are you going to kick me to the curb and not look back? What about making sure no one is after me? What about my heart? You can't go back to the Acqusitions place without it, can you?"

"You think I'd actually rip your heart from your chest?" He shook his head in disdain.

"How else would you get it? But could you kill me first?"

"Kizzy," he said through a tight jaw.

"What? I'm flying solo here. I don't know what to

think anymore. I thought you kind of liked me." She tapped her chest with the stake. "I mean, I like you, Bron. And more than because you said you'd protect me, and you've saved my life. I want to understand you so I can continue to like you."

"Werewolves and humans..." He shook his head. "It's complicated."

"Why? You just said you're exactly like us most of the time."

"Most of the time." He rapped his thumb on the steering wheel. His jaw tightened. He blew out a frustrated breath. "You pulled away from me this morning when we were kissing. Can you tell me it wasn't because you were disgusted remembering me in my werewolf form?"

"No. Yes. Maybe? Bron, I had a moment where I realized I was kissing a werewolf. That kind of freaked me out. Because, really? I told you about the outhouse scare. So, yeah, I reacted. But I'm over it now. You're cool. And I don't expect to ever kiss you when you're all wolfed out, so there is that."

"There is that," he said sharply.

"What's your problem? I'm the one making the monumental effort to understand and accept. And yet you remain closed and uninterested in any sort of sharing."

"The kind of sharing you're interested in is—Kizzy, when a werewolf takes a mate, they bond for life."

"That sounds kind of romantic. How long is a werewolf lifetime?"

"We can live three or four centuries."

She whistled. "Cool. That must be—hmm, kind of tough, when I think about it. Do you have a driver's license? How old does it say you are?"

"Acquisitions secures new documents such as driver's

licenses and passports for me when I need them. It is a challenge existing for so long in a society that likes to document every damn bit of information about a person."

"I get that. I suppose you have to change your identity every so often?"

"Not so extreme as that. But I change up my birth location and sometimes middle names. I let the experts take care of the details."

"That's a good thing to have. Someone watching your back."

He pulled into the McDonald's parking lot, which was packed. It was close to the breakfast rush.

"So you and the human thing," she said. "Is that why you're playing it cool with me? I'm not looking for happily-ever-after. I just like you. Can't a girl like a guy without committing? I mean, the dating scene has evolved over the years. You are aware that in the twenty-first century the meaning of friendship can be defined in so many ways?"

"I am aware of the changing social mores. People have friends with benefits, they hook up, they have sex without commitment. I understand all that and am glad society has advanced over the decades. And I like you, too, Kizzy. But humans are— Very well, if you must know, I swore off relationships with human women a long time ago."

"What's a long time ago?"

He thought about it a few seconds, then said, "1860."

"Wow." Another spin of the stake and she caught it smartly. "What's wrong with human women? And don't tell me you've been a monk since then?"

"My work comes first. Always. But sex is necessary to a man's sanity, if not his emotional health. When

I feel the, uh…urge, I find others who can serve my needs."

"Paranormals?"

He nodded.

Kizzy tilted her head against the cab glass behind her. She knew that werewolves were creatures ruled by the moon. Or so the myths told. But now that she was sitting next to an actual werewolf, it was her opportunity to set the record straight. "Is that a full-moon thing? And what is bonding?"

He exhaled, and she saw his fingers flinch toward the radio.

"No, we're going to do this," she said, turning the radio completely off. "The line for the drive-through is long. We've got time. And I've got questions. You're stuck with me, like it or not. If you answer my questions, I'll let you kiss me again."

She knew the tease probably wasn't as appealing as she hoped it would be. If he'd sworn off human women? What was that about?

"For a kiss, eh?"

"Promise I won't even flinch."

His smirk was sexy even from side profile. "Well, then."

"That won't encroach on your swearing off human women vow, will it?"

"Kissing is good. Especially kissing you."

Good answer. The man had won himself some points. And she was willing to award said points to him because she did like him. Very much. "Okay, then. Sex during the full moon?"

"Werewolves are compelled to shift the day before the full moon, day of the full moon and the day after. It's never wise to shift so often, especially since we share our world with humans. It was different a few centuries ago when the densely populated cities were fewer and farther between. We've adapted. Most of my species have taken to only shifting on the night of the full moon. The other two nights we can quench the need to shift by having sex. Lots of it. Until we're sated."

"Wow. So two days out of the month you have to get your horny on?"

"That's a way to put it, yes."

"Never with a human woman, though? What if that's all who is available?"

"You would be amazed at the proliferation of the paranormal species living within this mortal realm."

"I'm sure I would be. I never would have expected vampires in Thief River Falls. Or harpies, for that matter. Okay. So tell me about bonding. Is that like a till-death-do-us-part, happily-ever-after thing?"

"It is. We marry just as humans do, and a werewolf generally takes one mate for life. We prefer mating with our own species, but the ratio of female wolves to males is much lower. Many of us take a different species as bride. Some even marry human women."

"Heh. So we're not so bad after all. And then how do you bond?"

"We have sex in our werewolf form with our mate."

"Ah." Kizzy let that one sink in. Two werewolves going at it in shifted form? That would be crazy, and she didn't want to think about it in detail, but it made sense. A werewolf and some other creature like a vampire or demon or whatever? Could still make sense.

A werewolf and a human? Hmm…

"It's biologically possible," he provided. "And anatomically, as well. You've seen me in my shifted form."

Yes, and though it was dark, he'd had the body of a human, though more powerful and muscled. His hands had been paw-like, and yet he'd had fingers as well, tipped with long vicious claws. She'd not noticed his feet. Or a particular part of his anatomy that would prove his claims to things being anatomically possible. Torn jeans had still clung to his frame…

"So you're anatomically all proper and right, then?"

"Really, Kizzy?"

"Come on, I'm curious. Deal with it."

"I've a cock when in werewolf shape, yes. I'm pretty sure it's remarkably human-like too. Though when I'm in werewolf form my mind is ruled by the animal, so I don't generally sit about pondering my junk."

Kizzy couldn't help a little laugh, but she felt no mirth. "Sounds not right to me. A wolf and a human?"

"I am half animal, half man when in werewolf shape. I don't need to sell you on it. It's not ever going to happen with us. Promise." He winked at her.

And Kizzy held back a sigh. Sex with Bron was definitely on her radar. Not when he was in animal shape. But there were other werewolves who married humans? That had to make for an interesting bedside manner.

"So you're not sexually attracted to me?" she tossed out.

"What?"

"No desire to have sex with me? In your human form?"

"You just put it right out there, don't you?"

"Don't tell me you're a prude. Twenty-first century

girl here. And you're a big boy. We can talk about sex. It's okay."

"I know it's okay, and I'm mostly comfortable with this conversation, but everything about you surprises and challenges me."

"Good for me. But you're changing the topic. So much for 'mostly comfortable.'"

He sighed, then gestured with a thumbs-up. "I'd do you. Is that what you want to hear?"

"It is. I'd do you, too. Just so you know. Oh." Her phone vibrated, and she tugged it out. "Nightcat approved me."

"What does that mean?"

"That means…" she said as she scrolled through NightCat's Twitter profile "… I can now read all of his Tweets. Give me a few minutes. There's a lot. Hmm… He's named us both, Bron Everhart and Kizzy Lewis. That's weird that he knows so much."

"If he can communicate with others, and they are reporting to him, it's not implausible."

"Yes, but I haven't lived in Thief River for a while. I'm pretty much a stranger in town, just as you are." She scrolled up a few more Tweets and read a startling entry. "Everhart should be home with his wife?"

Heart dropping in her chest, Kizzy looked to him.

"What's that? Does it say that?"

Her mouth dropped open, and she almost let out a peep, but she was smart enough not to respond to his surprises with anything he'd take offensively. But really? "Are you married? You were just telling me about bonding…"

"Kizzy, relax. How does he have that information?"

"I don't know. Is it true? He also Tweeted that you've

pissed off the soul bringer. What's a soul bringer? But wait!" She stopped him just as he was opening his mouth to reply.

He pulled up to the speaker and a voice asked for his order.

"Wait for what?" Bron asked her.

"I think we'd better get the food and then sit down at a table," Kizzy said. "We've got a lot to talk about."

Chapter 11

After a couple sausage McMuffins and three orange juices, Bron wasn't compelled to immediately jump back in the truck and drive Kizzy home. The sky was bright, and they sat at a yellow plastic table out back of the restaurant near a thatch of woods that sported red-bark pines. The air smelled like freedom and lacking responsibility. And his inner wolf howled to go for a run.

One thing about all the traveling he did, he had to make time to get out in the open—away from the job—and surrender to the "being one with nature" thing. It was necessary to his very soul.

Three days. Then he'd let the wolf out. And in two days he'd need to have sex all night to sate the need to shift. If the mission continued on its course, running less than smoothly, he anticipated Kizzy still being around. How to handle that one? Their conversation had confirmed they were both interested in one another in a sexual way. He'd love to get busy with her. She was gorgeous, smart, and when she kissed him, he forgot himself.

And that was more dangerous to his well-being than going after a wraith demon unarmed. Because intimacy, well…it wasn't his forte.

But he owed her some answers because she'd put up with a crazy man dragging her all over without telling her much, save that he had been tasked to take her heart from her chest. That was unconscionable. But would she be forever pursued for her Purgatory Heart?

The sun glinted in Kizzy's eyes, and he noticed the freckles on her nose. Then he realized she was watching him watching her. And all he wanted to do was stare at her endlessly, maybe touch the few strands of hair that the wind blew across her forehead. Trace those freckles. Kiss her lips. Grasp for that relentlessly aspiring freedom. But there were reasons he'd never feel completely free, unyoked from the mistakes of his past.

And she deserved to know that reason.

"The wife," he muttered and clasped his hands before him.

Kizzy set down her soda cup and propped her chin on the back of her hand, giving him her full attention. No judgment in her brown eyes. No revulsion either.

"I married in 1840. Was married to my wife for fifteen years. Well…" Longer than that, considering he'd never officially divorced Claire. "I haven't heard from her since 1855. And…I never allowed myself to check up on her. To see if she's still alive."

"What? You just…left her?"

He nodded. "I had to. I was banished from my pack. And I was the pack leader at the time."

"Really? I guess that makes sense. Wolves run in packs. You were pack leader? I get that vibe from you. Go, alpha male."

"We alphas tend to have egos the size of football stadiums. Useful for standing as a leader and vowing to protect all. Not so useful when it comes to understanding the intricacies of an intimate relationship. I committed a grave crime against my wife and the pack. I was forced to leave. When a wolf is banished, he is tortured and the physical scars remain. And then he's forced out on his own, a lone wolf. No other wolves will associate with him if they know he's been banished."

"You don't have any werewolf friends?"

He shrugged. "A few I trust and who know they can, in turn, trust me."

She nodded, taking that in. "What did you do to your wife?"

"I had an affair," he offered. And it felt much easier saying it than he'd anticipated. Over the centuries he'd thought about it on occasion but had never allowed himself to dwell because that would reduce him to misery, self-blame and stupid regrets. "With a human woman."

"Oh. Is that taboo for werewolves? But you said some marry human women."

"Some do. And it's not taboo, per se. Having a child with a human woman can be, if you are the leader of a pack and are married."

Kizzy's jaw dropped. "You're a father?"

"I was."

"Oh, right, I'm sure if she was human she's long dead now, but once a father always a father."

"Kizzy, she—" He blew out his breath and braced himself for the horrible truth.

This was too much, too soon. But at the same time, the words spilled out because they needed escape from the cage in his core that he'd held locked for so long.

"I kept the child and the affair a secret, though I visited them often. The child, her name was Isabelle, was very smart. Too smart. One snowy winter evening a carriage arrived at the pack compound, and Isabelle was delivered to our doorstep. She told me her mother had died in a house fire. Isabelle had the wits to grab her mother's pearls and hire someone to bring her to me."

"Smart kid. I'm so sorry about her mother."

"Yes, well. With a human child standing in the compound I had to reveal all to the pack. And to my wife. Their disapproval was unanimous. All voted to have me ousted through banishment, and I had to agree. It's what I, as pack leader, would have commanded of any other wolf who had committed such a crime.

"I tried to talk to my wife, Claire, but she wouldn't allow it. The last words I said to her were Isabelle's name and that I hadn't intended for it to happen."

He scrubbed his hand across the back of his head and confessed quickly, "I was an asshole back then. Egotistical. Thought I ruled the world and could do as I pleased with whomever I pleased. It was sort of necessary to head a pack as an alpha. I was a force."

"I can see that in you."

"Really? Because I've changed considerably."

"I can see that, too. You've an innate but controlled sense of command about you. You own the ground you stand on. You won't take shit from anyone. And your word is fiercely honorable. So they forced you to leave the pack?"

"It's a sort of ritual, the banishment. The wolf is strung up before his pack members, and each of them go at him, in werewolf form, with their claws. Claws dipped in wolfsbane to ensure the wounds will scar and forever mark. It took hours. And during that torture I only hoped that Isabelle was safe and not being tormented by any of the younger pack members.

"After the ritual, I must have passed out. Blood loss. For most of the night I lay on a cold dirt floor in my own blood. And when I woke, I was allowed to clean myself up, pack some supplies and then was sent away on foot. When I asked to take Isabelle along with me, I was told she'd been sent away the day before, just as I was being brought to punishment."

"But you said it was winter," Kizzy said quickly.

Bron nodded. Bowed his head. His heart crushed, and he sucked in his upper lip. The cage was squeezing tighter. Why had he thought telling her this would be wise? The memory was so painful. His heart froze as cold as the night had been.

"It was January," he offered quietly, clasping his hands together to keep from revealing his shaking fingers. "Below zero weather, I'm sure."

"OhmyGod."

That gasp said so much. And Bron felt her distressed realization deeply. For the moment, he was transported back to that windy winter morning, the snow whipping across his face. His skin cold, yet his heart so much colder at the sight of what he'd found.

"Four hours after setting out from the pack compound I found Isabelle in the woods beneath a thick, exposed tree root. Frozen." He pressed a hand to his mouth and strained to keep the tears from his eyes.

And when Kizzy rose to stand beside him and leaned over to embrace him, he did allow a few tears to slip. Couldn't stop it. He'd loved Isabelle. And because of him, she had suffered. Her lips had been blue, her eyes frozen open in an accusatory stare up at him.

"She was an innocent," he whispered. "They had no right. But I was the reason she died. And so I've avoided human women since then."

"But it could have been any woman," she said softly. "Yes? You shouldn't blame all humans."

"Were Isabelle born to any other species she might have been accepted by the pack. If not for the affair, of course. Isabelle died because I was stupid and greedy and thought I could have anything I wanted because I was the pack leader. I told everyone else what to do. And I did care about my wife. I just didn't respect her as any woman deserves."

Kizzy's arms bracketed his chest, and she tilted her head to his shoulder. "So you punished yourself by becoming a virtual monk? When will you have suffered enough?"

"Never," he managed. "Isabelle deserves my constant penance."

"She's gone, Bron."

"Not from my heart."

And he stood, shrugging out of Kizzy's warm and welcome embrace, and marched to the back of the truck, needing to distance himself from her sweet, gentle understanding. From the fact that she hadn't cringed when he'd told her how cruel he had been to his wife. Why was she so…nice? So accepting of everything? She should run away from him. He could only bring her trouble. As had been proven thus far.

The passenger door slammed, and he turned to look inside the truck cab. Kizzy waved and gave him a warm smile.

What was that saying about drawing to you that which you needed most? Even if it annoyed the hell out of him, it was something a person was supposed to examine. No one entered another person's life for no reason. A man should either take that person's presence as a blessing or a lesson.

So what was Kizzy? A lesson in how to resist yet another human woman? Or a blessing come to forgive him his sins against his innocent daughter?

By all the gods, if he could go back and change that night, he would. He'd sacrifice his life to give Isabelle hers. He'd struggled over and over with this for years after walking away from the pack. Decades. And then he'd pulled up a shield of emotionless, monk-like resolve. And that was how he'd survived to this day.

So he'd put it out there, and he wasn't sure how he felt now. Better? Worse? Had she really needed to know? *Yes.*

Because something about Kisanthra Lewis made him want to be better. Made him want to rise up and meet her wondrous beliefs and show her that her fears were not all real. And he would. He needed to prove to her that werewolves could be kind and not monsters.

He gestured he was going inside the restaurant and bought two coffees to go, then returned to the truck. Kizzy kissed him on the cheek as she took the cup. "Thank you for telling me that. It means a lot that you trusted me."

"I don't want to talk about it anymore."

"I understand. I think we can head to my apartment. The Nightcat Tweeted that our location is currently unknown. That could be a good thing, yes?"

"Possibly the tracker is no longer sending out vibrations."

"Though he did mention the soul bringer again. That its wraith had been destroyed. Makes it sound like that demon with half a face was sent by this soul bringer person."

"I suspected it had been commanded by another force."

"What is a soul bringer?"

He shifted into gear and steered the truck onto the road that filed into the main part of town. "They were once angels. They Fell to this realm to become psychopomps."

"I've heard that term before. Aren't psychopomps the ones who usher dead souls to Heaven?"

"Above or Beneath. I have no idea why a soul bringer would be interested in your heart. I would assume he's already got entrance to Purgatory."

"Does he? You said Heaven or Hell. What if Purgatory is closed to him? Which still doesn't explain why he would want to go there. Do you think he sent someone to Purgatory by mistake?"

"I don't know much more than what I've told you. Were you able to learn the Nightcat's location?"

"He doesn't list one beyond the state, which is Minnesota. You think he could be here in Thief River Falls?"

"I'll place bets on it. Especially if he witnessed the

harpie attack. We may have to call him out. Can you do that with that Tweet thing?"

"I could."

"Save it. We'll drive by your apartment, but I think it wise we stay away for a little longer."

"Right. More motel beds. Love it."

He didn't miss the sarcasm. "Unless you prefer I drop you off?"

"No, I'm cool with not attracting too much attention. Let's pick up some new clothes at that Walmart just ahead and make a plan. And for sure, I need to buy a comb. I just checked the side mirror. Shouldn't have done that. I have Vampire Tilda hair."

He gave her a side glance. "Do I want to know?"

"Haven't you seen *Only Lovers Left Alive*?"

"I don't often have opportunity to watch movies."

"Oh, man, I love movies. Well, Tilda Swinton starred in a flick about centuries-old vampires. Her hair was long and white blond and always thick and messy, like it hadn't been combed in decades. I kept thinking to myself, she's lived centuries. Certainly by now she should have developed a grooming routine. Anyway—" Kizzy tugged out a clump of her decidedly tangled hair "—Vampire Tilda hair."

"A comb it is, then."

At the Walmart, Kizzy bought some shockingly cheap jeans, a toothbrush and paste, and a comb, and some protein bars and bottled water. They drove through town on Main Street. A glance toward the windows on her third-story rental did not indicate anything suspicious. Still, much as she was so over the motel rooms, she felt it would be safer to give it another day before attempting a return. They had the afternoon to sit around and do some research on soul bringers and to try and locate Nightcat.

Bron found a room at the edge of town. The receptionist recognized Kizzy and gave her the eye. They'd graduated the same year and had shared an interest in art. She sized up Bron from head to crotch and smirked knowingly. Kizzy didn't say anything beyond a friendly hello, but she did grab Bron's hand, kiss him on the cheek and walk out with the key in hand.

"Sorry," she offered as they strode toward the room. "I know what she was thinking, so I gave her something to think about. Couldn't resist."

"What was she thinking?"

"Oh, please, Bron. You may have been born in the nineteenth century, but you've been around. You saw that look she gave us."

"I did. I thought she was laughing inwardly at your Vampire Tilda hair."

"What?" Kizzy gaped. "You totally missed her eyeing you like a piece of meat? She thought we were lovers. Vampire Tilda hair?" She punched him on the bicep. "Teaser." They entered the room, and she tossed her bag aside while Bron headed to the window to scope out the area. "Seriously? No TV or movies?"

"I've had occasion to watch a movie or two since they started filming them in color," he offered.

In color? Mercy, the guy was an old man, and he didn't even realize it.

"A few months ago on a transatlantic flight," he continued, "I sat next to a four-year-old. She thought she was so clever to allow me to watch *Frozen* with her."

"You watched a kids' movie?"

Bron cleared his throat and, pressing one hand to his chest, belted out rather modestly, "Let it go, let it go!"

Kizzy's jaw dropped, but then she clapped her hands together. "I love you! Ha! No, I mean, I love that you just did that. Not like real love. Oh—hell. Just shut up, Kizzy." She sighed heavily at her faux pas, but then summoned a smile. "I bet it's pretty rare that you show anyone your spontaneous fun side."

He tugged down the brim of his hat, assuming his usual stoic profile. "I don't have a fun side."

"Dude, you just sang a line from a movie loved worldwide by four-year-old girls. I'd call that fun. And it really makes me want to do this."

She kissed him quickly. It was sweet and teasing. Long enough to taste him and feel him pull her closer, but short enough to spark the reminder that she needed to be cautious with him and his carefully guarded emotions.

"What was that for?" he asked. "Letting it go?"

"That. And you did say you liked kissing me. Are you going to pass up my kisses now?"

"Never."

"Another?"

"How about I run and get us something to eat?"

"You're hungry again?"

"Breakfast was hours ago. And, yes, I have a healthy appetite. While I'm gone, you go through Twitter and report back to me all the things we need to know. And then we'll work on a plan of attack."

"With kisses?"

He leaned in and kissed the corner of her mouth. "With kisses. What are you in the mood for?"

"Pizza. Lots of cheese."

"Lots of cheese, it is. I'll be back." As he exited he asked Siri for the nearest pizza place.

Chapter 12

The savory odor of tomato sauce and pepperoni crept under the bathroom door. Kizzy combed her hair and was going to brush her teeth, but she'd save that until after eating. Her daily clock had been screwed up, so—showering in the middle of the day? Seemed legit. Besides, she had washed some bits of grass out of her hair. Vampire Tilda hair, indeed.

Bron had left before she'd gone into the shower and… she'd left her new clothes out on the bed. She tucked in the towel at her chest and studied her reflection. The towel was thin, but it was long and went to her thighs. It covered all the important parts while still leaving enough to be desired. She could call out and have Bron hand the clothes in to her.

Or she could wander out and give him something to desire.

"Plan B, coming right up," she whispered with a wicked grin.

She strode out and caught him with a slice of pizza in his mouth. He looked over the triangle of cheese and sauce, and his eyes grew wider.

"Good?" she asked and sat on the end of the bed and picked up her own slice. "Extra cheese. Yes!"

He mumbled something that sounded agreeable. He sat on the other side of the pizza box. His eyes strayed toward her thigh, exposed by the parted towel. If desire had a scent, it was cheese and pepperoni. She liked making him uncomfortable.

And then she felt a wave of guilt. After everything he'd told her about his affair and Isabelle's death? What was she doing?

She set down the piece from which she'd taken a bite on the cardboard-box cover. "Be right back."

Kizzy grabbed the bag of clothes and returned to the bathroom to dress. So she'd played things wrong just now. Much as he'd given her the eye, it had felt off. She was out of practice. Who would have thought her first dive into dating after the accident would be with a werewolf? Wouldn't that give the chick at the reception desk something to gossip about?

She shook her head at her reflection in the mirror. Much as she'd spent years trying to convince others that the otherworldly existed, she wasn't stupid. She'd protect Bron's identity. He'd earned that trust from her.

The jeans were cheap but comfy, and she'd found a T-shirt with a *Game of Thrones* logo on it. Would winter *ever* come? Good enough for now.

She returned to the main room, picked up her slice

and sat on the chair, propping her feet up on the bed. "So now we work out the game plan, right?"

"Yes. This sitting about waiting thing is not my norm." He finished off another slice. "I need to move. Be actively involved in whatever the mission demands of me."

"You are actively protecting me. That's something."

"Sure."

So little enthusiasm in that reply. She brushed the pizza-crust crumbs from her fingers onto the sides of the chair, then tossed her wet hair over a shoulder. On the pillow sat her camera, so she picked that up and clicked through the most recent shots.

"It's a marvel, the cameras nowadays," Bron said, picking up another slice.

"Nowadays. OhmyGod, you really are an old man." She couldn't help a chuckle.

"I prefer mature."

"I'll give you that. You look like a thirty-year-old. So, were you around when cameras were invented?"

"I think they were invented just before I was born. I didn't have opportunity or the interest in one until around, hmm…1880? Give or take a few years. It was a camera obscura. About this big." He held his hands to encompass a square shape the size of a hardcover book. "I didn't know how to develop the photographs, nor had I the time, so I took them to a friend who owned a photography business close to Hyde Park in London. It was a lot of work, and as I've said, I never stayed in one place for long, and toting along one of those big things wasn't practical. I didn't get my next camera until probably the 1950s. A Kodak."

"Black and white?"

"You bet. I favor the black-and-white images over color."

"Memories?"

"No, just more impactful. The eye doesn't get distracted by thousands of colorful details. Though I do like the cameras nowadays that transfer the pictures directly to the laptop. Technology." He shook his head in wonder and leaned back on his hands. But one slice of pizza remained in the box.

And now Kizzy noticed Bron didn't look at her so much as scent her. Yes, she could tell when he was reading things around him. His nostrils flared, and his eyelids shuttered. He could probably read the world by scent. Cool werewolf stuff.

"What's that like?" she asked. "Your senses? I notice you smelling things a lot."

He closed the pizza box and got up to set it outside the door, leaving the door open to stand in the threshold. The summer afternoon offered the occasional *whoosh* of a passing car on the highway and a scatter of crickets nestled somewhere within the unmown grass edging the motel parking lot. The promise of rain thickened the air.

"I navigate by smell," he said. Brushing the thick hair from his eyes, he closed them and tilted back his head. "I start close and move out. Garlic and oregano in the pizza. Your mint toothpaste and the chemicals lingering in your hair from the motel shampoo. Your skin…smells warm."

"What does warm smell like?"

He shrugged, eyes still closed. "You know it when you scent it. It's good. Sweet. Sensual." He let that word hang between them. Kizzy could feel it brush her skin as if he'd touched her. "And then there's the tarmac stained with various oils from decades of parked cars. Stale beer in the garbage can down near the registration office. Animal droppings in the grass. Mold growing on the poplar trees across the highway. Gasoline. Building materials. Birds. Bees. Ozone. I can smell it all."

"That must be overwhelming."

He stepped back inside and squatted, this time sitting in the threshold, his long legs splaying out across the loud blue carpet before him. "I can turn it down. Zone out the nuisance smells and focus on only those most important. Like you."

His smile was easy, and it stayed on his mouth for a while as his eyes wandered everywhere but to her.

"My coming out in a towel before bothered you," she guessed. "I did it on purpose."

"I knew that." His smile widened, but more so, his eyes glittered with an unspoken challenge. "And it didn't bother me. I'd consider it a tease if I weren't familiar with you. You weren't teasing. Were you?"

Now he looked at her with those piercing blue eyes, and Kizzy's heart fluttered like a hummingbird's wings.

She shook her head. "Nope, not teasing. But then, I remembered what we'd talked about at the McDonald's."

"Ah." He bowed his head.

"I don't want to misstep with you, Bron. I told you already that I like you. I like what's going on with us. I mean, the part where we're not running from villains. Talk about a crazy first date. And I really do apologize about my reaction after kissing you when we were on the bed. Everything is happening quickly. And I like that. It feels natural. One day I was walking through the park with my camera, I turned around and there you were. Ohmygosh. There you were."

"I was tracking you."

"Right. But that's what my mother once said to me."

"What?"

"I'd turn around and he would be standing there."

"He?"

She nodded.

"I'm not following, Kizzy."

"You don't have to." Because he might think her crazy if she did explain that one. Mom had been right. Because there he had stood. A man she might like to have in her life. Yes, really. A *werewolf.* Was Bron the man her mother had predicted would be there for her someday? Still too soon to tell. But she wanted to keep him around long enough to find out.

He bent up his knees and propped his elbows on them, hands hanging loosely before his legs. Sunshine glossed his hair. It looked rich and thick and so decadent. She could happily get lost in his hair.

Kizzy wasn't sure what he was thinking right now as his brows narrowed and he awaited her explanation. Should she recant her confession? Did it make him uncomfortable? She knew he had an aversion to human women. But to carry it for so long? Since the mid-nineteenth century? Seemed as if it was time for him to get back into the swing of all a human could offer him.

Which probably wasn't much. Werewolf-on-werewolf sex was most likely the ultimate for him. Pair him with some other kind of paranormal creature, and he'd probably be just as happy. But a boring old human?

Why was she so concerned about his love life?

Holy Hannah, she wanted sex. And she wanted to get it on with Bron. She never should have kissed him.

That intimate connection had sparked a flame that she was now aware glimmered within her.

It had been almost a month since she'd hooked up with a cute young plastics artist in Brussels. They'd had supper and drinks, but she'd decided against going home with him. Hadn't liked his smoking. So she'd seriously gone without sex for eight months, and right now, she was horny. She needed some touching. She wasn't looking for a relationship or a ring or even forever. Sometimes she just needed to get close to a man and lose herself in him. Didn't everyone crave human touch?

"Bron? What's going on inside that brain of yours?"

"Too much."

"I understand. Oh, man, do I understand." She shifted on the chair. Her body hummed for his attention. And parts of her were relaxing and growing moist. She could imagine his beard gliding along her thigh, his mouth getting ever so close—

"You might understand a little but not all," he said.

"Hey, it was just something I needed to put out there. We are adults. We both know sex can happen without happily-ever-after. I'm feeling needy and—okay, the truth?—horny. And—"

"Kizzy."

His abrupt tone made her clutch the front of her shirt.

He tilted his head in a "come here" gesture. "Don't tell me what you want. Just show me."

She wasn't going to argue that invitation. Sliding off the chair, she walked over and knelt before him. "Seriously? Right here, with the door open?"

He pulled her to him with a hand to the back of her head, and the kiss chased away further protest. What had she been protesting? Who cared! His mouth on hers made everything else unimportant. And he went up on his knees and somehow managed to lift her as he stood and kicked the door closed at the same time. He laid her on the bed and crawled over her body, without breaking the kiss.

But he had asked her to show him, so she pushed his shoulder down, turning him onto his back, and climbed over him. She unbuttoned his shirt and glided her fingers over his chest. The short black hairs were soft and thick but didn't disguise the incredible hard muscles that pulsed with his movement.

"I like all this," she said and kissed his chest. "You're like a big loveable bear."

"I prefer wolf." He propped up on his elbows and kicked off his unlaced boots.

"Do you howl when you come?" she asked, and then felt a little embarrassed by the question. "Sorry."

He pulled her up to kiss her. "I guess you'll find out, won't you?"

His tongue dashed across her lips, and she followed the tease, pressing her mouth to his and dancing her tongue with his. He tasted only a little like pizza and more like the outdoors. Fresh air. He was a creature of nature. And this time, to think about creatures didn't offend her. She wouldn't allow it to.

He kissed her again quickly, then asked, "Are you on the pill?"

"Yes."

She almost asked him if it was okay that she was human, but then nixed that. Why bring it up if it might only make him think? Mindless was the best way to experience sex. No, not mindless, but unfocused and lost in the sensations was a good vibe to have.

Mmm, like the gentle tickle of his fingers gliding up her arm and to her shoulders, where he clutched her hair beside her jaw and held her against his deep and lingering kiss. The command of him deepened her desire and melted her muscles. She straddled his hips, and the summer breeze blowing in from the open window crept up under her shirt, whispering between her breasts, where her pulse beats thumped. And lower, between her legs, her body hummed in aching want.

Shoving the shirt up over his shoulders, she wanted it off him as quickly as possible. Skin against skin, baby. He tossed it to the floor. Mercy, those pecs were hard and tight. She aimed her greedy touch for his pants, unbuttoning, unzipping and searching beneath the taut, hard landscape of his lower abdomen and a thick tuft of dark hair.

He lifted her shirt, and she peeled it off to reveal her breasts. Bowing his head, he kissed the top of the surgical scar and then glanced up to her when she gasped.

"No one has ever done that before," she whispered.

"It hurts me that you had to suffer because of another man's anger."

"Let's not talk about that."

"Do you want me to not touch you here?"

"No, it's okay. I trust you."

She pressed her hard nipples against his chest, and he moaned and glided his hands up the backs of her thighs to cup her derriere. Firmly, as if she were his and let no one think otherwise. She nuzzled her mons against his groin and felt the tickle of his pubic hair and his hard erection strain against his jeans.

His hands slid down her jeans and quickly tugged

them off. He tossed them aside and suddenly flipped her onto her back.

"Whoa!" Kizzy cried. "I thought I was supposed to do the showing?"

He shoved down his jeans. "I have a pretty good idea of what you want."

His erection sprang free, and she gasped. Because it was gasp worthy. She reached for his penis, thrusting up from a dark nest of curls, and clasped it firmly. It was hot and solid, and she briefly thought of the stakes he'd wielded to kill the vampires. Oh, man, please, let him slay her with this weapon.

"You see," he said, kicking aside the jeans. "I knew you'd be interested."

"This is nice. What am I saying? It's awesome."

He lowered over her, pressing the thick rod between them as he kissed her breasts and suckled her nipples. He danced kisses along her scar as well, and it felt as though he were sealing away all the darkness behind the reason for getting that scar in the first place. Sweet. Caring. Right.

Kizzy closed her eyes and ran her fingers through his soft hair. As decadent as she'd guessed it would be. The sensation of his mouth at her nipple strafed through her system, bringing all systems to ultra-alert. And the added tickle of his beard over her skin sweetened the feeling. Her core hummed and her toes curled. Her scalp prickled at every lash of his tongue over her skin.

"You do that so well," she whispered. He sucked a little harder, gently teasing her with his teeth. "Mmm, yes."

Wrapping her legs about his hips, she rocked her loins against his, eliciting a throat-deep moan from him at her breasts. He thumbed a nipple and squeezed it, and she responded by pulling his head down to show him she liked it a little rough.

Rolling her hips, she worked her aching clit up against the hot column that jutted against her folds. Wet and wanting, she slicked against him, and that made him swear against her breast. She liked the rough sound of his desire, of his want, of his failing control.

The stoic protector was losing himself in her.

She gripped his penis and squeezed the head of it, noting the thick fold of his foreskin that had slipped down beneath the corona. A few tugs up and down seemed to coax it impossibly harder. Then she pulled her tightly coved fingers the length of him. He was so thick. She pressed him against her clit, slicking it and sliding it lower to tease at her opening.

"Kizzy…" He pressed his forehead to her shoulder. She'd assumed control of him, and she wasn't about to renege. "Please."

He pushed his cock through her circled fingers and she squeezed firmly, spurring him to push faster. One of his hands made its way down to her clit, and his thumb slicked over that sensitive, wanting part of her.

"Yes," she hissed. "Inside me. Now."

She guided him inside her while he rubbed and teased and pinched her clitoris. His entry was hot, determined, solid. He burned into her, and she felt him fire through her body. Clinging to his arms, she dug in her nails, and he hissed at that but only increased his speed, thrusting, searing, finding his way into her soul.

"Kizzy, you are so tight. Good inside you. Have to… come…"

"Yes," she gasped because she felt the orgasm building inside her, and if he came then, she would, too. She was on the pill. No worries. *Just make it good.* So good. And hot. "Faster, Bron."

He leaned up on his palms, meeting her gaze. His jaw tight, the ecstatic agony on his face must have matched her own. She pressed a hand against his chest and curled her fingers into the hair. And with one hard, deep thrust, he chuffed out a shout. His body shuddered, his hips trembling against hers. He came hot inside her, and Kizzy closed her eyes as the climax surged through her. Her shoulders pressed into the bed, and she cried out. Above her a magnificent creature shared her joy.

Chapter 13

In the morning, Bron rolled over and snuggled up next to the warm, naked body stretched out beside him. Kizzy's hair spilled over his face, and he inhaled the soft sweetness of it. This wasn't Vampire Tilda hair. Not by a long shot. Lush and full, it felt like a retreat into a place he'd like to spend a lot of time.

He didn't move to tug her closer. It was early. Not five yet. They'd had sex until the sun had set, and then they'd pulled out the cell phones and tried to track Nightcat, to little success. So, more sex it had been. Kizzy had drifted to sleep just before midnight, while he'd lain watching her for a while.

Now he wanted her to sleep. She'd been through a lot in the past few days.

As had he. What the hell was he doing? Sleeping with a human? That was okay. The occasional one-night stand with a human woman could be overlooked. Nothing would ever come of it.

But was this thing with Kizzy nothing? A guy didn't lie in bed watching the woman he'd just had sex with for no reason. And if he was honest with himself, he didn't want it to be nothing. Maybe? He shouldn't have had sex with her.

No, skip that stupid guilt stuff. Casual sex was not something he beat himself up about. As she'd said, it was something they'd both wanted. People hooked up all the time without picking out wedding stationery and tuxedos. It was a natural urge that he was pleased to have fulfilled with her.

Pleased? What a way to think about it. It had been hot, sweaty, messy and all kinds of right. And he wouldn't regret it. Nor would he dwell on what was to come next. He'd let it go. Play it by ear. See where she went with it.

Yeah, that was the way to do it. Let the woman take the lead. He had enough to worry about with some potential cat-shifting familiar reporting his location to any paranormal who had a Twitter account and urging them to rip out Kizzy's heart.

And the soul bringer. How did a soul bringer figure into all this? If gaining the key to Purgatory meant letting out souls to begin some kind of hell on earth, that made little sense to Bron. Hadn't the soul bringer put them there in the first place?

He wondered why the director hadn't gotten back to him regarding the mission. Surely it would be canceled. He'd check his email when he got up.

But for now, with darkness still filling the window and the compelling warmth of Kizzy seeping into his pores, he was content to kiss her between the shoulder blades and close his eyes as he nestled his cheek against her skin to breathe her in.

Kizzy rolled over into a kiss. She hadn't planned it, but he was right there, and her lips had simply migrated toward his. It was a slow, lazy kiss that didn't open their mouths. Bron felt great. Right. Strong and powerful. He moved his hand along her back, urging her to snuggle against his body, and she tangled her legs with his.

Drawing his fingers down the scar on her chest, he tapped it softly. "You're perfect."

She didn't know what to do with that compliment, so she went with a sigh and kissed his neck. His erection beat a few taps against her belly, and with a laugh she answered the call and shimmied up to adjust her position and allow him to glide his penis between her legs. He hugged his face against her neck, kissing her as he moved within her, with slow, sure, measured thrusts. She hadn't been quite wet, but that problem was quickly resolved as he thumbed her nipple, sending a shock wave of erotic energy directly to her core. It was as though he'd lit her on fire, and she would gladly burn them both to oblivion.

"'Morning," he muttered and tilted his head to kiss her under the chin.

"Good morning. Do we have to go out into the world and fight creatures today? Can we just stay here? Doing this. All day?"

"As my lady desires."

And he came quietly, shuddering against her, clutching at her hips, her arms, her hair. And with a kiss to the side of her mouth, he pulled out and rolled to his back. "Gotta brush my teeth so I can kiss you properly," he said.

"How about we meet in the shower?"

"It's small."

"We'll fit."

"Give me a minute first."

He dashed off to the bathroom, and with the door closed, she heard him pee. Gliding her hand over the sheet, she mined the remnants of his body heat, then pushed her nose into his pillow and inhaled. God, he smelled good. Wild, even. The shower started, and she got up and tiptoed into the bathroom. Bron was just entering the stall when she noticed his back.

"OhmyGod." A swallow choked her, and she slapped a palm over her mouth.

"What?" He turned under the shower stream, the water soaking his hair over his forehead. He offered a hand to her. "Kizzy?"

"Your back. I didn't notice it last night. Bron?"

"Ah." He rubbed a shoulder and tilted it forward, though she couldn't see what she'd just seen with him facing her. "I told you about the banishment. The scars left behind have worn smooth over the years. Probably why you didn't feel them."

"Turn around." She joined him under the warm shower stream. "Let me touch you."

"I don't know… It's nothing, Kizzy. The past."

"Please, Bron." She moved around behind him, and he allowed it, pressing a palm high on the shower wall.

A lattice of scars covered his upper and lower back. How she'd not noticed last night was beyond her, but then she hadn't been behind him, only beneath him and on top of him. She dared to touch a thick red line slickened with water. It wasn't raised, as she'd expect from a scar, and felt rather smooth, though the skin was red and clearly showed trauma.

"Werewolves heal remarkably quickly. Except wounds poisoned with wolfsbane," he commented, pressing a hand to the shower wall and bowing his head forward under the stream. "I forget about them most of the time. Until a woman notices them."

"So you don't walk around on beaches with your shirt off?"

"We haven't known each other long, but I wager you can guess I'm not much of a beach bum."

"I do know that. More of an Indiana Jones kind of wolf. Why the wolfsbane?"

"To ensure scars. So I will forever wear the mark of a banished wolf."

She swallowed hard. Tears mixed with water. He was so unemotional about it. But she imagined he'd had a long time to get over the pain of it. "Do they hurt?"

"No. Sometimes I'll stretch my back muscles oddly and feel a twinge. That's when I remember. And…think about Isabelle."

"I'm so sorry." She wrapped her arms about his torso, her fingers gliding over his rigid abs, and hugged her cheek against the awful scars. "I wish I could make it better for you."

He chuckled softly. "It was a long time ago, Kizzy."

"But you still don't feel as if you've been forgiven for what happened."

He nodded, and his back muscles flexed against her body. "You hit that one right on the mark." His words came out softly. He was remembering.

And she simply held him there beneath the warm

shower spray. She was no one to provide forgiveness. A person had to do that for themselves.

Would she ever allow herself to forgive that night of the accident?

Bron's hand slid up and traced her scar. "I wish I could smooth this for you, but I suspect you would not be the same woman you are today if you had not gotten it. And that woman is amazing."

And that observation made her want to forgive, so she could be that person he suspected she was.

It was well after noon when Bron suggested they find a place to eat because they could not survive on sex alone. Kizzy was inclined to agree, though she bet she could last until nightfall, fueled exclusively by sex. Every muscle in her body felt deliciously achy, and her limbs were stretched and well worked.

Pulling on a pair of jeans and the *Game of Thrones* T-shirt, she watched as Bron drew up his pants, adjusting his semi-hard erection to the left. He cast a wink over his shoulder at her. "What?"

"You're cute," she said. "A sexy wolf of a guy. But I didn't hear you howl once when we were having sex."

"Didn't want to wake the neighbors. In a few more nights I'll howl."

"Is that when you said you needed to have sex so you wouldn't shift into a werewolf?"

"Yes. I thought I'd have this mission completed and be back home in Germany by then. I own a vast wooded lot close to the French border. Lots of forest in which to wolf out. It's my go-to place for the full moon."

"What will you do if you're still here on the night of the full moon?"

"Head for a wooded area. Pray there are no campers."

"You wouldn't attack them?"

"Kizzy." He tugged on a short-sleeve gray canvas shirt. "Don't you know me better by now?"

"Right. You wouldn't harm a human. But when you are a werewolf, are you like, in your man's brain? How does that work? How do you know not to harm someone?"

"I'm sort of a man/beast in that form. I think as an animal, but I also have thoughts as a man. It's hard to explain. I can't really understand human language, but the tone of it comes across to me. Nor can I speak. As a wolf on four legs and scampering about? I'm all animal. If I were around you in that form I'd recognize your scent and that you mean something to me, but that is all. In werewolf form, I'd know you."

"I mean something to you?"

He paused as he was lacing up his boots. "Hmm?"

"You just said I meant something to you."

"I did?"

She nodded.

"Yes, well… Yes," he offered decidedly, "you do." He pulled on his other boot and laced it up, then grabbed the panama hat and placed it at a smart angle over his brows. Tugging the truck keys from his pocket, he said, "You'll have to recommend a good place to eat. I'll bring our stuff out to the truck. We'll swing by your place after we eat lunch."

And he strode out, without another comment about what she meant to him. But he'd admitted it. And that was enough for Kizzy. Because she wanted to mean something to him. Which made her believe she was falling for him. Love? It was a difficult emotion for her to define. She tended to avoid the word simply because people used it so freely.

Admiration, respect, trust, honor, integrity. Those were the things that attracted her to a man. And Bron possessed them in spades. He was distant yet loving. Focused yet able to confide and expose his darkest secret to her. And if that wasn't enough, he had sung "Let It Go" to her. She didn't even know what to do with that one. It was a good thing, no matter.

The scars on his back had faded over the centuries, but to know that he had suffered hurt her heart. It was a suffering he had brought upon himself, but no man should have to find his daughter dead. No matter what he had done.

The man held much guilt for that. She could relate. He had been broken and scarred, as had she. And she wasn't sure she could fix either of them. Well, she didn't want to fix Bron. He had to do that for himself. She just wanted to be a part of him.

"Kizzy?"

"I'm coming!"

She picked up her camera bag and her makeshift suitcase/Walmart bag and recalled his warning that she must erase the photos she'd taken of him in werewolf shape. She would. But perhaps she'd send copies to her computer first. It would be insane to toss such amazing evidence. He wouldn't have to know. And no one else would either. The photographic evidence of a werewolf would be her secret.

Chapter 14

After lunch at the local Chinese buffet, Bron parked the truck before Kizzy's building in the center of town. He stared up the side of the three-story structure, which boasted a café on the main level, a craft shop on the second and apartments on the top. The brick front was laced with a climbing vine that had turned crimson with autumn. A clatter of bikes were chained up to the street pole.

"What do you think?" she asked.

"I'm not sure. You haven't had anything come after you for a day."

"That's something. I seriously don't think I can do another cheesy motel room. I'm starting to feel like Sam or Dean."

"Why would you feel like a man?"

"Sam and Dean hunt monsters and stay in cheesy motel rooms."

He narrowed a brow. "You *know* monster hunters? Weren't you talking about those men earlier?"

"Probably. They are on a TV show," she offered with a kiss to his cheek. "They've got nothing on Bron Everhart, the Retriever with the sexy abs and Indiana Jones hat. That's another movie—"

"I know. I've seen that flick. Preposterous, but good entertainment."

"You must get all the entertainment you can handle from your job."

"That I do." He pushed the driver's side door open and got out. Before closing the door he said, "Stay behind me."

When Bron swung around the front of the vehicle, she noticed he carried a bowie knife. Not cool in this small town. But he didn't swish it in front of him, so she'd give him the benefit of his cool, calm discretion.

Kizzy felt like the curious heroine following the intrepid hero into danger as they walked through the doorway and down the long, narrow hallway to the stairway at the back of the building. It was cool in here, thanks to the brick walls. The back door opened to a teeny courtyard, where the landlord, Mrs. Davidson's hydrangeas still burst with pale violet petals.

"Top floor?" he asked.

"Yep. Only apartment up there. Here's my key." She handed him the brass key chain, which featured the demonic symbol Sam and Dean both had tattooed on their left shoulders. So she was a fangirl.

Bron took the stairs two at a time, and she scrambled up after him. She didn't know what she looked forward to more. An empty apartment so she could relax and change into her own clothes. Or making a peanut butter and jelly sandwich. Or even taking a shower in a clean, noncheesy bathroom. But dare she risk any of that? If nothing waited for her in the apartment, that didn't mean something might not eventually show up. With claws.

Bron stuck the key in the lock and opened it. He gestured for her silence and to stay by the door, with a finger to his lips while he walked in and checked the place out.

Feeling nervous standing alone by the door, Kizzy crept in until she stood in the living room that featured windows all along the front wall and which looked over the newspaper office that sat below and across the street. Nothing seemed out of place. The rental wasn't accented with knickknacks or a lot of decorative items. Dishware was minimal, set in the open cupboards. Though the landlord had prettied up the place with a spider plant hung between the two front windows. It was frothy and thick and must have weighed thirty pounds. As per instructions, Kizzy had dutifully watered it upon arrival.

Bron returned from back in the bedroom. "Nothing. But I don't think we should stay long. You check Twitter again?"

"Doing it right now. There's food and drink in the fridge. Help yourself." Though they'd just eaten, she could never not offer hospitality. One did not grow up in Minnesota without getting the "nice" label attached to them.

Bron stood before the windows, searching the area. Ribbons of gray dashed the sky. It was still early in the afternoon, and it hadn't rained yet.

Nightcat's Twitter stream hadn't posted anything

new since yesterday morning. Last post stated no known location for the Purgatory Heart.

Kizzy sneered at the cell phone. She hated being referred to as an object. Although they weren't exactly referring to her, but rather, just her heart. A heart *not* in her body.

Did it have to be out of her body to provide the gateway to Purgatory? Maybe it could function intact?

Panic caused her to say quickly, "I really want to keep my heart." She met Bron's curious lift of brow. "I don't want to die. I especially don't want anyone to rip out my heart. There's got to be some way to make this all stop."

"Hey." He wrapped his arms around her and snuggled her against his lean, hard body.

The hug felt great, and she hadn't realized she'd missed feeling the beat of his heart against hers so much. It had only been a few hours since they'd been in the motel making love. She needed him again. Around her. Inside her. Within her. He satisfied a craving she never knew she could have. One for such intimacy that, she felt, without it, it wouldn't matter if she no longer had her heart. She didn't want to need it, but damn her, she did.

"I'm not going to let anything hurt you," he said and kissed the crown of her head. "You can keep possession of your weird handprinted heart. I'll make sure no one has any reason to want it."

"And how will you do that? Why does someone want to go to Purgatory?"

"If there's a soul bringer involved, it could be for any reason. Nothing on Twitter?"

"No. Do you think it's safe to take a shower? I crave

the water pressure and changing into my comfortable jeans."

"Go for it. I'd join you but I should keep an eye open for…you know."

"You really think it's dangerous?"

"I don't know. Go." He kissed her quickly. "Do you have a laptop? I might go online and do some research on the soul bringer."

She pointed to the laptop sitting on the counter near a cereal box. "Beer's in the fridge. Give me a leisurely half an hour, and then I'll be back, refreshed and in my own clothes."

"Take your time!" he called as she sailed down the hallway to the bedroom.

Stripping off the bargain clothing, she decided she didn't ever want to wear the seven-dollar jeans again, so after they'd been washed she'd donate them. In the bathroom she turned on the shower to warm it up, then tugged out the little refillable bottle of orange-scented body wash she always tucked in her travel bag. That would give the werewolf's senses something to devour.

While the shower pattered, Bron found a beer in the fridge, thankful it was a dark Belgian ale, and tilted back half in one swallow. That hit the spot. He'd never have pegged Kizzy for a beer fan. Maybe she might like to try the authentic craft brews in Germany, and he might like taking her around to try them.

Did that imply a date in the future? The concept of dating wasn't even on his radar. But spending more time with Kizzy was alluring. Of course, he didn't have the time for it. Not when he was gallivanting across the world. Though, she did seem open to travel.

She'd come here from Brussels. Europe must be her home base. But she must have traveled to her hometown for a reason. Friends? The site of the accident? He guessed she wasn't as ready to begin the carefree traveler's life as she thought.

The street she stayed on was a main road just a few blocks down from the central shops and city buildings. He didn't see anything in the sky or notice any suspicious individuals walking the sidewalk below, but he sat on the foot-wide windowsill anyway and kept a casual watch as he dragged the laptop onto his lap.

First line of business? He typed in Kizzy's name, and her blog scrolled on to the screen. "*Other Wonders*," he muttered the blog title. The header was a shocking picture that he initially took for faery wings silhouetted by a pink-and-violet sunset.

He squinted and tilted the screen back for a better view. Wow. That really was some fabulous photography. She'd captured the intricate veins of a tree leaf, made virtually clear from the backlighting. It really did look like a faery wing, because it didn't resemble a butterfly or dragonfly. And a swish of blond that simulated faery hair must be some kind of moss hanging in the tree.

The top post was titled, "Sunny Outlook." The pictures were of bright yellow flowers he had no name for, yet they could be daisies or sunflowers. Set between the long green flowers' stems were a pair of eyes. Gold eyes that looked ready to pounce.

Or *were* those eyes? He tilted the screen again and studied the photo closely. Could be some kind of dried seed pods making up the eyes, but they looked so realistic. Like an animal or creature that lurked in myth and legend.

Yet another photo, rendered in black and white, featured a misty forest. A beam of sunshine swept down, but within the mist perhaps an elemental or forest sprite zipped by.

How cool was it that she'd taken to finding the otherworldly in common nature?

"Impressive," he said.

His cell phone rang, and he answered even as he typed in a new search for "soul bringer." It was the director. "Everhart, you still at the sight?"

"Yes. Keeping watch over the subject. There's been increased activity from many trying to put their hands on the heart."

"And a soul bringer, eh?"

How Pierce knew about that wasn't something Bron would question. Acquisitions boasted an elaborate database, and their network threaded worldwide. With witchcraft involved in Systems Tech, anything was possible.

"Haven't made contact with that particular subject yet, but I've heard about it. You have anything on a cat shifter?"

"No, but, listen, Everhart, if you are unable to somehow deactivate the Purgatory Heart, we'll have to alter the mission to find and finish. Got that?"

"Uh…deactivate?" he muttered, even as his heart dropped to his gut and the laptop slipped from his grasp to land on the windowsill with a thunk. Wouldn't deactivating a beating heart mean the same as finishing it? "I'm not sure I follow."

"Make it useless. Unable to open the door to Purgatory. You've rendered items useless on previous missions."

Yes, but that had involved breaking them or using a spell to obliterate the object to ash. He wasn't about to do that to Kizzy's heart. But if not, the mission would be altered to find and finish, which meant he would have to finish her. Either way, it didn't look good for her. Or him.

"Understood?" The director waited for his reply.

"Uh…yes," he muttered.

"Deactivate the heart and get your ass back to headquarters. I'll hook you up with whatever new job we have upon your return." The connection clicked off.

Bron stared at the phone until the screen went dark. Exactly how his heart felt. A worrying darkness falling over it.

"Ah, you found the beer. Good call. I think I'll have one, too."

Kizzy breezed by him in something so short he bet the bottom of her ass showed. He didn't want to look at her. Because when he did, she would know what was going on in his brain. She had a weird sense of his emotions.

And yet he couldn't avoid drawing in the delicious aroma that clung to her. Oranges and steam. He didn't have to look to mentally curve his fingers beneath her bottom and draw her closer. To press his nose against her thigh and inhale as he curled his fingers around and between her legs.

Deactivate. That word aggravated the sensual fantasy. Only three instances in his service to Acquisitions had he been issued such orders. And he'd fulfilled them without question. Because that was what he did. He was a Retriever. And if an object, or a person related to that object—or who *was* the object—presented problems, then he took care of it, as commanded.

He kept a bowie knife with his supplies. All he needed to do was shove the blade into her heart…

Kizzy kissed his cheek, and he startled. He stood abruptly and paced to the center of the living room before the L-shaped beige sofa and scruffed fingers through his hair.

"Bron? What is it?"

He swung a glance at her but quickly looked away. He didn't want to look into her trusting eyes. But, hell, that T-shirt she wore was so low in the front it revealed the delicious curves of her breasts…

Deactivate.

"There's something wrong. Tell me."

He squeezed his eyelids tightly, but no matter how hard he wished, he could never turn back time and erase the director's phone call. Nor could he erase the car accident that had almost killed Kisanthra Lewis yet had branded her heart as a beacon for any and all paranormals with the morbid desire to use it as a wicked gateway to Purgatory.

"Bron?"

"There's nothing wrong. I just…wow." He spread his arms before him to take in her figure. "That's hot."

"This old thing? It's my travel nightshirt. Just wanted to put on something comfy after being stuck in jeans for two days straight. It's getting threadbare."

"Nothing wrong with that."

Her smile beamed. Best to focus on the sweet citrus skin than the direct order from his boss. He'd think about that later. Had to. He couldn't tell her his mission had changed.

But could he fulfill the new command? He'd never disobeyed a command. Of course he would do it.

"I wish I had something with lace," she offered and tugged at the frayed shirt hem. "I would love to seduce you."

He hooked his hands at his hips. "You don't need lace to do that."

"Oh, yeah?" She drew a teasing finger along her lips and scampered up to him. Bron shoved the phone in his back pocket and curled his hands around her hips. His fingers touched skin, and he curved them around to cup her buttocks. "Maybe a quickie before we buckle down and put our heads together over the important stuff?"

He answered her with a kiss and lifted her into his arms. He knew the bedroom was down the hallway and strolled into the white-walled room that looked gray in the afternoon light. Cinnamon filled the air. On the windowsill, a jar of oil with thin sticks jutting out of the narrow neck must be an air freshener. A bed and small chest near the door were the only furnishings. The open closet door revealed but a few items. Perhaps she *could* handle the traveling life?

"You live sparsely," he noted as he set her on the bed and climbed over her.

"I pared down all my belongings and started living from a few suitcases after the accident."

Yes, eight months ago she had died. Bron imagined dying on the operating table could prove a strong catalyst for starting over and venturing off to greater experiences. If he had never activated the tracker and found her, would she be safe now from all those who sought her heart?

Including him.

"Kiss me, Bron, and save those deep thoughts for later."

He smirked at her stunning ability to read his mind.

"I can read you," she confirmed. "If you're not eating or driving or talking to me, you're on the job." She tapped his temple. "Mentally."

"You picked that up, eh? Sorry." He pulled the night-shirt over her head and spread his hand across her stomach and bent to her breast. "I'm focused now."

He sucked in one of her tightened nipples and toyed with it until he felt sure he was commanding a symphony of her moans. She sighed and glided her hands over his shoulders. His muscles flexed, just a normal reaction to having his back touched, even though the scars did not hurt, as he'd told her. She'd accepted his banishment. It meant nothing to her, a human. It had meant the end of what he was at the time and being faced with starting anew.

Oddly, this moment felt like that start for which he'd been waiting for so long. And yet, he must end it by destroying her heart.

No. There must be another way. Damn him, why had he gotten involved?

"Lover?"

Her voice lured him from desperate thoughts. He wouldn't question this moment. Going with it felt right.

He hooked a hand under her thigh, coaxing her leg up and around his back as he leaned over her on the bed. Kizzy spread her hands across the bed and let him do what he wanted to do. And he wanted to move lower, tickling his wet tongue down her stomach, circling her navel and then teasing the diagonals between thigh and mons.

His big, wide hand covered her pussy, and she tilted up her hips to meet the promising pressure. She clasped at his shoulders, then her fingers danced in his hair, gripping and pulling gently, then pushing a bit when he moved lower, and his mouth kissed her moist, wanting apex.

"Mmm, Bron."

His tongue dashed her clitoris, and he didn't just flick and go. He stayed there, circling, knowing from her rising hips and faster breaths that he had found the right spot.

"Oh, mercy," she gasped. Clutching the bedspread in tight fingers, she closed her eyes and soared into the exquisite giddiness of orgasm.

The sound of her pleasure stabbed at the director's voice, chasing it from his thoughts completely. He was here with this woman he cared for, and that was all that mattered right now.

Chapter 15

Kizzy pulled on the pair of Rock & Republic jeans and a faded red T-shirt that clung to her figure and revealed a bit of cleavage with the V-neck. It was close to suppertime. The hazy kind of evening light she loved filled the apartment, glancing off the laptop screen. It was the golden hour. Perfect for photographing outdoors.

While Bron showered, she nestled onto the windowsill and checked her emails. Confirmation of the bank transfer for the one-week rental in Romania had been attached. She looked forward to exploring the Romanian landscape. If she couldn't get a picture of a vampire there, she didn't know where it would happen.

"In your own hometown," she muttered.

Because, holy Hannah, those fangy guys must be everywhere. She shivered at the memory of being chased under the willow tree by the vamp—and nearly bitten—

but then relaxed to know Bron was just down the hall. No singing in the shower? She had been looking forward to hearing another Disney tune.

Her Twitter stream was so active it scrolled continually, so she clicked on Nightcat to read his Tweets specifically.

"Oh, no." His latest Tweet, posted forty-five minutes ago, reported that she was in Thief River Falls, possibly staying somewhere on Main Street.

"He knows where I'm staying? This is bad in so many ways." A shiver lifted goose bumps on her arms. "I've got to get out of here."

Not wanting to rush Bron out of the shower, she instead readied herself. Tugging her backpack from the closet, she quickly packed the few T-shirts, jeans, panties and the one bra she traveled with but rarely used. She'd grab her toothbrush, comb and toiletries when he was done.

Next, she pulled the SD card from her camera and uploaded all the pictures she'd taken in the past few days to her laptop. Giving each of the three lenses a quick polish with a soft cloth, she then packed them in the camera bag, which was padded for banging around on her many adventures. A credit card and a hundred dollars in cash she stuck in a back pocket.

Bron strolled out of the bathroom whistling, towel wrapped about his hips, and aimed for the bedroom. She ran up behind him and showed him the Tweet on her phone.

"Shit. We have to leave," he said.

"I'm packed and ready to go. It's all on you, lover."

He smiled at that moniker and then quickly dressed. Kizzy grabbed her toothbrush. "I'm packing up everything. Don't intend to return here, even though I've got another few days on the place. It might be a backup plan if we need it."

"That's a good idea." He grabbed her as she spun about the living room collecting her things and kissed her. "You're good at the fast escape."

"I've had some training the past few days. And you know, I'm all about the no attachments. Ready to dash at will. It's kind of how you operate, isn't it?"

"That it is. I don't own much and always carry the basics with me. Turn off all the lights and…" His gaze fell onto the open laptop. Kizzy grabbed it and shoved it in her backpack. "Right. Let's do this."

She followed him down the hallway to the front door. Bron opened it to a young man poised to knock. He reached back to stop Kizzy and turned to whisper, "Be careful."

She wasn't sure why. Looked like a delivery boy. He held a black box about the size of his head and presented it to, not her, but Bron. "This is for the werewolf," the guy said.

Whoa. Not a greeting she would ever expect to hear from a delivery guy. Who could have no idea who was renting for merely a week. He knew something.

Bron peered into the guy's eyes, and now that Kizzy looked closer, she noticed they were white, no irises visible. Creepy.

"What is he?" she whispered.

"Human. And, I can only presume, under a spell," Bron said as he took the package. "Who gave this to you?"

The man shook his head. "I don't have a name."

"Tell me what he looked like," Bron asked.

"I'm only allowed to give answers to the right questions."

Bron swore under his breath and stepped back, protecting Kizzy with his stance. He shook the box gently. "Can you tell me what is in the box?"

The man shook his head.

"Ask him *what* gave it to him?" she said over Bron's shoulder.

"The soul bringer," the man answered rotely.

"You asked the right question," Bron said as he pulled the twine from the box.

It fell away, and Kizzy collected it before it hit the floor. The box was topped with a cover that Bron could simply lift up and off, but at his heavy sigh she sensed he'd rather not.

"Is this dangerous?" he asked.

The guy didn't answer.

"What does it smell like?" she asked, now noticing a definite distasteful odor.

"Blood," he said.

"Then it can't be a bomb." He turned a questioning look on her. She shrugged. "I'm nervous. And that guy is creeping me out. Why are his eyes like that?"

"Apparently the soul bringer has bespelled him to his bidding. When he walks away from here he'll likely forget everything. Will you be set free once I've opened the box?" he asked the man.

"Yes."

"Just open it," she encouraged and clutched Bron's arm. "If it was dangerous he'd be running, yes?"

"Or that could be a means for the soul bringer to clean up loose ends."

"No, it's okay," she said. "I mean, I have a feeling it's

not going to explode. He wants my heart in one piece, right? Hold it out and I'll take the top off."

He clutched the box to his gut, eyed the delivery boy, then nodded. "Fine. But be slow. Careful."

Wishing she dared to take a photo, Kizzy let her camera hang at her chest as she went for the box top. She was scared, excited, freaked and—her girl gene that loved to open gifts felt as if it was Christmastime. Carefully she lifted the box lid with her free hand. Underneath, folded red tissue paper concealed the contents. On top of the tissue lay a white card with one word on it.

"Trade?" Bron read the word. It had been followed by a question mark. "Trade for—ah."

"My heart?" she guessed. "You think?"

"Let's see what he has to offer."

"Wait." She grasped his hand before he could fold back the tissue paper. "You wouldn't really trade my heart, would you?"

He shook his head. "Never."

Spoken without pause and with a truth she could read in his eyes. He had her back. She could trust him. She relented, and he pulled open the tissue to reveal…

Bron swore and reacted, gripping the delivery boy's throat with his free hand and shoving him against the threshold. "What is this about?"

"I don't have that answer," he squeaked out. "Wrong question. Can I go now?"

"You're not the one asking the questions. I am," Bron growled.

"What is it?" Kizzy asked.

"Give me the cover."

"I want to see what it is."

"You shouldn't." But when she clutched the cover

to her chest he met her gaze and relented, holding out the box.

Kizzy pushed aside the red tissue. Now she could smell the meaty odor, and it looked like a piece of meat, actually. Then she really looked at it. "OhmyGod. It's a heart."

Bron grabbed the cover from her and put it on the box. "Give this back to your master." He shoved it toward the delivery boy.

"I'm not allowed to leave until the gift has been accepted."

"I don't accept it!"

"Just say you do and let him go. He's being controlled," Kizzy said. "We'll figure this out."

"It's a poor joke," Bron muttered. "Very well, I accept it. Go!"

The delivery boy nodded, and just as he turned, Kizzy said, "Wait! Whose heart is this?"

"I have that answer. It belongs to Claire Everhart." With that, the guy made a quick exit, running down the stairs.

Bron stumbled and landed a shoulder against the wall. He stared at the box held between his bracketed hands as if it really would explode. "No."

"Who is—wait. Claire is—" Kizzy quickly put two and two together. "You said you hadn't seen your wife since you were banished. Claire was her name, right?"

"Yes," he hissed and sank to his knees beside her.

Chapter 16

Bron clutched the black box with the cover on top of it to his chest. He didn't know what to do, how to feel, what to believe. His mouth was dry. His skin felt clammy. Did his heart even beat?

How could it be his wife's heart? He hadn't seen Claire since the nineteenth century. Though he'd occasionally wondered if the legalities of such an absence negated their marriage vows over time. He had never hated her. Had genuinely cared for her. And even when he had hurt her by having an affair with another woman and she had screamed vile words at him, he still respected her.

And then he'd moved beyond that part of his life. Since that first assignment for Acquisitions he had always focused on his work and rarely looked back, save to mourn Isabelle's cruel demise.

And now the soul bringer would threaten him with this. What was this? He had no proof the bloody organ inside the box was Claire's heart.

It didn't matter. It was *someone's* heart. But why would the soul bringer take a stab at him in such a personal manner when it was Kizzy's heart the bastard apparently wanted?

Perhaps the soul bringer believed Bron would actually trade Kizzy's heart for…what? His wife was now dead. Bloody hell, he held her heart in a box! There was nothing on the earth he could imagine that would be worthy of a trade for Kizzy's heart.

The gentle glide of Kizzy's hand down his shoulder startled him to the present moment. "Talk to me," she said softly.

Coming back to reality, he looked left and right. He sat in the hallway against the wall of her apartment. The front door was still open. Twilight darkened the air and shadowed his lover's face. But he saw the question in her eyes, more so than worry or fear. She needed him to stand up and be the protector.

"We can't stay here. He'll find you." He stood and, with the box under an arm, stepped toward the threshold.

"Bron, no matter where we go, they seem to find us. How can we possibly hide?"

Soft brown eyes entreated him. She was right. The Nightcat had spies everywhere, capable of communicating in real time via Twitter. And apparently, the soul bringer had his own means to flush them out.

Bron had no supernatural methods to fend off such devious observation. He possessed no magic. His only strength was in his physicality and his claws. But perhaps there was a spell that could hide Kizzy from those who had a fix on her heart? Why hadn't he considered that earlier? He knew a handful of witches. And he did know a witch who lived in the area.

He clutched the box tighter, and his eyes fell to Kizzy's chest. He wasn't willing to rip out her heart and hand it over to the soul bringer to bring this to an end.

Yet he'd been charged to finish the mission. And he'd never before disobeyed an order.

Hell. He didn't know what to do. He held his wife's heart? The woman he was starting to care about possessed a heart that a vicious soul bringer sought?

And where was his heart?

Bron had never thought he had the capacity to care since Isabelle had been cast out into the winter night and left to die. What a horrible way to die, alone, and without her father's protection. He'd not shielded her. The only reason she had walked the earth was because of his indiscretion. Yet he had loved her the moment she had been born. Had tried to see her often, even though his love for her mother had faded, and she, a human woman, had turned vindictive against him because she had wanted his love so desperately. He should have protected Isabelle. He should have been a better man.

He was incapable of using his heart for good, of loving.

"Whatever is going on in there—" Kizzy tapped his temple "—has to wait. There's something clawing at the living room window." She bent to grab her backpack, stuffed with her clothes and the laptop. "And it has wings."

He rushed down the hallway and into the living room. Another harpie? Since when were harpies so abundant in the mortal realm? Faery was their native habitat. Dark or malefic magic might conjure them to another realm. Or something even more powerful? They had to have been summoned by the soul bringer.

"Is there another way out of this building?" he asked, turning to stride to the front door again.

"There's a back courtyard."

Bron backtracked into the kitchen and pulled open a narrow drawer by the stove. He grabbed a large chopping knife and handed it to Kizzy. "You'll need this." He tugged out the bowie knife from his boot and grabbed her hand. "Let's go."

"I'm right behind you."

"Siri, find the closest witch!" Bron commanded his phone as he slipped alongside Kizzy's building, his eyes to the sky for the harpie.

"Really? Siri is in on the whole paranormal thing?"

"I have names categorized by species in my contacts."

"Remind me to scroll through your contacts some time. What a trip!"

The phone dinged, and Siri announced the nearest witch was an hour and a half away near Lengby.

"Excellent." Bron shoved the phone in a pocket. "I know that witch."

"Is that so? Right, you mentioned you were familiar with the area. Old girlfriend?"

No time to explain. He still carried the box with the heart in it. Not what he wanted to have in hand, but he certainly couldn't leave it in Kizzy's apartment. Or toss it to be found by a garbage man. The police would

have a field day over such a find. He had t̶
it. And—if it truly was Claire's heart—say g̶

When there was time.

Overhead a shadow swept through the night sky
circled as if a vulture stalking dying prey. He pulled
out the bowie knife and nodded that Kizzy stay behind
him. When the harpie swooped down into the alleyway,
he ran toward it.

Kizzy didn't want in on the harpie action, so she
clung to the brick wall and kept an eye out for passersby
who might witness the man engaged in a knife-against-
talon battle with a winged creature. She desperately
gripped the kitchen knife, praying she wouldn't have
to use it to protect herself in something so terrifying
as hand-to-hand combat. How did the paranormals do
it? Exist amongst the humans without discovery? No
wonder Bron was so closed off. It was a self-protection
instinct.

A slash of talon was countered with a stab of the
blade into the birdman's underbelly. Blood spilled out,
but it was too dark for Kizzy to see what color it was.
She gripped her camera—when a commotion behind
a big blue garbage container averted her attention. She
swung around, the knife thrust out before her.

A black cat peeked at her from behind one of the
dumpster wheels. Its gold eyes took her in—with intent.

"That's weird," Kizzy said. "Cat's aren't usually so
concerned with humans." In fact, she'd expect the thing,
if it were feral, to dash off at first sign of a human.

It was still looking at her, dividing its attention between her and the harpie fight, which she hoped Bron

was winning. But now curiosity nudged her to creep toward the cat. Could it be?

"Here, kitty, kitty. I'm not going to hurt you." She would never harm an animal; but she wasn't about to abandon the knife.

The feline meowed and darted down a narrow aisle between two brick buildings. It paused and looked back at her. Another odd cat move. She'd had a cat when she was a teenager. Felines were the kings of selfish entitlement. They could care less what humans did.

With a leap, it tried to climb up the stack of wood pallets that blocked the aisle. Its claws took it up halfway, then it slipped.

Kizzy lunged for the animal and slipped her hand about its belly. Expecting a vicious swing of claws, she dropped the knife and gripped its forelegs together with one hand, holding it securely against her gut.

"I think you and I have something to chat about, Nightcat."

The cat growled and hissed at her.

"Nope. Not going to intimidate me. And I think we both know that I know who you are."

Out in the main alley a brilliant blue glow burst and then all went dark. Kizzy rushed out to see Bron standing over the fallen harpie, blade in hand. His biceps pulsed with frenzied energy. At his feet a pile of dark feathers glowed with red embers. He turned to her, noted the cat and tilted a wondering gaze at her.

"Grab the box," she said. "I know an empty warehouse just down the street we might be able to get into."

Five minutes later they wandered through a dark abandoned brick building. The structure had served many a purpose over the decades, from flour mill to aside, then clasped his hands about his legs to protect his privates.

"Haven't got any clothes," Bron said. "Maybe he'll be inspired to talk fast so he can shift back and get the hell out of here, eh?" He walked over to the shifted cat and stood over him. "You Nightcat?"

"Yes." The man bowed his head. "Don't hurt me, man. I am not comfortable around your sort."

"My sort." Bron chuffed out a quiet chuckle. "Why do you think it's okay to broadcast this woman's location for any insane paranormal to go after her and try to rip out her heart?"

"I...I have to. The soul bringer makes me. He says it'll wear you two out. Make you crawl to him."

Kizzy noted Bron's clenched fists. She didn't want him to hurt the guy but sensed he was not averse to violence. Nightcat seemed harmless; he cowered before Bron. She almost felt compelled to lean over and pat him reassuringly on the thick thatch of black hair on his head. Almost.

"He put a spell on you?" Bron asked.

The cat shook his head. "Not that I know of."

"Then stop Twittering or whatever it is you do."

"The soul bringer will kill me if I don't help him."

Bron gripped the cat's hair and jerked his head backward. "It's either that or I kill you." He released him roughly. "I'm trying to protect this woman, and you are making it difficult. Way I look at it, I get rid of you, the problem is solved."

"You'll still have the soul bringer on your ass." The cat sniffed the air. "What's in the box?"

"None of your damn business."

"Doesn't smell like lunch, that's for sure. It's from

the soul bringer. I can smell him on it. He means business."

"Then why doesn't he come talk to me face-to-face? Why not rip Kizzy's heart out himself?"

Kizzy shivered and clutched her arms across her chest.

The cat smirked. "He can't touch the heart. Soul bringers deal with Above and Beneath. Purgatory is forbidden to them. If he wants to get in, he'll need a guide to operate the portal."

"The portal being my heart?" Kizzy asked.

"Exactly. Apparently harpies are not sufficient means to take out hearts. But they provide a good scare, eh?"

"Why does he want her heart?" Bron asked. "I know it gets him into Purgatory. But if he is forbidden, why does he want to go there?"

The cat shrugged. "You got me. Maybe he sent a soul there by mistake and needs to get it back?"

Bron stepped back and rubbed his jaw. The cat eyed the doorway. Kizzy stepped closer and blocked his path to a quick escape. Would he really run off in the buff?

"What do you think?" she asked Bron.

"I think the cat is better off dead."

"No! I'll stop Tweeting. Promise. But then I've got to go under to save my furry ass from the soul bringer's vengeance. He's a mean bastard."

"You have his name?" Bron asked.

"Blackthorn Regis," the cat provided.

"That'll help." Bron clasped Kizzy's hand and tugged her away from the cat. "Go," he said to the familiar. "Best of luck on staying away from the soul bringer."

The cat stood, cupping his privates. "You got a coat or something I can borrow, man?"

"Nope."

The man sighed and wandered toward the warehouse entrance. Kizzy glanced away from the sight of his naked backside. In the glow of the moonlight he shifted down to the black cat and scampered off.

"If I see one more Tweet," Bron called after him, "you will die!"

An angry meow faded with the cat's retreat.

"And how will we find him to kill him?" Kizzy asked as Bron turned to her.

"I've his scent in my nose now. I could track that feline anywhere within a twenty-mile range. I'll know where he is. Now, to get to the witch." He grabbed the box, then took her hand and strode out of the building.

"What do we need a witch for?"

"To put up a protective shield so the soul bringer can't track us. Including his minions. You cool with that?"

"Is there another option?"

"Nope."

"Then I'm cool."

Outside the building, she tugged him to a halt and pulled him into a hug. Kissing him, she lingered on the warmth of his lips. All that mattered to her was that she lived. Because then she could kiss him again. And have sex with him again. And, simply have him again.

"We make a good team," she said.

"Don't dream for things that can never happen, Kizzy."

"Why not? That's what makes dreams so wonderful."

And with a shrug and a forced smile, she strode

ahead of him, her heart falling because he didn't believe in them. She should not. But it was too late. The werewolf from her nightmares had slipped into her dreams.

Chapter 17

Kizzy drove by virtue of the fact that Bron had simply climbed into the passenger side and quietly handed her the keys. While Siri directed her down a dark country road toward the witch's home, she couldn't help but feel her heart break for Bron. He held the black box on his lap. Eyes closed and head bowed, his silence gripped at her empathy.

She couldn't imagine what he must feel. And then she could relate, in a manner. She had lost a boyfriend. No matter how she'd felt about Keith on the night of the accident, she had once cared for him, and losing any soul before its time was a tragedy. Though relating to losing someone you hadn't seen for over a hundred and fifty years, such as was Bron's case, was a little difficult. And he'd had an affair, which had resulted in a child.

No one was perfect. And she wouldn't judge him. He was holding his wife's heart in a box on his lap! But she suddenly had an idea. She knew this road. And just ahead...

Kizzy turned left, contrary to Siri's monotonous demands to make a corrective U-turn.

"What are you doing?" he asked.

"I've been in this area a few times. High school keg parties. Used to have to hide them in the woods. There's a special spot close by, if I recall my midnight excursions well enough." She pulled over beside the ditch and turned the engine off. "Trust me?"

"I don't know why you need to go tramping through the woods in the middle of the night. Is this about your closure thing?"

"Nope. It's yours." She tapped the box. "I thought maybe you'd like to give her a proper burial."

He opened his mouth to say something but then did not. Instead he nodded and got out, box clutched in his hands. He reached into the truck bed, where a utility box stored stuff such as his extra clothing and boots, and pulled out a small, foldable camp shovel.

He followed her down the dry ditch, stomping tall grasses, and hiked through a short stretch of knee-high milkweed and into the woods. Less than five minutes in, Kizzy was rewarded for her night navigational skills. A stream burbled crisply. Moonlight beamed through the tree canopy. The air smelled fresh and untainted by society. Whimsy abounded. If she squinted and looked through her lashes, she could see the faery dust in the air.

"This is—" Bron stopped at her side and took in the scene with a long glance in all directions "—wondrous."

She clasped his free hand. "And magical. I have some amazing pictures of the stream that I took in high school. I also used to come here when I was *not* partying. I think the trips here were what really got me interested in photography." She tapped her camera. "I'm going that way to take some pictures with the moonlight beaming on the stream. I'll leave you to yourself."

He slid a hand along her cheek and pulled her in for a kiss. It was slow and sweet, and she couldn't help but feel like a damsel standing beneath the moonlight with her hero. Her werewolf hero. A man who had been punished for something he had done so long ago and was still being punished today. She wanted to free him. Bringing him here was a small first step.

"Thank you," he said.

"Take your time." She stroked his beard. "I'll be just that way. Catching faeries."

"If you catch them they'll harass you and your loved ones forever after. Just take pictures, okay?"

"Deal." She wandered along the stream's edge, not turning back when she heard the shovel hit the rocky earth.

Faeries? Maybe. Well, most certainly. Though she'd never seen one, she had felt their presence.

Once she'd walked about three hundred yards away from where Bron was digging, she found the perfect cove. Verdant moss frosted the rolling earth, and even the tree roots that pushed up from the ground were mounded in lush moss. Delicate white flowers dotted the emerald carpet and red-capped amanita muscaria mushrooms sprouted at the base of an oak. Possibly Faery did exist here.

Kizzy squatted and began to snap pictures. She had

sensed faeries most of her life but only ever thought to have seen them out of the corner of her eye. Whether that was because it was in keeping with the mythology she'd read, or truth, didn't matter. She believed. And those beliefs were currently being proven every second she breathed.

Losing her balance, she caught a hand in the moss, and her fingers sank into the plush green. Surrendering to the fantastical moment, she lay down and pressed her cheek to the moss, inhaling deeply and exhaling with a smiling sigh.

"It smells so good out here. I could have been a faery," she said and then laughed. "Though I'm not sure what I'd do with my wings. Bron must know so much about all the varied creatures that live on this planet." She sat up on the moss and leaned against the tree trunk, cradling the camera in her hand. "I'd love to pick his brain. Get to know him much better."

Even better than skin on skin? While sex was awesome, learning a man's mind was the real turn-on. Kizzy was attracted to intelligence and honor. A man who was not satisfied to stand still and exist, but who was drawn to explore and learn. To help others.

Was Bron that man? Traveling because of his job also implied a quest for knowledge, but it did appeal to her hunger for movement.

"A wanderlust," she said. With Bron by her side.

And he was helping others by taking dangerous magical objects out of circulation to lock them away. Maybe? So long as he didn't rip out her heart, she was good with that definition. And she'd still keep him by her side.

Date a werewolf? It was not a ridiculous notion. They

would make a perfect pair. She, a believer who did not question his otherness. And he, a powerful and honorable protector who had only her best interests in mind.

He'd been sent to claim her heart. Instead he'd become a part of it.

And who was she, getting all romance and roses on her crazy self? She wasn't in the market for a boyfriend. She hadn't considered dating since the accident. Hookups worked just fine for now. For some reason, mourning Keith had meant not going out with friends when they invited along that "extra" guy and certainly not making eye contact with the sexy stranger in the Starbucks as she used to once do.

Of course, she did believe that love found the person. It wasn't the other way around. If it happened into a person's life, it was meant to be.

One day you'll turn around, and he'll be standing there.

The fact she couldn't get that long-ago whispered prediction from her brain now had to mean something. And Bron had been there when she had turned around in the park. How cool was that?

Bron's footsteps neared, and she patted the moss beside her. He accepted her offer and sat down, legs bent. He stabbed the shovel into the loamy moss beside him. His fingers were darkened with dirt, which he rubbed at, then gave up. He tilted back his head and took in the moonlight.

Kizzy wasn't sure how to ask if all had gone well with burying the box. She knew he would offer information if he felt inclined. Inhaling, she drew in his masculine scent, the dirt from his hands and the warmth of his body. She leaned against him, shoulder to shoulder.

She wanted to kiss him but, again, decided to let him make the first move. This moment was too perfect to spoil with words. And when he clasped her hand, she felt sure the glint of moonlight above them was speckled with faery dust.

After a while he said, "Tomorrow is the night before the full moon."

"Yep." Okay, completely off subject. Nothing wrong with that. She did want to get this important topic out there and explained. "Do you, uh…think you might need some help with that sex thing you told me about?"

He smirked. "Are you offering?"

"I am."

He kissed the back of her hand, then clasped it loosely against his chest as he gazed over the stream. A lazy ribbon of silvery water glistened with moonshine. "Find any faeries?"

"Maybe. I won't know until I review the pictures later. They have a sneaky way of flittering in and out of view. Whether or not they get captured on film is entirely up to them." She nuzzled her nose into his hair and kissed the base of his neck. "And how are you?"

He shrugged. "I just buried my wife's heart. She was an innocent. She died for no reason other than some bastard's means to goad me. And it worked."

"What does that mean?"

"I will kill the soul bringer."

She was about to protest, but it didn't feel fair. He'd been wounded directly in the heart. She didn't know the way of his kind or of any paranormals. Perhaps such extreme vengeance was the norm for them. Did they not have laws? Courts? A justice system?

"Claire deserves vengeance," he said. "God knows

I was not a good husband by seeking love away from her arms. We were an arranged marriage, you know?"

"Really? So you didn't pick one another? Did you know one another before you married?"

"Only met once. Our respective packs wanted to join forces. We were chosen to marry and seal the bond between the packs. I was made leader. We thrived, the new pack. It was a good thing."

"What's it like being the leader of a pack? How many wolves are in it?"

"There were an average of thirty at any given time. I was the alpha, chosen because, after our former leader had been killed by demons, I'd slayed them all—eight powerful corporeal demons who had escaped from Daemonia. I won the principal position, and I'd not let any others defy my authority. You might say I was power mad. I liked being in charge. In having others look up to me. I've learned since, that was ego, and ego can be a stupid distraction for what the soul desires."

"Your soul desired being a lone wolf and traveling the world?"

"I didn't know it at the time, but, yes, I believe my actions, the affair, were a direct catalyst to putting me on the path I now walk."

"Lone wolf Retriever. Are all the Retrievers werewolves?"

"No. Acquisitions hires myriad species for the Retrieval team. Comes in handy when a specific species may be needed to finesse a retrieval or deal with the locals. I've met all sorts, both human and paranormal, in my travels. I've learned a lot."

"I bet your wife would have been proud to see the man you've become."

He exhaled. "She would not have. Claire preferred me growling and in control. Stepping on others for the good of the pack. Her idea of a man was the ultimate alpha. A chest beater who would take a man down just for looking at him the wrong way. I imagine she may have hooked up with the new pack leader after I was banished."

"You never once looked into her welfare? Tried to learn what had happened to her?"

"I figured I owed her the respect of never contacting her after what I'd done. And I was angry over Isabelle's death. The pack could have prevented it. They could have kept her safe until I was released."

"I'm sorry." Kizzy squeezed his hand. "You've lost much."

"It is my past."

"A past that's been resurrected."

"For reasons I can't begin to grasp. I don't understand why the soul bringer believes I would be amenable to his threat. A suggestion to a trade after he killed my wife? What reason do I now have to hand you over to him? If anything, I am even more determined to protect you to ensure that yet another woman doesn't fall to his brutal treatment."

She spread a hand across his chest, resting it against the hard, steely muscle. His heartbeat was strong, solid. "I would have liked to have seen you as the alpha wolf standing at the head of your pack. I saw a glimpse of your animal nature that night the wraith demon was after me."

"I am not that wolf anymore, Kizzy. I am kinder, gentler. More thoughtful."

"And you wield a stake and crossbow just for the

fun of it? Surely your travels must land you on some amazing adventures. Are you faced with life-and-death situations?"

"All the time," he said with a smile. "Just because I have mellowed doesn't mean I don't seek the adrenaline and excitement. And sometimes weapons are very necessary. I am still a wild creature. I need the freedom. It is my nature."

"Your penchant to seek adventure excites me."

He waggled his brows at her.

"Not that way. Well, maybe a little. Okay, a lot. I like your wildness in bed. I like to think of myself as adventurous, as well. But snapping pictures probably isn't quite what you consider excitement."

"The photos you could take on my adventures would capture gorgeous scenery. I confess I checked out your blog. I'm impressed."

"Why, thank you. That means a lot coming from a real werewolf."

"So long as I don't see any pics from my fight with the wraith demon up on your blog I'll continue to be impressed."

She crossed her heart with a fingertip. "Promise."

"I should have already destroyed that camera by now. It wasn't a direct command, but I consider it a mark against my service history with Acquisitions."

"I wouldn't want you to get in trouble. But this camera cost a lot. What if you watch me erase all the pictures?"

He eyed her carefully. "Have you downloaded any to your laptop?"

"Maybe—" She pressed fingers to her mouth at the escaped confession. "Bron, you've got to let me keep the interesting ones. I will swear on my heart I will never publish any of them." She crossed a finger over her heart.

"Not good enough. But we'll have this conversation again. After the threat has been eliminated."

She'd take that. For now. She was just thankful he hadn't already destroyed her camera.

"You think we should head to a motel and try for the witch in the morning? It's getting late."

"No. She'll be up." He checked his cell phone. "It's only eleven. I know this witch. She never sleeps."

"How do you know her?"

He shrugged. "Do I have to say?"

"Oh? So she's a lover?"

"Former," he corrected. "I was in this neck of the woods a long time ago. Decades, surely. Looking for a chronomancy totem, if I recall correctly. Witches can be very useful."

"Oh, I bet. Should I be jealous?"

"Jealousy would imply you've made a claim to me."

"Oh." But she had. He didn't think she had, or he didn't want her to? Hmm…

"Have you?" he asked with a side glance to her. "Claimed me?"

"I imagine you would never allow anyone to claim you. You being a lone and adventurous wolf. But I wouldn't mind knowing you for a while. Promise, I won't try to tame you."

She stood and tugged his fingers, but he pulled her down to straddle his legs and kneel. "Kiss me in the moonlight, Kisanthra. Make a claim if you wish."

An offer she hadn't thought him capable of. She wasn't about to refuse.

Kizzy kissed her werewolf lover and promised him everything she'd said. That she wouldn't try to tame him. And that she would stand back and admire his wild and free heart. Because in doing so she could only grow wilder and more free alongside him. And untamed sounded perfect to her right now.

"You're mine," she whispered against his mouth. "My wolf."

Chapter 18

"So if you know this witch, then you know the area?"
Kizzy asked as Bron navigated the dark country road
paralleled by sky-reaching white-papered birch.

"It's coming back to me." He reached over and turned
off Siri. "Just ahead, if I recall correctly. You scared?"

"Of visiting a witch? Should I be?"

He shrugged.

"Dude, I've been chased by harpies, wraiths, vampires and have got a soul bringer on my ass. One little
witch isn't going to move the meter over to panic mode
now. Besides, I have a sexy werewolf to protect me."

When he smiled she wanted to grab him and make
out with him. But before she could act on that desire he
turned down a gravel road overgrown with weeds and
pulled before a dark cottage that captured her attention.
It was run-down, and the tree branches stretched over

the roof as if to hide it from prying eyes. No light in the windows. It looked like an abandoned shack the hapless teens always fled to in the horror movies.

Yikes. So not welcoming. And she prided herself on not being hapless.

"What's the witch's name?" Kizzy asked.

Bron closed his eyes, seeming to ruminate on that one, then sang softly, "Eglantine, Eglantine, oh how you shine."

"Bedknobs and Broomsticks!" she said, utterly awed that the big alpha werewolf had a thing for Disney movie tunes.

"Saw it when it first showed in theaters," he said. "See? I know a thing or two about popular culture."

"I wouldn't call a movie from the 1970s *current* popular culture, but I'm not taking off points for your knowledge. Any man who sings me songs from Disney movies scores bonus points."

"I'll take them."

He jumped out of the truck and gestured she lead when she walked around to him. "You go first," she said. "Because, uh…you know her."

He grabbed her hand and pulled her in for a kiss. His tongue made a quick dash over her teeth before he cupped the back of her head with a hand to hold her against him. Every part of her body wanted every part of his body to master her, own her. She'd never felt that way about a man before. And the feeling did not frighten her so much as promise the adventure she craved.

Breaking the kiss, he bowed his forehead to hers. "You have my permission to be scared at any time.

What you've been through? Most human chicks would have been a puddle by now."

"I will not puddle." But she had to keep reminding herself she could be brave as they walked up the cobblestone path overgrown with tangled weeds that smelled acrid and deadly. "I will not puddle," she whispered.

Bron knocked, and the door instantly opened. Kizzy startled but didn't step back. To say the resident was a hag was putting it lightly. Bent over and dressed in dusty, tattered black, her gray, uncombed hair snarled this way and that. A long warty nose hung over her mouth that revealed no teeth in the gums.

The witch lifted her head with great effort and eyed Bron. "Oh! Shit."

The door slammed shut.

Kizzy eyed Bron, who merely smiled and said, "Give her a minute. She didn't expect me."

"I—okay. That woman was the epitome of witch. Seriously, she looked like a picture you would see in a dictionary under the word *witch*." She threaded her arm around Bron's bent elbow. "I'm not puddling, but I might feel a slight mist coming on."

The door again opened to a burst of interior light that was so bright Kizzy blinked a few times before she could make out the hag. Er, not a hag but a glamour girl sporting platinum-silver hair, gorgeous black lashes that framed bright blue eyes and a youthful smoothness to her skin that belied her seeming octogenarian age.

"Bron Everhart," she declared as if Auntie Mame herself. "It's been ages! Come in, come in! Let me look at you."

Bron gestured for Kizzy to cross the threshold first, and she did so cautiously. The witch was completely focused on the handsome werewolf who entered behind her. And why not? The guy was sex on a stick.

She took Bron's hands and looked him over. Kizzy noted she wore all white, and the foyer of her home was…huge. Sparkling white marble stretched as far as she could see. A grand crystal chandelier hung overhead, a centerpiece that belonged in a castle ballroom. A staircase ran upward two flights and curled to the right. What the…?

She turned to look over the ramshackle stoop where she'd just stood, but the door slammed shut before she could see into the darkness and ascertain they had indeed walked up an overgrown path to a decrepit shack.

The witch smoothed a palm over Bron's cheek and glided down his beard in a move that tweaked Kizzy's jealousy. "Always so stoic and handsome. It is so good to see you."

He leaned in and kissed both her cheeks. "It is exquisite to see you, Eglantine."

So that really was her name? Cool.

"Have you missed me?" she eagerly asked.

Bron thought about that one a few seconds. "No. You did send me off with no means to counteract that nasty attraction spell."

"You needed that spell to draw in the siren," she stated matter-of-factly.

"I did. But it took weeks to wear off. And my next assignment was in Wales, on the beach. I won't even go into how many sirens I had to fend off after that. But I will always adore you, you know that. Let me introduce Kisanthra Lewis. She's a—"

"A human." The witch turned to Kizzy with baffled wonder and a flutter of her long lashes. She was so gorgeous Kizzy figured she must have pulled on some kind of witchy glamour after seeing who it was knocking on her door. "Bron, I thought you didn't do humans."

"I, uh… Kizzy has the Purgatory Heart."

"Oh? Oh." The witch placed her hand over Kizzy's heart. It was a gentle touch, and the light in her eyes felt like nothing less than a sweet grandmother looking after her, but still Kizzy's fingers stiffened at her thighs. "Mustn't fear me, darling. Any friend of Bron's is a friend of mine. I can feel the handprint. Who touched your heart so deeply it's been forever scarred?"

"It wasn't a deep love," Kizzy said. "He was… possessive. Wouldn't let me go. Even in death."

"Interesting. Yes, yes, a bit of malice wavering out from within you. Come in. I was entertaining guests when you knocked, but they can wait a bit. They need to cool down. Let me treat you two to some tea."

"No henbane tea," Bron said as he followed the witch into a spectacular room filled with plants and flowers and white marble columns. A burbling fountain tucked in somewhere Kizzy couldn't quite place.

She marveled over the utter impossibility of it all. It was as if a Victorian tea room in a glass-walled conservatory had been plunked in the middle of a dark and wicked forest. She loved it. Had it always been here? Even when she'd been partying with friends in high school? Weird. And a little creepy to consider now. But as her eyes fell over the lush flowers and she breathed in the humid freshness, she forgot to be scared.

Darn. She'd left the camera in the truck. Probably for the best. Bron would not like her to take pictures of his former lover's wondrous country retreat.

With a snap of her fingers, the witch produced from

thin air a round table laden for tea with pastel cakes arranged on a tiered server. Delicate white china set for three. The aroma of the tea lured Kizzy closer.

"Smells like chocolate," she said.

"And bacon," the witch said.

"Bacon?" Bron asked.

"I'm trying something new with the chocolate tea cakes, darling. You know, bacon makes everything better. Or so they say. Now sit!"

Kizzy did so and had to keep herself from appearing rude by grabbing for the treats.

"Full moon in two days," Eglantine noted as she poured them tea and sat between them. She pushed the tray of sweets toward Bron, and he selected a tiny cake decorated with a real violet and set it on his plate. "Does she know?"

"I do," Kizzy spoke up bravely. "Bron's a werewolf. You're a witch. I've got harpies and vampires after me, and a soul bringer."

Eglantine's tea spoon clanked against the china. She cast a worried look at Bron.

He nodded. "The soul bringer wants her heart, for reasons I cannot comprehend."

"Is she a job?" the witch asked him.

Again, he nodded. "I had no idea the heart I was tasked to retrieve was inside a living human's chest. And the director…" He sipped his tea.

"The director." Eglantine rolled her eyes and waved a dismissive hand before her. "Ethan Pierce is an idiot. I bet he wants you to find and finish, eh?"

Bron sipped even more tea and only offered a noncommittal shrug. Because to say "not exactly" would require too much explaining that Kizzy did not need to hear.

"Uh-huh." The witch turned to Kizzy. "How long have you had the handprint on your heart, darling?"

"The car accident was eight months ago. My boyfriend was the driver. He died during the crash. I died on the operating table. My heart stopped beating for six minutes. Afterward, the doctor told me about a weird scar on my heart, but I had no idea it would culminate in…this."

"Quite the boyfriend to possess the spiritual energy to grasp your heart from Purgatory. You must have been there with him."

Kizzy set down her tea. "You think so?" She'd not considered that. She'd always assumed, upon death, she would go directly to Heaven. Not that she was so perfect and sinless, but she'd never committed a grave crime against another human. "I don't know what to think about that."

"Don't think on it too much, darling. All that religious babble is just that. The real places are quite compelling and much harder to get into, I'm sure."

"We've come to ask your help," Bron said. "I used a tracker spell to locate Kizzy. Lillian Devereaux crafted it."

"She's an excellent Light worker. With a touch of the Dark to round out her edges."

"Yes, and I have since destroyed the tracker because I was told it would send out vibrations. Paranormals of all sorts have had a bead on Kizzy's heart and want it. They still do, even with the tracker out of the picture."

"Ah." Eglantine sat back and clapped her hands as if to command a grand procession of waiters. Instead she raised both hands and simply said, "Protect these fine souls from the eyes of those who wish them harm."

She then picked up her teacup and sipped.

Kizzy looked to Bron, who lifted his flower-topped tea cake in a toast to her and said, "There you go."

"So simple as that? I don't feel any different."

"The best magics are like that," Bron said with a smile at the witch. "Thank you, Eglantine."

"Anything for you, love. Now." Eglantine moved aside the teacup and her plate and placed her hands on the table before her. "What troubles me is that a soul bringer is in the mix. My magic won't hold up long against such a powerful being. Why does a soul bringer want her heart? It isn't as though he's access to Purgatory. He can't even touch her heart. It would burn him alive. Or rather, I should say, burn him to death."

"Really?" Kizzy leaned forward. "The delivery guy said the same thing about him not being able to touch my heart. But it's a gateway to Purgatory, so we assumed he wanted to go there."

"He'd have to send a champion in his stead. Must be something most valuable if he's willing to afford the risk."

"I wondered if he needed to get someone out," Kizzy said. "Maybe he put a soul there by mistake?"

Eglantine shook her head adamantly. "Soul bringers are not allowed into Purgatory. The Toll Gatherers would shred him to bits."

"I know little about the Toll Gatherers," Bron said. "Tell us what you know about Purgatory, Eglantine."

"Love to. As you must know, Purgatory is where human souls are sent to atone for their sins before they can move on to their Heaven. There are twenty Toll

Houses, and at each one the soul must atone and compensate for their sins. The Toll Gatherers are demon, and they are nasty bastards. It's not all gardens and roses like the Catholics believe. Purgatory will put the soul to the test. If it fails, it's on to Hell, or rather, Beneath. Myself…" She brushed the gorgeous sweep of white hair from her face and over a shoulder. "I look forward to meeting Himself and tempting him for a turnaround."

"You are not destined for Beneath, Eglantine. You are the kindest witch I have known."

She balked. "Doesn't look so good on my witchy resume, does it? Kind. Ugh." She turned to Kizzy and propped her chin in hand. "So are you and Bron a thing?"

"Uh…" Kizzy laughed softly. "We're more than friends." Feeling a blush ride her neck, she met his eyes to see his reaction, and he smiled. Approval. Whew!

"He is quite the lover. If I were forty years younger…" The witch sighed. "The disadvantages of choosing mortality, eh?"

"You can *choose* mortality?" Kizzy asked. "Does that imply you could choose immortality?"

"Why, yes. We witches can live forever so long as we perform the immortality ritual once a century. It involves eating a beating vampire's heart. Not for the weak of stomach. But that's not what turns me away from immortality. I've only ever felt I have a century in this current incarnation of soul. I look forward to a reincarnation. It'll be a hoot. But that means I experience wonderful, handsome lovers over the years, such as Bron, and then must stand by and age as they remain so young and virile."

"You are gorgeous," Kizzy offered. "Just because you're getting older doesn't mean you have to stop taking lovers."

"Oh, I know that, darling. Hans and Gustave are upstairs waiting on me. So let's make this quick, shall we? Tell me, Bron, have you contact with the soul bringer? Do you have a name?"

"Blackthorn Regis," he said.

"Ah. Oh." She tapped a perfectly manicured finger against her cheek. "I had thought that one had taken a human lover. A sin eater, in fact. Heard things like she had softened him, actually made him feel." To Kizzy she said, "Soul bringers are quite without emotion. They were once angels, you see. Fallen specifically to ferry the dead, day in and out. Seems a tedious job."

"So the soul bringer has a lover or girlfriend who is human?"

"It's what I've heard about him. I thought it was true. Well, no matter. But you know, darling…" She clasped her hand warmly over Kizzy's hand. "The soul bringer can take out a person's heart without killing them. Something to think about should worse come to worst."

"I don't understand. If someone takes out my heart, I'm pretty sure I'm dead."

"No. The soul bringer's magic can give you life. It could be very similar to the life you have now. You might never notice you're missing your heart."

"But I want my heart. In my chest! It is mine."

"Yes. And why give it away just to save your life, eh?"

The witch stood and leaned over to kiss Bron on the

cheek. "As I've said, I was previously occupied when you two arrived."

"We should be going." Bron stood. "Thank you, Eglantine, for the protection spell."

"It will make the two of you invisible to any wishing you harm. But as for the soul bringer, well, I'd start to panic after twenty-four hours. That's about as long as I suspect my magic will hold against one so powerful."

"It'll give us time to make a plan," he said. He took Kizzy's hand as she thanked the witch. And they found their way out of the witch's estate.

And found themselves standing before a ramshackle cabin on a dark and miserable night. Rain spattered the overgrown weeds and vines. Bron gripped Kizzy's hand as they ran to the truck.

Chapter 19

Rain pummeled the windshield. The flick of the wipers made a rhythm in the absence of music on the radio. They didn't talk much on the way to the motel. Bron's thoughts were occupied with what Eglantine had said about the soul bringer having a human lover. Could he somehow use that against the soul bringer? It wasn't as though he had the stomach for ripping out the lover's heart and taunting the soul bringer with it. An eye for an eye? No innocent should ever be involved in such devious means. Though he could have no clue if the lover was involved in the quest for Kizzy's heart.

It had been good to see Eglantine again. Such a glamorous woman, and she wore her age well. She must be in her eighties. He loved that she wore the hag glamour to answer the door and kept her home warded as a decrepit old cottage. Kept away curiosity seekers.

He had led a blessed life and had gained many friends and lovers over the years. He regretted the affair that had shattered his marriage, but then he had been young and foolish. Claire truly had been much better off without him.

Poor Claire. He'd buried her heart and said goodbye to her. The very last person she may have wished to touch a part of her was him. That he'd found himself keeper of her heart—in the worst manner possible—must be serving her some crazy karmic backlash. Because he did believe she had been the one to put Isabelle out on that cold winter night.

And now there was Kisanthra Lewis, the pretty woman who dozed on the passenger seat beside him, who could stand up to hags and harpies and did not back down from a vampire. Could he welcome Kizzy into his life? For a little while? He had never thought of a woman in terms of spending time with her for months, even years. That he'd like to have her in his life for more than a few nights of sex and companionship was a given. In all his decades he had never met a woman who had given him such a thought. And that was remarkable. If a little unnerving to his established routine of living alone and free.

Kizzy could follow him across the world as he fulfilled his missions. She, taking photos, and he—well, he wasn't exactly following orders now, was he?

Find and finish.

Eglantine had mentioned it. And in that moment he'd noticed Kizzy's attention rivet to the witch. With hope, she'd not remember what had been said, and he could move on. Because he hadn't been ordered to find and finish. Yet. Deactivation was the same process. He wouldn't fool himself on that. There had to be a way to fulfill the mission *and* keep Kizzy alive.

Eglantine had mentioned the soul bringer could take out her heart without killing her. Hmm...

Once at the motel, he carried a drowsy Kizzy into the room and set her on the bed. She curled into sleep, and he pulled off her shoes and then he got undressed.

"Thanks," she whispered as he snuggled next to her. "For everything."

She slid her body against his, and he shivered at the heat of her and pulled her close. He slid a hand up under her shirt, caressing a breast and stirring a wanting moan from her.

Kizzy unbuttoned her jeans and shimmied them down and off. She put a leg over his hip, and with a bend of her hand, directed his cock inside her. He pumped slowly, eyes closed and their mouths touching and then not. Climax wasn't important. Falling asleep inside her meant the world to him.

The soul bringer couldn't find that bedamned black familiar. Had it left the area? Something was up. And he didn't know how to use social media. Those tiny buttons on those tiny devices. Ah!

He'd thought sending the werewolf's heart in a box would have lit a fire under the Retriever. Apparently, he needed to try a new tack.

Time to face his only hope for Nova's salvation.

Kizzy woke to sunshine and an amazing realization. "Bron!"

He stood in the bathroom and leaned back from the sink, toothbrush wielded near his mouth. He was naked, and his cock was half-mast. What a teasing image to wake to.

But her dream! No werewolves this time, only a witch and a promise.

She scrambled off the bed and into the bathroom. "The witch said the soul bringer can take out a person's heart without killing them."

She clasped her fingers over her heart and nodded encouragingly at him.

Bron eyed her a few seconds, then shook his head. "Don't even think about it, Kizzy. You wouldn't be the same. I'm not sure how, but—"

"No!" She grabbed his toothbrush and kissed him, getting a peppermint-laced squishy kiss. "Your wife."

He swiped his mouth and took the toothbrush from her, rinsing it. Then he leaned a palm on the vanity and eyed her fiercely. Things were going on in his brain. She liked watching him think. Then suddenly, he reached the same conclusion as her.

"You think?" she asked.

"It's possible. It didn't occur to me…" He looked in the mirror briefly, then grabbed a clean towel from the rack on the wall.

"She could still be alive. If the soul bringer took out her heart without harming her—"

He cut her off with an abrupt, "I need to think about this, Kizzy."

"Yes, do that." Sensing the sudden wall he'd put up, she clasped her arms across her chest. He was disturbed by the idea of his wife possibly being alive, she could sense it. "You going to shower?"

He nodded, but she could tell his mind was deep in thought, and if she invited herself into the shower he probably wouldn't even notice her. There were far greater things to concern himself with now.

She kissed him quickly and left him in the bathroom.

Fear that some strange creature would come knocking on her door was gone. With the witch's protection spell she could relax. She plopped onto the bed and picked up her camera. She regretted not taking photos last night. What a unique experience. Tea with a witch!

But elation aside, she had to focus. If the protection spell only lasted twenty-four hours, they had work to do. Like find the soul bringer. She tugged the laptop onto a pillow and opened it up. A search for Blackthorn Regis didn't bring up anything, save a few references to Regis Philbin. Completely wrong guy.

She wondered if Bron had access to a secret online network that cataloged paranormal creatures. Wouldn't that be cool? Surely the Acquisitions place he worked for must have a computer database.

On the nightstand, his cellphone rang. She eyed the iPhone, knowing she shouldn't answer. It would go to message. Maybe? Queen of discretion, she was not.

She grabbed it. The screen simply read Director. Bron had mentioned something about a director. His boss?

Without thinking, she hit the answer button and said hello and asked to take a message because Bron was busy.

"Since when does Everhart have a secretary? Who is this?"

"Kisanthra Lewis."

"I see. I thought he had finished that job. Where is he? Why are you answering his personal phone?"

"I'm sorry, I—"

The bathroom door opened, and Bron strolled out in a mist of steam.

"I'm sorry I answered your phone." Kizzy handed it to him. "It was a reflex action. It's your director."

He snatched the phone so rudely she tugged her hand away and clutched it to her chest. Feeling as if he'd just struck her, she filed into the bathroom and closed the door. So she probably shouldn't have answered his phone. But he didn't need to be a jerk about it.

Grabbing a towel for the shower, she muttered to herself, "Give him a break. He just buried his wife's heart and said goodbye to her, and now there's a possibility she could be alive."

He must be going through hell. She'd cut him some slack.

After a long, hot shower, she towel dried her hair and slipped into her jeans and a clean T-shirt from the things she'd packed while at the apartment. Bron was not out in the room, but the rental truck was still parked outside the door. He must have gone for a walk or, she hoped, to scavenge for some breakfast at the diner across the parking lot.

And, yep, there he was, striding toward their room with a food bag in hand.

"Gotta love that guy. Wolf. Werewolf. Wow. I'm dating a werewolf."

Maybe. Or it could just be a fling. Of which, she was okay with a fling. She didn't need to get serious. And Bron didn't seem in a position to get serious with anyone, especially with the looming possibility his wife could very well be alive.

What would a reunion bring about? Would they hug and forgive one another and resume life as a married couple? It had been over a century and a half. Surely, Claire had moved on, as Bron had suspected. Did the law even allow for marriage vows to remain intact after such a long separation? She felt inclined to Google that, but the warm breeze beckoned her to remain in the open doorway.

Bron spied her waiting and lifted the bag. "Pancakes and sausage."

"Great. I'm hungry. You think we can go back to my rental today? Since we've got the witch mojo thing going? I'm all about clean sheets and water pressure."

"Yes, we should. In fact—" he handed her the bag and patted his pocket for his phone "—I should give Certainly Jones a call. He works in the Archives. Keeps records of anything and everything paranormal. He'll be able to tell me what I'm dealing with. Let's eat, then head into town."

Half an hour later they rolled down the main street toward the city center. And Kizzy dared to speak about what had been niggling at her all morning. "I'm sorry about taking that phone call, but your director didn't seem very happy with me."

"It's unprofessional to allow someone to use my phone. I should have said something to you."

"No, it was my fault. It was common courtesy that I should have let it ring through to message. But he said something about finishing the job. And then I remembered Eglantine said something about your mission being find and finish. I thought you said your mission for the Purgatory Heart was find and seize? So I take it that has changed? And if so, are you supposed to finish me?"

His fingers clenched about the steering wheel, and

his jaw pulsed. She wasn't about to let him clam up this time.

"Bron?"

"I was given orders to deactivate the heart," he hissed abruptly. Nothing else. No eye contact. Attention fixed on the road before them. They crossed the bridge that passed over the Red Lake River.

"I see." Kizzy swallowed and drew up her legs before her chest to clasp them tightly. "When are you going to do it? How? Oh, don't answer that one."

"I'm not going to do any such thing."

"But you just said—"

"I promised I would not harm you, Kizzy. And I meant that. Have you so little opinion of my honor that you actually believe I could do such a thing?"

"Sorry. But if it was an order…?"

"I'll have to figure a way around it."

"Why not tell your director that you don't kill?"

He winced.

"I see."

Because he was not a man who lied easily. And he'd probably had occasion to kill over the years. She'd witnessed as much already. He'd killed the wraith in self-defense, as well as a handful of harpies and vampires. If he had let them live, they could have harmed others. So it had been a good call, right?

Kizzy pulled up her backpack from the truck floor and hugged it to her chest. She wanted to be home. Even if it wasn't her actual home, the rental in town felt like someplace safe and familiar.

And for just a few blessed moments, she would really like to have never heard of werewolves and witches and soul bringers.

* * *

Bron followed Kizzy into the apartment, and before she could veer down the hallway and retreat, most likely from him, he pulled her in for a long hug. He wanted her to know he was there for her.

"You can trust me," he said as his fingers glided through her soft hair, clutching and caressing. "I don't want you to fear me."

She nodded against his shoulder. He sensed an utter lack of trust in her.

"Kizzy, I need you to know that I care about you. I've never felt this way about a woman before."

"Really?" When she looked up to him, a tear glistened in her eye.

He touched the tear, and it spilled down her cheek. "Did I do that?"

"Maybe. I don't know." She chuckled softly and sniffed away another tear. "I think I've hit the wall with all things creature and crazy. I really… I need a little time to myself. I want to wash my face and—whatever. Go ahead and use my laptop. Will you give me some time alone?"

"I will. Do you want me to leave the apartment?"

"No," she said quickly. "Just give me an hour to get right with the world, okay?"

"Do whatever you need to do. I'm not going anywhere. Promise."

"Thanks."

Bron wandered out to the living room and stood before the window. Looking out at the sky, the buildings faded out of his peripheral vision. It wasn't even noon, but he could see the shadow of the moon in the sky.

"Tonight," he whispered. "I'll need to have sex all evening to keep back my werewolf."

It couldn't have happened at a less opportune time. With a soul bringer after Kizzy's heart, he had to be on his game. He had named himself her protector, and he would do just that. No one was going to touch her heart.

But what sort of challenge would a soul bringer present?

He tugged out his cell phone and scrolled through the contacts until he found Certainly Jones's number. CJ was a dark witch based in Paris. He headed the Council's Archives, which was basically a keeper of all paranormal knowledge and the mother branch that headed Acquisitions. Some muttered that Acquisitions was the Archives's dirty little secret. But the Archives' contents didn't simply arrive, waiting to be filed and collated. Someone had to obtain the stuff, by trick or by trade. Oftentimes, more violent methods were employed.

If CJ didn't have an answer, he could look it up for Bron. He'd helped him numerous times over the years when Bron went up against creatures about which he had no clue.

"Everhart," CJ answered. "Where are you?"

The dark witch knew Bron was a wanderer and rarely stopped into one of his home bases.

"The States. Minnesota, actually. Tracking the Purgatory Heart. I've found it, but now I've got a soul bringer on my ass."

CJ whistled lowly. "Tough luck, buddy."

"Really? Tell me what I'm dealing with?"

"First of all, you should know my sister-in-law Libby is engaged to a former soul bringer. He got his soul back a few years ago and is now mortal, but the guy was strong and powerful when he was fully charged. You know they are angels?"

"I'd heard something about that. Did they Fall?"

"Not purposefully, but rather they were forced to Fall as a mission to ferry souls. It's a hell of a job. Ferrying souls to Above or Beneath all day and night. Gotta be boring. Another name for them is psychopomp."

"Yes, I'm familiar with that term."

"They are emotionless sons of bitches. And usually work a territory. Can twist a man's head off and toss it aside as if a softball. But that's only if you piss one off. And like I said, emotionless, so it takes a lot to make one angry. Generally they do their job, ferry souls. They don't interact with the population, either mortal or paranormal. Not usually. So this one is after you for what reason?"

"Apparently he wants this heart that will give him access to Purgatory. But I've learned he can't touch the heart, or actually enter Purgatory, so why he wants it is beyond me. I need to know how to fight him and stop him."

"Not much you can use against one of them. His original halo, which fell away when he Fell to earth, can be used to restore his soul and make him mortal. But you'll have a hell of a time locating that. It could be anywhere, and the soul bringer doesn't usually know where it is. You'd need a professional halo hunter if that's the route you want to take. My theory is that many halos sank to the bottom of the ocean."

"I'm not much for deep-sea diving. Next option?"

"If you can get your hands on a Sinistari blade, that will probably wound him, slow him down a bit, but not sure about ultimate death. They are equally as power-ful as the Fallen."

"Interesting. I had my hands on a Sinistari blade a few years ago. And now I think of it, the blade should be in the Archives."

"I can take a look for it."

"I'd appreciate that, CJ. I'll text you an address, and you can send it."

"Will do. You know this soul bringer's name?"

"Blackthorn Regis."

CJ's hiss chilled Bron's heart. The man had seen many things, had even spent time in Daemonia, one of the most despicable, demon-infested places in exis-tence. To hear his reaction to the soul bringer's name did not bode well.

"That's odd," CJ finally said. "I'm sure I have re-cord of him hooking up with a mortal sin eater not too long ago."

"But I thought you said they were emotionless? Doesn't a hookup imply romance?" And yet, Eglan-tine had said much the same.

"Generally. Let me look into this and get back to you. If he has a mortal girlfriend, that's his weak spot right there. Means the guy has feelings now."

"Perfect. The sooner you can get back to me, the bet-ter. He's close, and he's made it known he's willing to kill to get the heart. And Kizzy is an innocent."

"Kizzy?"

"Uh…" Bron shoved a hand over his hair and made a wobbling gesture with his hand, even though CJ couldn't see it. "She's the one with the heart. I'm pro-tecting her."

"Since when do Retrievers protect? I thought you

guys just grabbed the goods and got the hell out of there. Oh. You didn't know the heart was intact, did you?"

"That detail was not mentioned when I accepted the assignment. And a guy can't very well rip the thing out of her chest."

"A guy could. Because he has done things like that before."

Yeah, so CJ knew him well.

"You always make the wise decision," the dark witch encouraged. "Talk soon, man."

"Thanks, CJ."

Oh, yeah. A little time to herself definitely served to improve her mood. The cinnamon-scented oil rising from the nearby diffuser jar served to give Kizzy some clear thoughts. She'd stripped to her underwear and crawled into bed, even though it was afternoon. She wasn't tired, just confused by the push and pull in her heart.

It pushed her to run to Bron, arms open and ready, yet it pulled her back at any mention of the weird or violence that may occur because of his job. He was supposed to deactivate her heart. She could imagine only one possible way to do that. And while he'd sworn he would not, it wasn't every day a girl learned her lover had been assigned to kill her.

Stuff like that only happened in the movies. And in stories.

Like vampires and witches and angels and…werewolves.

She sighed and sat up, hugging herself as she gazed out the window. Could she trust him? Did she really have a handle on the situation? When had her life become so much more than a lost boyfriend and the desire to put him in her past?

This new man in her life was everything Keith had not been. Bron was larger than life. She wanted to follow him across the world. And she did trust him.

Exhaling, she nodded and said, "I do. He won't hurt me. I won't allow it to happen."

Having decided that she would take control of her crazy life, she rose and pulled on a T-shirt and jeans. Her man sat out in the living room, likely wondering what the hell was going on in her brain. She needed to reassure him. And the only way she knew how to do that was with food.

Bron picked up his ringing phone to read a text from CJ.

Sinistari blade is currently dispatched in Rome. Will not have access for days. Sorry. Regis has sin eater girlfriend, Desdenova Fleetwood. Good luck.

No blade? He'd have to make do.

He tucked away the phone and turned to smile at Kizzy, who had just called him to the table. An early supper was disguised as breakfast, because she'd only had a few items in the fridge. She set a frying pan with eggs and sausage on a copper trivet, laid out plates and filled glasses with orange juice.

"Was that important?" she asked.

"I contacted a dark witch who heads the Council's Archives. He gave me information about the soul bringer. He may have a weakness that won't require hard-core weapons to bring him down."

She paused from forking a fluffy cloud of eggs into her mouth. "Which is?"

"He has a girlfriend. A sin eater, as Eglantine had suspected. The soul bringer is an unfeeling, emotionless thing. If he has a lover, then I can only suspect he's changed. And any man who is in love is weak."

"Have you ever been in love?" she asked. "I mean, I know you were married. And you had the affair. But was it love?"

Bron tilted down the whole glass of orange juice, taking a moment to gather his wits. She just came out with anything she wanted to know. Which he shouldn't mind, but every little bit she learned about him… Well. A man could only protect himself for so long before the inevitable emotion did bring him down and open up his walls.

Could he hope the soul bringer's defensive walls had fallen because he may be in love?

"If you don't want to say," she tossed out, "it's okay. I shouldn't have asked."

"I thought I was in love," he said quickly. "I thought I could love my wife. I did for a while. Maybe. I'm not sure. And then I thought I loved Isabelle's mother, but I realized it was more a means of exerting my freedom from the entire pack. I liked the idea of leading the pack, but actually assuming responsibility was something I wasn't yet prepared to do. I think that's why I did what I did. Instinctually, I knew I would be found out."

She reached for his hand and tapped his fingers. A reassuring touch.

"But I did love Isabelle," he said. "I should have spent more time with her. Been a real father to her."

Kizzy clasped his hand and smiled a small, comforting curve. "You did your best."

"Did I? I'm pretty sure I did as I pleased and was taken to task for it."

"Yes, but now that you know better, you do better."

"You have an inordinately high opinion of me. You should be careful."

"Why? Do you intend to break my heart? Or just steal it?"

He smirked. "There will be no talk of stolen hearts. Yours will remain exactly where it is."

The door buzzer rang, and Kizzy got up. Bron stood immediately and gestured she stay by the table.

"We're safe," she said. "We've got the witch's protection spell, right?"

"Still," Bron offered. "Sit. I'll get it."

He strolled down the hallway, but before he reached the door it crashed open, the doorknob crushing the Sheetrock inward. And in the threshold stood a tall, dark-haired man sporting a whiplash grin.

"Blackthorn Regis," Bron guessed.

Chapter 20

Kizzy stood up slowly at the sight of the tall man standing before Bron. Coal-dark hair spilled to his shoulders. He was deceptively slender, for she sensed he was powerful from the manner he stood in the doorway, head tilted forward, shoulders back, hands posed as if to grip a pistol for a shoot-out. He didn't move to attack.

Bron stood equally as prepared, feet planted. He'd placed himself between her and the man.

A soul bringer? Who had once been an angel. Wow. And yet… He wanted her heart.

She shivered and backed away from the table until her legs hit the windowsill behind her. Her eyes darted about in search of a weapon. Didn't Bron carry a knife on him at all times? She didn't see it. He must have taken it out of his boot. Would the stake in his holster have any effect against a soul bringer?

"I thought it time we had a chat," the soul bringer said to them both. He had a touch of a British accent, or so it seemed from his pure intonation. "Won't you invite me in? I can't harm either of you. Or even touch you. I can feel the witchy protection spell. It stings as if bees to my skin."

Glancing over his shoulder, Bron studied Kizzy's gaze. She gave him the slightest nod. If the soul bringer couldn't touch them, they should be safe. And she did want to get this hashed out. She trusted Bron would protect her, yet she sensed even he wasn't 100 percent sure how to face this particular opponent.

"Have a seat," she offered, gesturing to the table. She rushed to grab the breakfast plates and set them in the sink.

The soul bringer's approach felt as if a cool winter wind had blown beneath the windowsill, and she shivered as she turned to find him sitting opposite where she had been. Bron stood beside him at the table, eyes intent on the enemy. It felt wrong but strangely convivial.

The soul bringer sat. Dressed in a black damask vest stitched with gold threading, and a black shirt beneath and paired with black leather pants over Italian loafers, he looked out of time. Rather dapper, actually, but not dandyish. She would not doubt he could destroy them both with ease.

Bron did not sit but instead held the back of the chair with a tight grip as he leaned forward. "Talk then."

Kizzy carefully settled onto the chair across the table from their guest. Her skin flushed as the soul bringer's black eyes moved over her. She could sense his power. Feel it like electricity crackling across her skin. Or perhaps that was the protection spell doing its job. She hoped so.

Where was her camera?

"I can feel your heart beating swiftly," the soul bringer said to her, his eyes burning into hers with precise aim. "Who clasped it from Purgatory and tried to bring you down?"

"You talk to me," Bron said, dragging the chair out from the table and planting himself before the soul bringer. "She's not your concern."

"She is my raison d'être. Are you her protector now? You, who traveled across the ocean to rip the heart from her chest."

"That will never happen," Bron said. "As long as I live."

The soul bringer smiled a straight grin. "Your death can be accomplished."

"Don't you have some souls to ferry?" Bron asked tightly.

The man shrugged. "I am on holiday until this matter gets taken care of."

"This matter? You want something from Kizzy, and I've told you that will never happen. End of the matter. Anything else you want to discuss before I request you leave?"

"I wish to make a trade. I've already given you the means to securing that trade. You have your wife's heart?"

Bron smashed his fist on the table, and Kizzy's entire body stiffened. Would he shift to werewolf and take the guy out? *Could* he shift during the day? Was it a moonlight thing?

"You had no right," Bron said tightly. "Claire was an innocent."

"Yes, but it did serve to summon your attention." The soul bringer leaned back in the chair, crossing his arms. "I will give you your wife in trade for the Purgatory Heart. At which point you will have the opportunity to replace her heart, and she walks away. Alive."

Bron gaped.

The soul bringer grinned. "You thought she was dead?" He shook his head.

"The witch said you could take out hearts and keep a person alive," Kizzy said. "Where is his wife?"

"Kizzy," Bron admonished tightly.

She had lost her fear of the evil sitting across the table from her, which wasn't necessarily wise. Bron's severe glance tethered her back to reality. She clasped her arms across her chest but sat up straighter. She wasn't puddling now, nor would she ever. And she would show them both that.

"Why do you want to enter Purgatory?" Bron asked. "I'm given to understand that is impossible for you."

"What I can and cannot do is not your concern, werewolf. But what I will do to your wife should be." Blackthorn rapped the tabletop. "Tomorrow morning at nine, out past the farm supply store. There is an abandoned silo and former hardware warehouse that the human woman will recognize. By then I sense the protection spell will be depleted, for I can feel it drain from you both even as I sit here. Bring me this woman with the Purgatory Heart intact, and I will hand your wife to you. Best you retrieve her heart. After I release her, she won't have much time. The heart must immediately be returned to its rightful position."

The soul bringer stood and swept around to stroll down the hallway. Kizzy and Bron held each other's stares, mouths open. The front door slammed shut, startling them both from their frozen states.

"She's alive," Kizzy offered with hope. "Your wife."

Yet speaking those words cut into her heart. She shouldn't feel jealous. And Bron had admitted he'd never truly loved Claire, but now he *had* to save her. Honor wouldn't allow him to do otherwise. Nor could she ask him not to.

She clutched a hand over her chest. Would it be the last time she felt her racing heartbeats?

"If she is alive, he must be keeping her somewhere," Bron said, standing and pacing to the window. "Most likely the warehouse where he wants to meet. You are familiar with it?"

"Yes. It's about four miles out of town. Used to host snowcat races in the winter until the city cracked down on the bonfires as a safety hazard. What are you thinking? Rescue mission?"

"It's the only option."

"But if the soul bringer doesn't willingly release her to you, maybe you won't be able to put her heart back? I don't think we can simply grab her and run."

"We'll see about that." Bron strode past the table. Kizzy followed him down the hallway to the front door. He stopped before opening it and turned to her. "You stay here. I'm going to scout the warehouse."

"I'm coming with you. I don't want to stay alone. What if—"

"You are protected from all paranormals who wish you harm."

"You heard the guy. He said he could feel the protection spell draining. By morning it will be completely gone. Bron." She clasped his hands. "Maybe if you give him my heart, he'll do the same with me? Use it for whatever he needs it for, and then put it back in my chest. I could live. And you could save your wife."

"That's insanity. I don't trust the man. And I will not have another woman harmed because of my mistakes."

"This isn't your mistake." She touched his cheek, and he jerked away from her. But she insisted and stepped closer until he could look into her eyes. "I'm not your mistake. You just happened on to my weirdness. And because you're such an honorable man, you've been forced to make some tough choices. Now it's my turn to make a choice. It's my heart."

He clasped her hand and pressed his lips to her knuckles, closing his eyes. Shaking his head. "No, I won't. I can't. You… Kizzy…" He pulled her into his arms and hugged her tightly. "You mean so much to me."

The gasping plea filled her with hope. She meant something to him. As he did to her. They could join hands, turn and run as far from danger as possible. To live happily ever after? Not possible if they gave up on Claire.

"You can't let her die."

"I won't. I'll figure something out. But first and foremost, I will protect you. I swear it, Kizzy. Let me be your protector."

"You are. I adore you for that."

He smirked. "You don't even know me."

"You are kind and strong and loyal. That's all I need to know."

He bowed his head to her forehead. "And you are

smart, good and open to everything. I love that about you."

"I'm coming with you to get your wife's heart."

"I don't love her anymore," he said. "You need to know that. I'm not sure I ever did."

"I know. But you did care for her."

"I still care about her safety. And guilt will not allow me to ignore her."

"It's not guilt, but honor."

"If you say so. Let's go."

Grabbing her camera, Kizzy closed the door behind them, and they sailed down the stairs and out the back door into the alleyway where Bron had fought the harpie just the other night. No harpies in sight. No vampires, either, but Kizzy kept a keen eye peeled in all directions as they walked.

"I should go to the warehouse first," Bron said.

"The soul bringer will be watching for you. Let's return to the woods to get the heart first. You'll need it. *She* will need it."

"Why do you care so much about a woman you've never met?"

"I would hope if I were in her position, someone would care enough about me."

He kissed her and smoothed his hand through her hair. "Thank you, for being the strange, wonderful woman that you are."

The rental truck rumbled off the gravel road and back onto the highway. The shovel clattered in the truck bed. Bron had forgotten to secure it in the utility box. But he'd found the black box, exactly where he'd buried it. His nose had led him right to it.

That wasn't the only thing his senses had tuned into. It was only late afternoon, and he was beginning to feel the stirrings of the moon's call beneath his skin. He needed to stop it if he were to stay in top form. But the only way to do that was to have sex. Lots of it. Tonight.

It was either that or drive out to the country and shift to werewolf for the night. Neither option was optimal. Though one of the two was preferable.

He reached across the seat and clasped Kizzy's hand. She held the dirt-smeared box with her other hand. She smiled at him. He could think of nothing better than making love to her all night. And that was the problem. He was horny, damn it. His focus was divided.

And then a terrible thought occurred. If he craved sex tonight, all other werewolves would, as well. Including his long-lost wife. What condition was Claire in, missing her heart? Had the soul bringer chained her up? Imprisoned her? Could Bron rescue her tonight and set her free to go satisfy her own wild cravings?

He shouldn't be thinking about having sex with Kizzy when Claire's life was at stake. And yet, would Claire even be thankful for his return? Had Blackthorn Regis told her he'd given Bron her heart, and her freedom hinged on him returning with it? Of course, he had.

And yet, what would happen when he did stand before the wife he had not seen for over a hundred and fifty years, holding her heart? If a trade were made, Kizzy's heart must be handed over. And yet, the soul bringer couldn't touch it. How had he gotten Claire's heart in the box? Out of her chest?

Bron was missing something. And he didn't like not knowing how to deal with a situation. He pulled up before Kizzy's building.

"Why here?" she asked.

"I've rethought our original plan. You'll be safe with the witch's protection spell. I'm going to check on the warehouse myself. No arguments. Take the box." He tapped the black box, and dirt flecked onto her lap. "Guard it with your life."

Kizzy nodded. "You'll come back?"

"I have to," he said. "Full moon tomorrow night. Tonight…"

"I'll be waiting," she said and squeezed his hand. "Do what you have to do."

She slid out of the truck and walked up to the building entrance and didn't look back before entering. Bron wished she had. Would he see her again?

He wasn't sure.

Chapter 21

He found the old warehouse easily enough. The countryside was thick with pine forest, but a stretch along the highway had been cleared where he suspected farmers must have once brought in grain after harvest. Now the concrete drive was cracked and weed-ridden, and the building's corrugated steel walls were intact in about 80 percent of the area. Windows had been broken out or removed decades earlier, perhaps to prevent—or because of—vandalism.

Bron had driven past the place and parked half a mile up the road on an old turnoff that went nowhere. The truck was hidden from view by the pine trees that gave off a sharp, clean odor. Gravel crunched under his boots as he walked along the opposite side of the road and stopped a quarter mile away. His vision was sharp, allowing him to see through one of the warehouse windows. Something moved inside. His chest tightened, and he sucked in a breath. He caught a glimpse of the soul bringer, dressed in black, pacing, talking on a cell phone. Of all things! But his focus veered to the cage that, within, sat a blonde woman, clinging to the bars, her gaze lost on something Bron couldn't determine.

"Claire," he whispered. And his heart tightened. Had he forgotten that pale, long hair that had once spilled over his face as they'd made love? What had it smelled like?

How many decades had it been since he'd even considered the life he'd once had as pack leader and husband? It was too long ago. He'd put all that behind him. And now his past had been resurrected for reasons that baffled him.

Where had the soul bringer found Claire? She could not have been living in the area. Or even the States. Though he could have no clue where life had lured her in the decades since he'd been forced out of the pack, shamed for his selfish act against her.

Who the hell was he to think he could have a chance with Kizzy? That he *deserved* a chance with her? Human or not, did it matter? The simple question was: Could he treat a woman well?

Over the years he'd lost much of that wild, young wolf he'd once been. His wild nature had been honed, polished. Not exactly tamed, but focused. Change had been inevitable. But was he capable of fidelity? That he even considered it now startled him. He hadn't known Kizzy long. Yet she had planted herself within his cautious heart.

He mustn't think like that. Shouldn't his wife deserve his consideration first and foremost?

He should just wolf out and go after the soul bringer. That might get his wife released. It also might injure the soul bringer, but Bron knew it was an uneven match. Even in werewolf form he wasn't designed to go against an angel.

And if he did steal Claire away, how to put her heart back where it belonged? He'd been told the soul bringer had to do it and quickly. Would she die the moment he took her away?

Bron rubbed his temple, easing at the twinge that threatened to become a headache. His discomfort was more than just that. His body hummed; his skin was extra sensitive. The day was growing long, and with that, the urge to shift to werewolf grew stronger. As well, the full moon urged him to mate in his were form. He had to choose between shifting or mating.

He didn't want to do either tonight when he should be getting Claire away from Blackthorn Regis. But he didn't know a way around things. Likely the soul bringer had thought this through. He wouldn't expect Bron to come charging in tonight as a werewolf, because he'd not have fighting in mind.

Yet if Bron felt the urge to shift or mate, then Claire would, too.

He focused on the cage again but couldn't see her now. The bars would prove a godsend for her sake. She would be desperate to mate, as well.

If Bron should go near his wife tonight, it would inevitably result in mating. They would have no choice. Their hormones and instincts would demand it of the two of them. And he didn't want that. Nor did she, he felt sure. Certainly not with the husband who had cuckolded her, the man who'd left her so long ago only to now trap her in a new nightmare.

So to protect her—in the strangest way possible—he'd have to let her sit alone tonight and hope she could not break free from the cage.

It was best for Claire.

Rubbing a hand over his face, he shook his head at the ridiculous option he'd decided on. It wasn't fair or just. Cruel, even. But he could not choose the other option. He would not force sex between him and Claire. Because he cared too much about what Kizzy would think of that. She wouldn't like it. Though he suspected she'd suggest it. Just to be understanding. She was too nice.

And caring. And…he wanted her right now. Because his body craved sexual satisfaction. He wanted to dive inside her soft peachy scent. Instincts demanded he heed that desire or else answer the call of his wild.

He glanced toward the warehouse. Rush in, stab the soul bringer. Grab Claire. Head out.

With no means to return her heart to her chest.

Tightening his jaw, he resisted the foolish charge to the vanguard. Patience was required.

"I'm sorry, Claire. I will return for you in the morning."

Kizzy hadn't been able to sit still. She paced. Turned on the TV but hadn't been interested in Dr. Oz's prescription for a healthy heart. Paced some more. Then decided she had to offer herself so Bron could free Claire. The soul bringer would put her heart back when he was done with it. Everything would be swell.

Because Bron thought he could save her *without* removing her heart. She knew that wasn't possible. She hadn't been dreaming about a werewolf ripping out her heart for no reason. It had been a portent. One she must now step up to fulfill.

She put on a red T-shirt, then shook her head at the reflection in the mirror.

"I'll need buttons," she muttered, pulling it off. "Easier access."

Then she shivered as she stood before the mirror half naked. It would hurt to have her heart ripped out. She didn't have to wonder about that. And it would hurt as much to have it put back in. Anesthesia, anyone?

She stroked her fingers down the scar already there. She'd never thought it ugly, only a new part of her. A new chapter to her story. And perhaps, a reminder of a regrettable moment. She should have waited to talk to Keith after they'd safely arrived home that night. But would it have mattered?

Would he have ever heard her truth? Or would he have ignored her for his own desires, as he had been so excellent at doing. He didn't have to steer the car into the ditch that night.

"It was his choice," she whispered.

Could she live with that? Could she move on and not let this bother her anymore?

"I have to," she whispered. "I will."

She grabbed a floral button-up blouse and pulled it on. "What happened with Keith and I happened. It's done. I can't change it. And now? I'm going to do this. It's what is best. Bron's wife will be set free. And I will not agree to do it unless I am also set free with heart intact. Win-win," she said to the mirror. "Right?"

Her reflection did not return an encouraging smile,

so Kizzy turned away and shoved her feet into the pair of red Vans. She'd have to be careful going to the warehouse. Bron could still have it staked out. But she couldn't risk meeting him along the way. She'd have to stake him out staking out the warehouse. As soon as he drove off, she'd move in.

"I can do this. I *will* do this," she whispered as she strode down the hallway toward the front door.

It was the only way to be free. And only she could do that for herself.

But when she opened the door a handsome man stepped in and swept her into a deep and wanting kiss. Gliding his hands along her arms, Bron lifted her wrists and pinned them to the wall above her head. He smelled like pine trees and fresh air. Deepening the kiss, he hugged her at hips, chest and thighs. His erection nudged into her hip, teasing her with an unexpected offer.

"Well, well. You're in a mood."

"That I am." He kissed her jaw, her neck and tugged at the rayon shirt collar with his teeth. "Were you on your way out?"

"Uh, nope?"

"You were on your way to look for me," he guessed.

"I don't think so." Yeah, so she wasn't a first-class liar.

And Bron was more perceptive than she could imagine. Right now he perceived that lashing his tongue over her skin and toward her breast would send shivers up her spine and coax her to wrap her legs about his hips. Had she been on her way out to do something important? The sensuous glide of his tongue over her skin dizzied her better senses. And she didn't mind that at all.

"Did you find what you were looking for?" she asked.

"Talk later," he muttered. "I'm hungry."

"We could go get a bite to eat—"

"I'm hungry for you," he growled against her ear.

There was no arguing that statement.

"Oh, I get it. Is this the part where we have sex until you're sated?"

"Yes. Any objections?"

Happy to oblige, she grabbed him by the shirt and closed the front door. Pulling him down the hallway, she led him into the bedroom. But the sudden thought that she wasn't the first to help him out wouldn't allow her to just dive right in. She turned and pressed a hand to his chest. "You've lived how long?"

"Almost two hundred years."

"And how many lovers have you had in those two centuries?"

"Kizzy. You don't want to talk about this right now."

"Please, satisfy the curiosity in me. I'll tell you how many I've had?"

"It doesn't matter to me. All that does is when we're together you are completely here. Mine." He kissed her soundly. "No one else's." He lifted her and kissed the base of her neck. "The past doesn't matter, nor does the future."

"So we're not thinking about tomorrow morn—" Another kiss silenced her.

Bron laid her on the bed and crawled over her. The predatory spark in his eyes didn't frighten her so much as stir her desires to a giddy thrill. Who cared how many lovers he'd had? Well, she did, a little. Just for curiosity's sake, of course. But he was right. Now was for…now.

Her shirt slid up, and his hot tongue lashed her bare breast. Kizzy squirmed and pulled him closer. He nipped her jaw and kissed his way up to her mouth. He ground his erection against her, and she tilted up a hip to meet that tease.

"Hard enough for you?" he asked.

"Let's take that big boy out to play." She reached down and unzipped him, carefully, and before she could shove his jeans past his hips, she gripped his penis with one hand and slid her other down to cup his testicles.

"Mmm, Kizzy, careful."

"Kick off your jeans."

"You're in a hurry."

"And you're not?"

"We've got all night," he said as he tossed his jeans aside and allowed her to pull him toward her by his cock.

"Then let's start with a taste," she said and bent to lick his erection.

As the night grew into morning, and their antics moved them all about the bed, the room, and even down the hallway for a slammed-against-the-wall session of heart-pumping sex, Bron's werewolf demanded he continue to seek sexual satisfaction even after the incredible orgasms both he and Kizzy shared. And since he didn't want to break out into a howler in the middle of the city, he answered that insistent call. With gusto.

Somehow they'd found their way into the living room on the couch. The TV was on, turned to a music station, and currently played an 80s dance tune. One of Kizzy's legs hooked over his shoulder as he kissed the sweet spot between her legs and lashed his tongue along the tender folds, finding a different reaction from her from various places he touched. Some places stirred up long, hungry moans. Another spot made her peep with desperation. This particular place made her grip his hair and tug, roughly, pulling him in deeper, demanding he give her what she wanted.

She tasted sweet and salty and wanting. Everything about her answered his needs. Needs he'd avoided for decades. Not like a monk. But cautiously placing himself to the side whenever he hooked up with a woman. Never once returning for the second night. Yes, even when he must feed his hunger the night before and after the full moon—which was often—he made sure to find a woman who was only interested in the sex. Not him.

And the whole avoiding the human woman thing? He couldn't, for the life of him, figure why he'd been so frightened of actually moving beyond that fear and allowing a friendship or even a short affair. It hadn't been the human that had caused all his problems; it had been his choices. Bad choices. That he would never make again.

"That's so freaking good," Kizzy muttered. "Don't stop, Bron. Don't…"

He wasn't about to disappoint this woman. Her breathless gasps coaxed him to circle his tongue about her clit. She'd come quickly, he'd learned, if he placed the firm, lingering tip of his tongue right…there.

Kizzy gasped out a delicious shout of climax. Her head slid over the edge of the couch, and her breasts heaved in the moonlight that beamed through the boulevard window. Her body tremored. Her stomach glistened with perspiration. Her fingers clenched for a hold, finding his hair.

And in that moment Bron knew he could not easily walk away from Kisanthra Lewis. She was gorgeous. A moon goddess. A sweet innocent who knew more than she should. A keeper of secrets, hoarded within her camera. A daring believer.

He loved her.

For the first time in his life, he might really be in love with a woman. Was that possible? Or was it merely lust?

Hours later his werewolf was sated. It must have been around three in the morning. Bron lay beside Kizzy, panting, coming down from yet another orgasm that had shook them simultaneously.

"Do you need to do that every month?" she said on an elated whisper.

"Either that or let my werewolf out. If I'm home on my property I opt for the run in the wild."

"Yeah, that was certainly a run in the wild. Wow!"

"You rethinking your agreement to help me out tonight?"

"Nope. Never. I like your wild. I think you even growled at me a couple of times."

"You liked it."

"I did." She rolled to her back and closed her eyes. Smoothing her hand across his stomach she tickled a fingertip through the dark hair growing up from his groin. "I'm going to have some good dreams now."

"Then I'll let you rest. I'm sated." He almost said "thank you," but that felt wrong. She hadn't just given him a gift or done something kind for him. She had shared herself with him. And that was worth more than a simple thank-you. He kissed her forehead. "Sweet dreams."

"For sure they'll be much better than the werewolf-ripping-out-my heart dream," she said on a drowsy tone.

"What?" He'd heard her correctly. "You think I…?"

"Huh? Oh. Sorry. I shouldn't have said anything, but…it's nothing to do with you."

"I don't understand. Kizzy?"

"It's just—I've been having nightmares since the accident. Couple times a month. Always this werewolf rips out my heart. And then…well the dream ends, and I never know if he eats it or if I live or what."

"Kizzy, why are you only telling me this now?"

"I did mention it earlier."

"Not the part about the werewolf."

"I didn't want to freak you out. It can't mean anything. They've been going on much longer than I've known you. And I assume it's metaphorical. I'm into paranormal creatures, so of course it would be a werewolf that would show up in my dream, since those were the only ones I was really afraid of." She yawned. "You've worn me out. 'Night."

"Good night," he said and kissed her again. But Bron didn't fall asleep as easily as she did. She'd dreamed about a werewolf ripping out her heart?

What strange portent had brought him into her life?

Chapter 22

Kizzy rolled over in bed and wrapped her arms around…the pillow.

She sat up and blinked at the morning sunshine beaming through the window. Forgot to pull the shades last night. Her body felt lax and warm, and she smelled like Bron and sex. A delicious blend of wild and salty. She listened but didn't have to wonder if he was in the bathroom. The door across the hallway was open, and the small bathroom was dark. And she didn't hear anyone tinkering out in the kitchen.

Her heart dropped to her gut. "He left without me. He's going to try and beat the soul bringer and save his wife. He can't do that!" She scrambled off the bed and grabbed some clothes. "He needs me." She stood abruptly and clasped her chest. He'd successfully dissuaded her from her mission yesterday. All night. But now it was a new day.

And… "He needs my heart."

There was no way around it. He might be able to wound the soul bringer with some of those weapons he wielded, but to ultimately win? Even Bron had been unsure he could stand against one so powerful. There was only one way for him to walk out of that warehouse this morning with his wife in his arms.

And while she should care less what happened to the wife, Kizzy couldn't stand back and allow an innocent woman to suffer for something that she could fix.

Besides, she could get her heart back after the soul bringer had used it as a portal to Purgatory. All would be swell.

That's what she kept repeating as she dressed, quickly brushed her teeth, swigged back some orange juice—ugh! After toothpaste!—and headed for the door. Gripping the knob, she paused and wondered about bringing along her camera. She shook her head. Too big. And it would be a distraction.

She opened the door, then rushed back into the kitchen and grabbed the small digital camera she used for backup and tucked it into her front pocket.

"I'm not a fool."

Bron dodged a wicked arc of black lightning that crackled above his head. Jumping to the right, he stood upright with the bowie knife held at the ready.

The soul bringer smirked. "I can do this all day, werewolf. Face it. You've not the speed or the skill to defeat me. Sure, you can take down most other entities that inhabit this mortal realm. But that's because they are of *this* realm. I am not."

Indeed, the man was angel. But he'd had to try. Repeatedly. And with everything he could muster. And without Kizzy at his side. He'd made the right choice by leaving her back home snug in bed. No harm must come to her.

With a sweep of his hand, he wiped the sweat from his brow. He glanced toward the cage set against the wall in the shadows. Claire sat inside. She clung to the bars, her darting eyes wide. Blond hair tangled down her back. Her white dress was dirty. Had she shifted last night? The dress wasn't torn, but she may have been forced to take it off before shifting. Pray, the soul bringer had not stood there watching. She had suffered enough humiliation as well as personal threat. Because of him.

He had to set her free.

"I heard you howl last night, wolf," the soul bringer teased Bron snidely.

"You kept her in the cage all night?" Bron asked, wandering back and forth like a caged animal himself. The blade handle hurt his bones, he gripped it so tightly.

"Don't you know a werewolf can't shift without its heart?"

Again Bron glanced to Claire. It may have been a strange mercy for her that she hadn't shifted. "I'm so sorry," he felt the need to say to her.

"This is your fault!" she yelled, summoning a twinge of remembrance, at the back of his neck. He had wronged her. Again. "Get me out of here!"

"There must be some bargain we can come to," Bron said, stopping his pacing before the soul bringer. "She isn't a part of this."

"I made her a part of it."

"But she's…" He couldn't say it. That she hadn't

meant anything to him over the centuries. That even now he only felt compelled to help her because she was the classic damsel in distress. No woman should be treated so cruelly. Someone had to rescue her. But care for her?

Had he ever loved Claire? Or had he simply been fulfilling a requirement to become pack leader? Had he fooled himself that he'd known love?

Yes. The affair had proven it. It was time to move on. And fight for something that he really could love. Like Kizzy. And the only way to do that was to right a past wrong.

"I know. I've heard the sad tale of your infidelity," Blackthorn offered. He crossed his arms and leaned against a steel pole. He was not broad in shoulder or wide with muscle. Slim and lean, he epitomized the slinking dark menace. "Love is tough, isn't it?"

"As if you would know," Bron spat out and resumed his pacing.

He'd come with a plan that he had known would fail. But how else to avoid bringing the woman he did care about into this mess? He just hoped to solve this before Kizzy woke and figured out what he was up to.

"I know love," Blackthorn said. "It is why I need that damned Purgatory Heart."

"Soul bringers are emotionless," Bron said. "You are a liar."

"I cannot lie. It's an angel thing. And I have learned to love since Desdenova came into my life."

Within a second the soul bringer stood before Bron, gripping him up under the chin. The black gloves he wore fit like a second skin. His coal eyes blazed with a cold fire. "My Nova died a week ago. She was a sin eater. Do you know what that means, wolf?"

Bron shook his head within the tight grip. If he could just slash far enough with the blade…

"Unfortunately, sin eaters are mortal, and something so repulsive as a drunk driver took her life. Upon her death she went to Purgatory. Sin eaters are destined to spend eternity in that place. They cannot reach Above without direct guidance from a soul bringer."

Bron kicked the man at the hip, which released him to land on his feet and stumble backward a few steps. He wielded the blade between them but did not move to slash. He wanted to hear what the soul bringer had to say.

"Then why did you let her go?" he challenged. "You could have brought her Above."

"I was ferrying other souls! I was not there when the car struck her, crushing the life from her as she was thrown from her feet and slammed against a brick wall. I could not get to her soul fast enough. With her last breath, her soul was instantly sucked into Purgatory."

"So that's why you need to get to Purgatory?"

Blackthorn nodded. He sucked in a stuttering breath. "I know love, wolf. And it is fierce. Do you know what they will do to my Nova in Purgatory? She is reviled for the multitude of sins she has eaten to allow sinners to pass into Above instead of Beneath where they belong. Not once in her lifetime had Nova sinned. Never. Always she kept a clean soul in order to take on the brunt of the evils she ate to cleanse others. And yet the Toll Gatherers will take their revenge on her for those stolen souls they were not given opportunity to torment. I must get her out!"

Bron winced to recognize the desperation in the man's voice. Perhaps the soul bringer had loved. Bron had always walked away before any degree of love could escalate in his life. His one-night-stand rule. And yet, yes, he had known love in the eyes of an innocent child.

And now to learn exactly why the soul bringer sought an entrance into Purgatory changed things. Minutely. He still wouldn't hand over Kizzy's heart.

I dreamed of a werewolf ripping out my heart.

Bron's heart had cracked when she'd told him that. He believed in premonition and portents. But did she?

And now he knew the enemy he dealt with had a weakness and could be ruled by emotion. Blackthorn Regis wasn't simply pure evil.

Which made him much more complicated.

"I thought you were not able to enter Purgatory?" Bron asked. Not so eager to simply react now, he relaxed his shoulders, yet maintained a defensive stance with feet apart, blade at the ready.

"Purgatory is closed to me. I'll worry about that when I get the heart."

"Did someone ask about a heart?"

Bron spun around at Kizzy's voice. "No! Get out of here!"

She marched across the concrete floor toward him. Bron shoved the blade into the sheath where he normally kept a stake and gripped her by the shoulders. The contact filled his senses with her essence and momentarily returned him to the bed they had shared last night. She smelled like sex and warmth and everything he couldn't live without.

So he was wrong. He did know how to love. Fiercely.

"No, Kizzy," he said so softly because he wanted her

all to himself. And, for some odd reason, he didn't want to disrespect Claire. "I won't let you do this."

"Then it's a good thing I can make up my own mind. You can have my heart!" she called to Blackthorn. "If you promise to put it back when you're finished with it."

"Of course I will," the soul bringer said.

"You won't be the same," Bron argued. He clutched her shoulders tightly, wanting to make her stop, to force her to turn away and run. But she was a strong woman who would not be dissuaded. He loved her for her strength. Damn it!

He turned to the soul bringer. "There's no way you can take out her heart without her suffering."

The soul bringer gestured toward Claire in the cage. "She's doing just fine. Although I must say, she is getting weak. The longer her heart remains out of her body—" he shrugged "—well, that's how it goes."

Kizzy dashed for the black box Bron had left sitting on the floor before he'd attacked the soul bringer. She held it up. "Give her back her heart, and then you can have mine."

"I believe we have a deal," Blackthorn said. "But no putting the werewolf's heart back until I've seen if your heart opens the doorway to Purgatory."

"No!" Bron grabbed the box. "Give Claire back her heart now. Or this won't happen."

"It can't work that way." Kizzy gripped Bron's forearm. Her eyes flashed with more of that incredible strength. She stood between him and Blackthorn, and he could see Claire out of the corner of his eye. The haggard wolf gripped the cage bars, her eyes a desperate plea.

"This is the only way it can happen," Kizzy said

calmly. "You know that. And the sooner it gets done, the sooner she can have her heart back and get the hell out of here. Look at her. I'm sure she wants that desperately."

"Yes, please," Claire pleaded. She had fallen to her knees and no longer clung to the bars. She was growing weaker, for her eyelids fluttered, and she was so pale. "Do it, Bron. You owe me this much."

When Kizzy turned up her gaze on him he swallowed. Double guilt trip? Hell. How could he allow this to happen? He'd sworn he would protect Kizzy.

She began unbuttoning her shirt, and he gripped her hand. "Stop it."

"I'm not going to strip. I'm just preparing." She swung a look to the soul bringer. "Will it hurt?"

Blackthorn shook his head. "I'll make it painless. As much as I can."

She looked to Claire, then stroked Bron's chin. "Is she angry with you?"

"What do you think?"

"Of course she is. But she'll forgive you."

He didn't need Claire's forgiveness, but he did need her absolution. For the love he had never been able to give her.

Kizzy took his hand and pressed it against her chest. She didn't wear a bra, and his thumb brushed the curve of her breast beneath the loose blouse. "Remember what I told you? There's already a 'cut here' line."

She tried to make light of the situation. He hated that she felt she had to save them all. She didn't have to do that. He could find a way. He had to. "Just walk away," he said. "You don't have to sacrifice—"

"I do. And you know that."

"No, I—"

"Bron," she whispered. Her shaking fingers stroked his beard. He could smell not fear but apprehension. She was so brave, and he admired that about her. So much he loved about her. "Even if I walk away right now, it will never stop. He'll always be after me for reasons I can never know."

"He is in love," Bron said, noting the soul bringer paid keen attention. "His lover died recently and is in Purgatory. That's why he needs a portal into Purgatory."

"So, what will going to her mean?"

"She is a sin eater and does not have a chance to go Above. She will be tortured eternally in Purgatory. If she is taken out of there, then Regis can ferry her soul to Above."

"Then you have to hurry!" She released his hand and turned to the soul bringer.

It felt as if he would never hold her hand again. Never feel the warmth of her on his skin. Never get to sing to her those silly little lines from movies that stayed with him because they reminded him that life could be fun if he sought it. Never know how much it hurt to love someone so much.

Was this a fierce love, then?

It was. The realization hurt because it was so bittersweet.

"Kisanthra," he whispered, as the soul bringer uncrossed his arms and opened them to her. "I love you."

"Oh, you are my hero. I love you, too." She turned and leaned over to kiss him quickly. Too quick. He missed her already, and she wasn't even gone. "So if you really love me," she said, "let this happen."

He exhaled.

She lifted a brow, waiting for his response with a tease of the coy lover he'd held through the night. If he wanted to win her, he must step back and let her do this. Curse his immortal soul, it would kill him, but he must. Because he loved her.

Bron nodded.

"Thank you. Let's do this," she said to Blackthorn. "But you promise when it's done, you will put my heart back, and I will walk out of here in the same condition as I am now? I mean, all good?"

"Your goodness has no bearing on the results of having your heart removed. If you are asking whether or not you will be alive and healthy? Then, yes, you will be so. But time does become an issue. Your hero must work quickly."

"I don't know what he has to do," Kizzy offered.

And in that moment Bron knew the answer. This day Kizzy's nightmare would come true.

He lifted his head and met the soul bringer's bullet gaze. A triumphant defiance held him frozen. He couldn't speak. Couldn't imagine what it would be like. Only knew this sacrifice was only just getting started.

"Bron Everhart will be my champion. He will be the one going to Purgatory," Blackthorn said. "Since I am unable. Blade!"

The bowie knife flew out of the sheath at Bron's hip and landed with a *shing* in the soul bringer's grip. "Get over here, wolf. You've just become my heart-plucker. Remove all electronic devices. They will prove a detriment in Purgatory. This has to happen fast."

"No, I…" His legs wouldn't move. He dumbly patted his pocket with the phone in it. *Remove all electronic devices* sounded so pedestrian. As if he were merely stepping onto an airplane security scanner…

He couldn't step up and rip out Kizzy's heart. All the armies in all the world couldn't make him. There was nothing…

He'd made a vow. He would not break that vow as he had with…

Claire sat in the cage, intently focused on the three of them.

"Please, Bron." Kizzy's brown eyes teared, and her hand extended, awaiting his. "You have to do this. You're the only one who can save us all. Claire. The soul bringer's love. And me."

Fuck. Three women depending on him?

When he felt sure he should fall to his knees and yell for mercy, Bron instead lifted his chin and stepped forward. Tugging out his cell phone, he absently handed it to Kizzy. He stook another step. He nodded once.

And the soul bringer dragged the blade down Kizzy's chest.

Chapter 23

The knife that cut open her chest did not hurt. In fact, Kizzy had to look down to see that the blade was actually against her skin. She did not bleed either.

The soul bringer stood, stretching back his arm, fingers gripping the bloodless knife. Bron then kneeled before her, taking in the long, open gape in her chest. He looked as if he could be sick. Tears dropped from his eyes. He clenched a fist before him. Kizzy wanted to hug him, to reassure him that she was not in pain, but all she could manage was a few tears, as well.

"Quickly, wolf," the soul bringer stated. "Pluck out her heart. Or I'll have to cut her open again."

"I'm so sorry, Kisanthra," Bron said. "I promised I would never hurt you."

"You're not," she reassured. "I'm not in pain. Just find the sin eater and come back to me. Promise me that."

He nodded. "I will. You are everything that I live for now. But I…how can I take out your heart?"

"Grip it," the soul bringer instructed. "And pull. Come on, wolf, she doesn't have all day."

"Back off!" Bron growled at the man.

Holding his hand over her open chest, his fingers shook, then suddenly he gripped his fist tightly and nodded once. He whispered, "I love you," then plunged his fist into her chest.

Kizzy sucked in a gasp. The weird, muffling sensation of something moved in her chest, yet she panted to breathe through it. No pain, just an odd sense of being possessed. Claimed. By a man who had just said he loved her.

And yet, the nightmare had just come true.

When he pulled out his fist, she felt something leave her. A warmth. Vitality. Life?

Bron's bloody hand held a beating heart. She gaped at it. That was her life. Out of her body. And yet, she was breathing. Alive.

For now.

"What is your woman's name?" Bron asked the soul bringer, "And how will I find her?"

"Desdenova Fleetwood is her name. She goes by Nova. She will be the only embodied soul in Purgatory. Slight of frame and dark hair. The most beautiful woman in creation."

"Yes, yes. They always are." Bron bowed over Kizzy. His teared eyes searched hers and then he kissed her mouth. "You okay?"

Probably not, but he didn't need to know that. "Hurry," she whispered. "I love you."

"She will be fine unless you drop the heart," the soul

bringer said. "It is your return ticket back to this realm. Now. Turn it to grip it directly over the handprint, and that should—"

When Bron turned the heart in his grasp, suddenly a brilliant white light exploded out from his hand, and then he was gone. Only a few blood droplets stained the concrete floor where he'd just knelt.

Bron had been gone twenty minutes. Kizzy wandered the floor, feeling better when she moved. She was light-headed. The cut on her chest had closed up, and she'd buttoned up her shirt. Somehow, she felt her missing heart as an emptiness in her very soul. It ached and pulsed in her core. And yet, nothing beat in her chest. No heartbeat. How wrong was that?

Had she done the right thing? Whether or not she survived this, she wanted to feel as if she had done the right thing. But that hinged on her trusting the soul bringer.

The man who held her life in his hands stood by the dirty window, his gaze seemingly on her and Claire, but Kizzy sensed he would close his eyes on occasion. Thinking deep thoughts? The asshole. He'd involved too many to save his girlfriend. His *dead* girlfriend. Wasn't like Bron could bring her back from Purgatory alive, was it? Of course, if her soul could be saved from eternal torture, then Kizzy supposed the trip was worth it.

Bron had been forced to commit an unspeakable act. It had killed him to pull out her heart. And he had sworn that was something he'd never do so long as he lived. Poor guy. She would never forget the look in his eyes as he'd held her heart before him. In his mind he had wounded her deeply, irreparably. So she had to stay alive to prove him wrong. When he returned he would put her heart back in her chest, and all would be well.

She remembered what Eglantine had said about the soul bringer needing a champion to go into Purgatory for him. If only they had known then what they knew now. Would Bron have agreed to do it all over?

Yes. He was that kind of honorable.

She hoped his trip would not take long. For her sake, and for the sake of the poor woman in the cage. The werewolf sat on the floor, her face tilted against a cage bar, eyes closed.

Kizzy spun about and faced the soul bringer. "Why must you keep her in that cage? It's not as though she can hurt you. She's weak. Should she and I join forces, we wouldn't be able to cause you an annoyance."

The soul bringer's eyes opened slowly. They were fathomless voids. With a smirk, he lifted a hand slightly and made a flicking motion with two fingers. The cage door swung open.

"Stay in here," he muttered. "I can only maintain your vita within a certain range. The farther away from me you get, the quicker you die. Both of you."

Kizzy rushed over to the cage. Claire scooted out from inside, but she was too weak to stand. When Kizzy took her hand and studied her face, the werewolf smiled at her and said, "I like you. You've got spunk. I tend to overlook humans with their weaknesses. What has made you so strong?"

Kizzy helped Claire to sit on the floor and lean against a rusted iron column. She maintained a firm hold of her hand. Touching another person seemed to ground her. To remind her that she was still alive.

"I've always been independent," Kizzy said. "But I

think dying eight months ago following a car accident really put my head on straight. I don't take bullshit from anyone anymore. Unless, of course, he's an asshole soul bringer."

Both women eyed their keeper, who kept one eye aimed on them.

"How are you?" Kizzy asked. "Are you okay?"

"If I may be so bold…why do you care?"

"I care because you are a fellow woman, and you are an innocent in this matter. Whatever went on between you and Bron centuries ago is none of my business. I want you to survive this and to be free."

She smirked. "Are you Bron's newest wife? Lover?"

"Not his wife. Lovers…?" She didn't need to lie to this woman, nor did she want to. "We are. Did you two ever…divorce?"

Claire shook her head. "The pack considered our marriage annulled the moment he was banished. Served him right. Unfaithful bastard." She sighed and chuckled softly. "I had thought I'd gotten over him and what he did to me way back in the nineteenth century. I have lived a good life. I remarried the new pack leader and had seven children. I'd completely wiped Bron Everhart from my heart. And now, look. My heart has been removed, and all I can think about is the man who originally broke it."

"He's told me a little about that time. This isn't an excuse, but I suspect he was a bit of a rogue. Untamable. Not much for settling down?"

"You nailed that one, sweetie. Unfortunately for me. I chose not to give him another thought the night he left the pack. Merely assumed he'd taken his bastard child and got on with his life."

"You don't know? Isabelle, his daughter, she died. She was put out by the pack in the freezing winter. When Bron was finally released from the compound, he found her, frozen to death."

"Oh, *mon Dieu*." Claire gasped and turned down her head. Her hands shook on her lap.

Kizzy touched her wrist, but the woman flinched away. "It's what he told me."

"I had no idea," she whispered frantically. "I…I was the one who ordered the girl put out. But I hadn't thought she would—as I've said, I never consider humans and their weaknesses. We wolves can survive the cold. Oh, mercy. I hurt him so cruelly."

Kizzy pulled the woman into a hug. "It's over. You have both survived. And when Bron returns from Purgatory, you can get your heart and walk away from him forever."

Claire nodded. "We were both terrible to one another. I must apologize to him. You…you love him?"

"I think I do. I said it to him. We've only known one another a few days, but…yes… I do." Kizzy clasped her hands before her mouth and smiled to think over the past few days and their whirlwind accidental romance amidst a crazy chase and run. "He's a brave and honorable man. I think he's changed since that time long ago when you knew him."

"That happens to a person over the centuries. He needed to grow up."

"He has. You would be proud of him."

"But the girl. Oh, I am so sorry." Claire sniffed back a tear, and Kizzy clasped her hand. The werewolf gave it a squeeze. "So how are you? Are you okay?"

"I'm weak, but I know Bron will find the sin eater and bring her back. We'll both be okay. He'll save us."

Claire clasped her hand tightly. Nothing else to say. They would hold vigil for the man who had touched their hearts in manners so opposite yet long lasting.

It didn't take Bron long to get a handle on the conditions of Purgatory. They were ever changing, vile, and not something a man could predict. One moment he trod sun-baked earth, sweating and struggling to hold the slippery heart in hand. The next moment he walked into the teeth of a blizzard, which singed his nostrils and eyes with an icy burn.

Clutching the heart to his chest to secure his hold, he stepped onto soggy ground. His boots suctioned into mud as red as blood. And the meaty smell made him wonder if it were not mud but in fact blood. He wouldn't think about it.

He saw…things. Dark, shadowy figments that were most often human shaped yet with black spaces for eyes, mouth and nostrils. Others were more solid, perhaps souls attempting to cling to the human form they once held? When he walked near one they swayed away from him, as if fearing his presence, and misted into nothing.

Damned eerie, the lot of it. He was sure he hadn't felt his own heartbeat since arriving.

And when he came upon a bridge that stretched into the foggy distance, he decided that must be the path to a Toll House. CJ had explained there were twenty that the departed soul must pass through. He didn't need to go there. And if the sin eater was not allowed to pass through the Toll Houses, then she would not be there either.

He tried calling out her name, Desdenova, and then Nova, but his voice echoed back to him, and the air thickened like pudding, clogging his throat so he struggled to take a breath. And yet, breathing felt…odd. Unnecessary. So he didn't try again.

He neared another soul. A mostly solid soul that appeared as a man in dark clothing. His arm was torn off, and his scalp was bloodied. Must have been what he looked like when death took him. And once closer, he was more misty than solid. He spied Bron—his black eyes averting to the heart—and his mouth dropped open.

"Kizzy's heart!" The soul lunged for him.

The creature jumped onto Bron's back and snaked an icy hand down to claw for the heart.

The soul bringer hadn't moved from standing before the window. Kizzy felt Claire's head heavy on her shoulder. She had fallen asleep, which was a good thing. Better than being alert and having nothing to do but worry whether or not she would ever again get back her own heart.

A heart that sat in a black box on the floor in the middle of the warehouse. As if a forgotten gift after the birthday party celebrants had left for cake in the next room. Could *she* put it back in Claire's chest for her? Probably not. But the need to do something more than sitting was strong.

She remembered the digital camera and tugged it from her pocket. Clicking a picture of the box, she then took a few of the soul bringer, silhouetted by the high sun beaming through the open window. He didn't notice. The camera mechanism was silent. These were photos she might never publish. Not without a wild explanation of what they really were.

What if she did publish them and people believed? Would there be hysteria? Fascination? Laughter? Was the mass population really ready to believe in all the creatures that only moved about on the silver screen and in the pages of books?

Publishing such photos was a big decision. She should not take it lightly. And she would not. But she couldn't stop taking the pictures; it was how she recorded life. As strange as it had become.

She hoped Bron got back soon, so she could record him. To commit him to pixels. To know that he was alive.

"It's been hours," she called across the room. "How long will this take?"

"You starting to think your hero has abandoned you?" Blackthorn taunted.

"If he gives up on me, he gives up on you, as well."

The soul bringer shrugged and turned toward her. Leaning against the wall, he crossed one ankle over the other and peered across the concrete floor at her. "I am not without mercy."

"Could have fooled me. You sent harpies after us."

"I thought they could get the heart out for me."

"Nice." Kizzy kicked out her feet before her, and when she wanted to put her hands behind her neck, she did not because that might wake Claire. "How'd you ever fall in love if you're so all about the lacking emotions?"

"Nova showed me what love is."

"A sin eater and a soul bringer." There were so many

wonders she had yet to discover. "How long were the two of you together?"

"It seems like mere moments, but I was allowed a few decades with her. I would give my life to have Nova back. Alive."

But if she had died, then Bron would be bringing back a dead woman, right? Kizzy wanted to ask, but as much as she hated the guy, she couldn't put that terrible question out there.

"I understand that. Love is great. I've been in love a couple times."

"I don't understand the human penchant to love so often," Blackthorn said. "A love so great should only happen once."

"You'd think. But love is so great because it has to be. It is wide and everywhere. It is our reason for being. It sometimes breaks, and then you get to find it again. That's the cool thing about love. You can never run out of it. There exists an endless source."

"Humans make up ridiculous explanations to ease their pain and suffering. I will only and always love my Nova."

"I'm sorry for your loss. I truly am. But you can hold her in your heart forever. Do you, uh…have a heart?"

He nodded and rapped his chest. "It is glass and does not beat. Nova used to tell me she could hear it pulsing when she put her head to my chest. I would slide my fingers through her hair and know she was wrong, but still I believed her."

He dropped his head, and Kizzy wasn't sure, but was he sobbing? Nah. Not a big strong soul bringer like him.

"You vex me, you humans," he hissed as he stood and

marched over to the black box. Grabbing it, he strode up to her. Kizzy flinched, which startled Claire awake.

"Very well," Blackthorn said. "She has suffered for no good reason. And she has served her use." He tore off the cover and thrust the box toward Kizzy. Inside, the heart pulsed slowly. "Take it out. I cannot touch an earthbound heart."

Tentatively, she reached inside and picked up the slippery organ. It was warm and pulsed even more, so that she had to hold it with both hands to not drop it. Stunning to look upon something so vital to a person's being.

"Oh," Claire said on a fading sigh. "Mine."

Bending over Claire, Blackthorn drew the blade he'd taken from Bron down her chest. Her ribs seemed to gape open in expectation of receiving the heart.

"Put it back in," he muttered as he stood over Kizzy.

"Uh…" Kizzy reacted. She pushed the organ back into Claire's chest. A bright beam of white light radiated out. And the cut sealed up, breaking off the glow. With an exuberant sigh the werewolf sat up straighter. Claire held a hand over her chest and nodded that she was okay.

"You know that was an act of love," Kizzy said to the soul bringer.

"It was a means to show I am not doing this to harm but merely to gain that which I most need. If I could have gone after Nova myself, I would have. But I am not allowed in Purgatory. And besides. There is only one way to gain entrance to Purgatory."

"With the heart?" Kizzy asked.

"The heart is merely a portal. Entrance requires but one condition." He smiled the tiniest smile and then announced plainly, "Death."

Kizzy nodded. Of course all souls in Purgatory were dead. Even the soul bringer's girlfriend had died to end up there. Keith was there. He'd died in the car crash.

Had she gone there when she had died on the operating room table? For Keith to have been able to clutch her heart? Maybe.

"He means Bron," Claire whispered as she massaged her rib cage.

"What?"

The soul bringer strode across the warehouse back to the window where he'd held post. When he leaned a shoulder against the brick wall and turned a switchblade smile on her, Kizzy gaped.

"Bron? But—no. He's not dead."

"Apparently," Claire rasped, "he had to die to get there. I'm sorry, Kizzy."

"But. No, that can't be. How can he find the sin eater if he's dead? And when he returns? He can't exist *and* be dead. No."

Kizzy touched her chest, knowing that there would be no heartbeat beneath, yet feeling as if what was missing raced toward a cliff. "You bastard!"

She lunged up to stride across the floor. When she was but five feet from the soul bringer he flicked his fingers, which lifted her from her feet and sent her flailing back to land on the hard, concrete floor.

Kizzy screamed a loud and soul-crushing sound that was heard for acres beyond the abandoned warehouse.

And it was felt in Purgatory.

Chapter 24

Bron heard the scream and knew it was Kizzy's voice. Was she here in Purgatory? Had the soul bringer somehow sent her in his wake? He wanted to know, to seek out the voice, but the bedamned soul riding his back proved a solid and insistent force. A soul should not feel substantial, and yet, its fingernails dug in at his shoulders painfully.

"Get off!" He shook his body, but the thing was weightless, and it mercilessly clung with its one arm. "Who are you?"

"You've got her heart. It's mine! I won't let her go!"

Ah, hell. This had to be the boyfriend. The bastard who had gripped Kizzy's heart from Purgatory and put her in this mess in the first place. Keith...something or other.

Clutching the heart to his chest with both hands,

Bron twisted and attempted to swing the soul from his back—when he stepped into an icy wall. Turning to crush the soul with a forceful shove against the wall, he was rewarded with a throaty moan. The fingers at his shoulders slipped away.

Scrambling away from the maniacal thing, Bron ran as quickly as the slick ice surface would allow. Ahead loomed a dark forest of what appeared steel trees. Behind him he heard the soul shout that he would *never let her go.*

Cursing this madness, Bron ran. And when he entered the forest, razor-edged branches cut his cheeks, shoulders and thighs. But before he could ascertain a safe passage, the ground dropped away, and he fell into a muddy pit lined with long black, gleaming thorns that oozed a metallic substance from their pin-sharp tips.

Checking the heart he held had not taken any damage, Bron stepped to the center of the pit. It was about twenty-feet in diameter, but he maintained a mere five-foot circle in the middle safe from the thorns. He could use them as ladder rungs to climb out, but perhaps for the moment he was safe down here from Keith's soul. He had no idea how strong or powerful the souls were. Keith was dead. A figment of the man he had once been. Right?

This mission had turned into a proper adventure. And he was just fine with that. Hang on to the heart. Beat off the souls. Let the shrapnel fall where it will.

"Wh-who are you?" asked a shivering voice from the darkness.

Panting and scanning the sky above for signs of Keith, Bron checked again to ensure he hadn't let go of Kizzy's heart. "No one," he gasped when he determined the voice didn't sound like a threat. "Just here for a stroll."

The owner of the small voice crept forward, and clinging to a pointed thorn, her face was revealed. Heart-shaped, pale, with long black hair. And she looked solid. Not like the souls he had seen since arriving. More calm than Keith's soul and expressly fearful. He could smell her fear as he had not been able to scent anything from the lost souls.

She was…embodied. The soul bringer had said she would be.

"Are you Desdenova Fleetwood?"

She gaped at him.

"I've been sent by Blackthorn Regis to rescue you."

"Oh, mercy. You must be his champion! I had hoped he would send someone to save me. I've been hiding in here. The demons. They want to take me to the Toll Houses for torture."

"You're safe. I'll get you out of here." Bron stretched his gaze up toward the gray sky. "I just need a moment to figure how."

With a banshee howl that stirred all sorts of things in the darkness, the insistent Keith dropped from above. The annoying soul of Kizzy's ex-boyfriend swiped at him. Bron lashed out—with the hand that held the heart. Keith snarled, revealing extremely sharp teeth for a dead soul, and snatched at the heart. The slippery organ loosened in Bron's grip and…fell away.

"No!" He could not return to the mortal realm without that heart. And by all the gods, he was its protector.

He loved Kizzy. Life was not worth living without her. And he had come so far. Beyond all his better arguments against hurting Kizzy to help the enemy, he was here in Purgatory claiming a dead woman for a soul bringer who had threatened Kizzy's life. He would not fail now.

Bron swung and punched Keith's soul, but his fist soared right through the figment. The soul misted into a black curl and spiraled upward toward the pit opening.

The bottom dropped out of the pit, and it grew longer and deep. Suddenly falling, his instincts kicked in. Shifting to werewolf, Bron pushed off from the spiked wall of the pit with a foot and free-fell, diving, wishing his body would soar downward faster and faster. He could smell the heart. It smelled like her. The human woman who loved him without question.

And when he paralleled the falling heart, the werewolf snatched it with a clawed paw, curling the deadly instruments carefully about the slick organ. With his other paw, he grasped blindly and managed to grip one of the steel stakes jutting from the pit's wall. The pointed tip tore his paw in two. He yowled and dropped his hold. Thinking to reach for a hold with his other paw, at the last minute, he put the heart into his maw, gently, and managed to secure a grip.

Hanging there, the heart a pulsing reminder of all that he desired and cared for, the werewolf pulled himself upward using only his paws. He climbed the thorns, one paw over the other. It took utmost control not to relax his jaws and bite into the heart. When he neared the top, the diminutive sin eater, who had climbed out using the thorns, reached for him with a tiny, pale hand.

As did Keith's re-figmented soul.

The werewolf slashed its healed paw across the soul, reducing it to dust. Then he leaped from the pit and studied the delicate sin eater. He towered over the woman. Opening his maw he let the heart fall into a paw. He turned it over and over.

"Whose heart is that?" the woman asked. "Is it our passage out of here?"

In his werewolf form he could not answer, though he knew from her pleading tone what she had asked. Unsure what to do next, the werewolf tossed the sin eater over a shoulder and began to race across the vast desert.

He howled to a moon that did not exist in this terrible, desolate land. A place in which he did not belong. And when he squeezed the heart so hard it almost burst, suddenly the werewolf was sucked out from Purgatory.

Bron landed on his feet, in werewolf shape, and staggered across the concrete floor.

Someone yelled and rushed toward him.

Aware the air was lighter, cleaner, and that he was no longer in that vile place, he dropped to his knees, setting down the human he'd carried over his shoulder. The woman he'd claimed in Purgatory did not stand but instead dropped into a sprawl before him, arms splaying out at her sides, eyes closed. And he felt inclined to do the same. He was weak. His breaths…did not come, and yet he was conscious.

"Bron?"

He recognized the female voice as his mate. Or one he would take as his mate forever should she allow it.

"Nova!" Some other voice, sounded male. The figure leaned over the one Bron had carried up from Purgatory. With a glance to him, the man said, "Don't tell him he's dead, unless you want to seal his fate."

Bron's werewolf heard the words, and yet in this animal form he had difficulty understanding them. And he wanted to return to his were form, but he was so exhausted. Even to think about shifting did not bring it on. So he collapsed, his head lolling onto the concrete. The heart pulsed against his chest.

"Is he really dead?" the female asked, and again, he didn't understand the words but sensed apprehension.

"As soon as he realizes he is dead, he will be," the male voice answered.

The sudden, immense relief at knowing he was away from that awful place and near others he sensed were friends allowed him to release his werewolf shape and return to were form. Unfortunately, he was naked, so he squatted and bowed his head as Kizzy wrapped her arms about his shoulders and hugged him from the side.

"Kizzy," he whispered. The name felt like gold to his soul.

"You did it! You found her. I knew you would." Kisses to his face felt like redeeming rain after a forty-day drought. And he had walked through such conditions while in Purgatory. "Oh, Bron, I thought I'd lost you."

"Why?" he croaked. "You didn't think I'd come back to you?"

Her sigh fell heavily against his cheek. "It's just… all that matters is you're here. You're solid. Real." She placed a hand over his chest and frowned, then shook her head and hugged him. "Did I tell you I love you?"

Remembering he still clutched her heart to his chest he carefully pulled it away and held it before him. The handprint was gone. Did that mean it was…deactivated?

He must hope for that.

"I dropped it," he said quietly. "Down a deep pit.

But I caught it before it hit the ground. I almost lost you, Kisanthra."

"Never." She hugged him so he almost toppled. "I'm yours. You have my heart, wolf. You really do."

"We must put it back. Where's the soul bringer?"

"Yes, we should take care of that before…" Tears shimmered in her eyes. He couldn't read her thoughts, but they seemed deep. "Uh, yes." She swiped away a teardrop. "Just yes."

Whatever it was she wasn't willing to say to him bothered him. And yet, he was so relieved to be back in her arms, he didn't linger on what was probably nothing.

The twosome looked aside to where Blackthorn knelt over Nova's body. For it was a body. The petite figure, dressed in black and with skin as white as cream, did not move. He didn't see her chest rise and fall with breath. She was dead.

"Can you bring her back to life?" Kizzy asked the soul bringer.

He shook his head. "It's never wise to bring a dead thing back to life. Much as I desire just that, I am no fool. She is gone." He stroked the hair from her face. "But now she is safe."

"But you said that Bron…?"

The soul bringer nodded. "As I've said to you, as soon as he realizes it…"

"I don't understand." Bron looked at her. "Kizzy?"

"Thank you for your sacrifice, werewolf," Blackthorn said. "You'll need clothes." With a gesture from the soul bringer, Bron was suddenly clothed in the pants, shirt and boots he'd worn into Purgatory. "And thank you, Kisanthra Lewis, for the use of your heart. Now I must bring Nova to Above before it is too late."

The soul bringer scooped up his dead lover into his arms.

"You have to put Kizzy's heart back first!" Bron insisted. He choked, finding it difficult to breathe. Was he even breathing? "What the hell?"

He'd endured much in Purgatory, but he was sound and of his body. The weird lack of breath must be some residual effects from his adventure.

"You can put it back in for her, wolf," the soul bringer said. "Do it fast. She won't have much time after I'm gone. Nor do you. The bowie knife is over there." He nodded behind him and then was gone.

Bron grabbed Kizzy's hands. "What does he mean by that? That I don't have time?"

"I don't know. What matters is you are holding my heart, lover, and I want it back. You know, because here is where it belongs." She pressed a hand over her chest. "But don't think that doesn't mean you are the one who has ultimately won my heart."

She leaned in and kissed him on the cheek, stroked his beard and sighed heavily.

Bron held the heart tenderly. "But to cut into your chest again... To cause you pain. Kizzy, I can't."

"You have to! He said I didn't have much time. And you..." Her eyes fell over him, and tears streamed down her cheeks. "I don't understand all of this. Maybe the witch can help." She picked up Bron's cell phone, which had been abandoned before he'd been sent to Purgatory. "I'm babbling. Don't listen to that stuff. Just...please?"

"A witch can help him," Claire called from across the warehouse. "You know one close?"

Bron eyed his former wife. He'd not seen her for ages.

She looked the same. Beautiful, ethereal even. And she was out of the cage, standing. Relief flooded him.

"The soul bringer put her heart back in while you were gone," Kizzy said. She turned and asked Claire. "How do you know a witch can help him?"

Claire shrugged. "It's my best guess. Hand me the phone. Do you have a witch listed in your contacts, Bron?"

"Yes, but I don't know what you two are talking about." He wheezed and clasped his chest. "What's going on?"

"Hurry, Kizzy."

"Yes, do it," she said, shoving his shoulder. "Please, lover?" She touched his cheek and then kissed him lightly. "I need you, Bron. Do this for us."

She dashed for the blade, and Bron stood, ignoring his own weird symptoms. Time was of the essence. Hell, he had not signed on for this when he'd agreed to find and seize a legendary object for Acquisitions. But he wouldn't change meeting Kizzy for all the fortunes in the world. Yet what was up with Claire's insistence they call a witch? She scrolled through his contacts.

"Bron!"

Attention averted, his instincts reacted. When Kizzy slapped the knife into his hand he winced and shook his head. Growling, he resisted dropping the foul instrument that could serve as much pain as a slash from one of his claws.

"You did it before," Kizzy said. Opening her shirt revealed an angry red line on her skin. "If you love me, you'll do it…" She gasped and wobbled. "I can't…"

"Kizzy?" Claire called. "Wait! Eglantine says not to put the heart in just yet!"

Kizzy began to fall, and Bron caught her about the waist and lowered her to the floor. Her eyelids fluttered. She gasped for breath. She looked at him with such wonder. And love.

The fluttery blouse she wore spilled up to reveal the bottom of the scar from the open-heart surgery. He pressed the knife blade to the red line. When the soul bringer had done this he had been able to staunch the pain. Bron had no such powers.

"Wait," Kizzy gasped. "The witch says to…wait…"

Bron studied the heart in his other hand, which still pulsed, but it seemed to be beating slower. It was dying. He had to do this. Now. "The soul bringer said we had to hurry. Kizzy, I can't lose you."

"No!" Claire shoved his hand away from Kizzy's chest. "The witch is on her way here. She said whatever you do, do not put the heart back in her chest if you…" Claire bent and whispered something into Kizzy's ear that Bron, despite his excellent hearing, could not make out.

"She's right," Kizzy whispered. "Not yet, Bron. We need to…" She sat up, helped by Claire. "I feel like I'm getting a second wind. I'm good. Thanks, Claire. We just need to chat a bit. Fill the time until Eglantine gets here."

The two women held such a stare between them, Bron could not understand what was up.

"Why must we wait for the witch?" he insisted. "You could die, Kizzy. The soul bringer said time was of the essence. I won't lose you. I cannot." He bowed his forehead to hers. If she died he wasn't sure how to continue.

She clasped his hand as Claire stood and wandered over to pick up the black box in which her heart had been contained. Giving them some privacy, as best she could.

"Trust me?" Kizzy asked him. "And hold me?"

He cradled her in his arms, her back against his chest. He bowed his chin to the top of her head and while he gripped her heart against her chest, he got lost in the slow, yet promisingly steady, beat of it. She smelled like summer and wild fields with a hint of orange. He closed his eyes and drew in that scent, thinking if he could drown in it, he wouldn't struggle for air, only happily die in her arms.

"I'm glad that tracker led you to me," she said.

"So am I. You've changed me. I never thought I could love like this." He eyed the knife he'd laid on the floor. "Why are we waiting? Kizzy, don't you love me enough to explain?"

"I… Sing to me," she said softly.

"Kizzy, this is no time—"

"That's what I love most about you. You're not afraid to show me the silly side of you. You must know more songs?"

He knew them all because he liked to sit in a dark theater and lose himself to the innocent laughter and adventure of a good faery tale. He didn't want to sing right now, because most of the songs he knew were happy. And life was not a faery tale, it was pain and anger and blood and betrayal.

He was not happy; he was enraged the soul bringer had reneged on their bargain. And now Kizzy insisted he wait to put back in her heart? What the hell was going on? He would not lose her. He must not.

But as he closed his eyes and concentrated on Kizzy's firm grasp, she whispered, "Please."

And a verse did come to him, so he sang it for her. "Oo da lolly, oo da lolly, golly, what a day."

Kizzy laughed softly. "Oh, my lover. Robin Hood and Little John sang that together. I love that movie. And it has been such a day. Is it wrong to love a man because he's a Disney fan?"

"About as wrong as loving a woman because she looks cute wearing a shirt with Sam and Dean on it."

She traced a finger over the heart, and it pulsed as if shivering at the realization of its owner's touch. "Not long," she whispered in a voice that was desperately weak. "So brave, my lovely wolf."

And her head dropped heavily against his arm.

Chapter 25

Panic traced Bron's spine. "I don't think she's breathing!"

"She is. She's just resting," Claire reassured from across the warehouse. She clutched the box as if it were a lost toy. "I know. I was in her position and felt the same."

"Why do we have to wait for the witch? What are you not telling me? What went on here while I was away in Purgatory? Claire, please!"

Dressed in a dirty white sundress, she dropped the box and strolled over to him.

With Kizzy's warmth in his arms, he could only hug her tighter. But in that moment he was able to see his former wife clearly. And to acknowledge that she had suffered because of him.

"I'm sorry," he said as she stopped before him and Kizzy and knelt to stroke Kizzy's arm. "I am so sorry."

"I forgave you when you were in Purgatory," she said. "Can you imagine? I've held such hatred for you in my heart for so long. I'd thought I'd put it all behind me. Until I saw your face again. You haven't changed much. Maybe a few new lines beside your eyes. A little longer hair. But still the same."

"I've changed," he managed. "Inside."

"Yes, I can see that through her eyes. She adores you. You have become a man worthy of admiration. Don't hurt her."

"More than I have already?"

"You've done what was necessary to save her life. And mine."

"But I still hold her heart," he insisted, feeling the pulse beats against his palm. "Tell me what you are not saying. Why are we waiting for the witch?"

Claire shrugged and looked aside. She couldn't face him? Was she going to lie to him?

With a sigh, she regarded him. "Magic is required to make the heart stick. Or that's what I understand from what Eglantine said to me on the phone. She's using a transport spell. Should be here sooner rather than later." She clasped his hand at Kizzy's shoulder. "How do you feel?"

"It doesn't matter. I can't worry about that."

"You should not," she said quickly. "Think only of her. I—" she stood and smoothed her palms down her skirt "—really want to go home. But I'm not sure how I got here in the first place. One moment I was walking down a country path in Lake Como to my cottage. The next? I was sitting in a cage watching that bastard soul bringer command a demon to rip my heart from my chest. Feels good to have it back, though."

A brilliant flash of blue electrified the warehouse.

"Ah," Claire said. "The witch."

Eglantine landed on both feet, a slender white gown gliding to the floor and pooling in a silken train about her. A tilt of her elegantly coifed head took in the warehouse. With a nod to both of them, she bent and began to draw a design on the floor with nothing more than the blue electrical pulse emitted from her hands.

Bron carefully set Kizzy's head down so he could stand. He didn't want to drop her heart, but when Claire suddenly gestured he hand it to her, he only clutched it tighter.

"You should go talk to the witch," Claire insisted. "Let me hold the heart while you do."

"I don't trust you."

"Oh, Bron, Kizzy told me about Isabelle's death. I am so sorry."

"It wasn't your fault."

"It was." She closed her eyes and sniffed back a tear. "Forgive me?"

He nodded. "We're good." But he still wasn't willing to hand over Kizzy's heart to the woman.

"Bron!" Eglantine called.

As for his heart…well, just when he'd thought it should be either racing or dropping in his chest, it did neither. In fact, he couldn't feel it. He pressed his free hand to his chest to feel for his heart beat.

In that moment Kizzy sat up, and their eyes met. She shook her head, asking him to ignore…something. What was going on? Why were they being so secretive?

Eglantine stepped out of the circle she had created. It glowed blue. She indicated he step closer, which he did, reluctantly, his head twisting to eye Kizzy and then back to the circle until he stood right at the edge. The circle, and the ruins drawn about the circumference, looked familiar. In fact, he'd seen this once before when on a mission to Zanibia to obtain a zombie antidote.

"This is a death hexing circle," he said.

And in that moment he knew why he couldn't feel his heartbeats. Why Kizzy had been acting so strangely. She knew. They all knew. Bron slapped a hand over his chest.

Claire grabbed Kizzy's heart from him.

"I'm—" he started to say what he knew was truth. *Dead?*

The witch shoved him hard, and he stumbled into the center of the circle.

"Just in time," Eglantine said to Claire. "Poor guy just realized he was dead."

"Now what?" Claire asked, bobbling the heart back and forth in her hands.

"Yes, now what?" Kizzy asked as she pushed up to stand.

"Now, you're on, darling," Eglantine said.

Bron's body hovered in the middle of the circle amidst a foggy dazzle of blue light. Arms flung outward and head tilted back, his eyes were closed. It looked as if an alien ship were about to suck him upward as he hung suspended a foot above the floor.

"Is he alive?" Kizzy asked the witch.

"No, he's dead. The hexing circle merely holds him in place while I work the real magic. And for that, I'll need your help. And your heart. How you feeling, darling?"

Kizzy wobbled as she stepped forward. "Like I've

had my heart ripped out and I'm one step away from death."

"Then we'd best hurry. Thankfully Claire was able to contact me in time."

Kizzy offered the most grateful smile she could manage to the werewolf, which was weak. And then she directed her gaze back to Bron. He'd figured out he was dead just before the witch had shoved him into the circle. How could she help him?

He meant so much to her. He was the man who had not laughed at her beliefs. He believed in her.

Now she had to believe in him.

"Give her the heart," Eglantine directed Claire. "But only after I've opened her chest."

Here it comes. The pain, Kizzy thought. The weird stuff. The—hell, she just wanted this all over. And for Bron to be alive. She'd suffer any amount of pain for that.

"How is this going to save Bron?"

"You'll provide your vita and make a direct connection to his heart and soul," Eglantine said. "Take your heart."

Claire handed the slippery organ to her, and Kizzy marveled for a moment over its weight and size. It really was about the size of her fist, and for all it had been through outside of her body, it still looked bright red and beat steadily. But no handprint! Must have been erased when Bron had used it to journey into Purgatory.

When she held it in both her hands she could almost feel the heart beating in her empty chest.

"Hold that aside while I open you up," Eglantine commanded. "Quickly, darling, Bron hasn't much time. Nor do you! Support her from behind, Claire, will you?"

Kizzy sucked in a breath and quickly unbuttoned her shirt, preparing for…whatever hell came next. The witch drew a blue line in the air before her. Something burned down her rib cage, and she felt air rush into her chest cavity.

"Now hold it close, so it connects," the witch instructed, "but don't put it all the way in. I need to bring Bron in on this now."

Hold it close? But not all the way in? What the…? Kizzy moved her heart closer until she felt it nudge her skin. The sudden connection of veins or arteries, or whatever it was, alerted her, and a jolt of awareness gasped out of her mouth. She could feel her heart beat throughout her body. It was back!

Almost.

Eglantine traced the side of her heart that was not within her, and then she drew out her hand and, with it, what looked like a glowing red vein. The witch drew it as if yarn from a skein to the edge of the circle. When it touched the barrier of blue electricity that contained Bron's floating body, the entire circle lit wildly and turned violet.

The witch began to chant something in a language Kizzy didn't understand. She could feel her life force rushing out toward the hexing circle. Behind her Claire held her by the shoulders, her body supporting Kizzy's weight. And when Eglantine suddenly severed the connection and turned to slam her hand against the heart and shove it completely into Kizzy's chest, the witch's wild green eyes glowed as she announced grandly, "So mote it be!"

Kizzy collapsed, slowly, Claire helping her down to sit.

The circle stopped glowing. Bron's body fell, but instead of landing in a sprawl, his boots touched the concrete floor, and he caught himself, balancing and standing up. Alert, he looked about. Slapped a hand over his chest. His eyes landed first on Eglantine, and he shook his head, wincing. "You always land me in some kind of far-out magical situation, witch."

"It wasn't my doing, love. I believe it was the soul bringer's fault. But she did save your life." She stepped aside to allow Bron to see Kizzy.

Claire moved away, as did the witch. And before Bron could move toward her, Kizzy pushed up and ran to him, crossing the etched hexing line on the floor, and landed in his arms. Their connection ignited the wicked blue electricity, and a wall of the magic flashed up around the circle again.

"Is that bad?" Claire asked the witch.

"No. That. Is love. Come along. Those two will be needing some privacy."

Chapter 26

They didn't bother to look around to see if anyone stood in the warehouse watching. Bron had felt the witch's departure, and he no longer scented his ex-wife. The only thing that mattered was the woman in his arms. Kissing him. Legs wrapped about his hips, she clung to him.

And he felt some kind of amazing electricity encompass them both. The blue light flashed about them, crackling and snapping at their skin. The more they kissed, the deeper violet the light became. Every touch felt like an orgasm. His werewolf shivered within, wanting to get out. And at the same time, it did not. He was solid in his body.

And not dead.

Nor was Kizzy without her heart. A heart that he'd held in his hands and would protect forever after. He'd noticed the missing handprint when he'd brought it back from Purgatory. He suspected it had been a one-time-only use for that particular magical artifact. And he'd inform the director the heart was inoperative and safe where it belonged.

"Kiss me always," she said against his lips. "Love me forever."

"I can do that," he said.

And he believed that he could.

A day later, the couple stood in the gray-tiled shower of Bron's New York apartment. Before boarding their flight, he'd alerted the maid service he was stopping in, and upon arrival, the place sparkled and champagne had waited in the fridge.

"I think our hearts kind of meshed when we were in the hexing circle," Kizzy said as she slicked her hands up his wet chest. "At least, that's the way it felt to me." She kissed him right over the heart.

Bron bowed his head to kiss her forehead. "So I have your heart now?"

"Do you want it?"

"Yes. You asked me to love you forever. Did you mean that?"

She nodded. "I know you're a lone wolf kind of guy. Was that okay?"

"More than okay. I don't feel so inspired to be alone now that you've gotten into me. And I gave Director Pierce a call this morning to inform him that the heart had been deactivated. He trusts my assessment that it's no longer an active portal to Purgatory. You can keep it right where it belongs."

"Whew. And what about the soul bringer and his dead girlfriend?"

"He got what he wanted. You needn't fear him coming after you any longer."

"But do you think he was able to bring his girlfriend to Heaven?"

Bron nodded. "I'm sure of it. All ended well for those two. Despite the bastard almost killing you, I'll give him a pass."

"He did it for love," Kizzy said. "Love always wins. So what's next for you?"

"Another mission. Always another mission. How would you like to travel the world with me, Kizzy?"

"I thought you'd never ask."

"There may be times when I need to go on a job alone. But as often as possible I will bring you along. I need you by my side. You are good for me."

She kissed him. "Will you let me photograph creatures?"

"Only if they are never published on that blog of yours. Although, someone may have a use for them. I could check with the Archives. CJ may be able to use photographic documentation of certain species."

"That would be cool. Kizzy Lewis, photographer of wondrous species. I love that. But I suppose I won't be able to put that on a business card."

"Absolutely not. No more than I can tell people I'm a Retriever."

"You told me."

"I couldn't have not told you. Believer that you are."

She slid her hands down and around his hips, pulling him against her slick body. "I suddenly have the desire to have sex with you in every country we can manage."

"That's a lot of places."

"I like a good challenge."

"Let's make it interesting and include all the States, too."

"Oh, yeah?"

"We've covered Minnesota and now New York."

"Two down, forty-eight left to go. And a whole lot of countries. Kiss me, wolf."

Their kiss lasted so long the water started to run cold, and when it did, the twosome spilled out and wrapped themselves up with an oversize towel in a snug, tight embrace that would see them through many countries and decades to come.

A year later...

Kizzy emailed the pictures she'd taken of the chimera in Kazakhstan to CJ at the Archives. Bron had been sent to retrieve an ancient grimoire guarded by a millennia-old witch. She'd had chimeras guarding her lair. Three of them. And their screams still rang in her ears. They'd pushed off from their castle perches. Magnificent wings had glittered with sunlight as they'd soared through the sky. That was right about the time Bron had ordered Kizzy back into the bespelled truck to wait for his return. She knew never to question him when in a dire situation. Besides, the new camera he'd gifted her for her birthday a few months ago was so awesome the zoom lens could pick up images half a mile away.

Tonight they stayed in Bron's Parisian apartment. She'd never been in the city before, and Bron's mission wasn't urgent, so he'd promised to take her on a river cruise in a few hours. She was excited for a quiet evening touring the dazzling city.

The bedroom door opened, and in strolled her werewolf hero.

"You get the dossier from the director?" she asked. Meeting him at the end of the bed, she pressed up on her tiptoes to kiss him.

"I'm to retrieve an alicorn from a demon overlord while I'm in town."

"Sounds perilous."

"Actually, I know the guy. Edamite Thrash. He sounds much more evil than he actually is. And I've already spoken to him on the phone. He is happy to hand it over, which I'll pick up in the morning. Tonight we're doing the tourist thing."

"It kills you, doesn't it?"

"To play the tourist?" He shrugged. "You know those lines drive me mad."

"But we've reservations for the cruise?"

"That we do. Another hour or so?" He checked his watch, then lifted her and tossed her onto the bed. "We've time to get naked."

"Come here, wolf." She crooked a finger, and he dove for her.

"I love you," he said as he crawled over her and bowed his head to kiss the base of her throat. "Without you I am nothing. I need your heart beating close to mine."

"You can have it close whenever you wish it."

"How about—" he leaned on an elbow and slid his hand down to his pants pocket "—we make it a permanent thing?"

Kizzy pushed up to lean on her elbows, not sure

what he was getting at. Until she saw the glint of silver as he held up the ring before her. A gorgeous diamond that looked too big for a girl who liked to travel spare and live off the land. Yet when she looked to Bron and saw the smile in his eyes she could only nod effusively.

"Is that a yes to forever?" he asked.

"Yes, of course. Forever."

* * * * *

I hope you enjoyed the story! If you're curious about the purgatorial objects, Google the "Museum of the Holy Souls in Purgatory" online. My stumbling on to that site one day served as the seed to this story.

If you'd like to read about other characters in this book, some also have their own story, and all are available at your favorite online retailer.

CJ and Vika's story is
THIS WICKED MAGIC

Libby and Richardt's story is
THE SOUL MAGIC

Blackthorn and Nova's story is
THE SIN EATER'S PROMISE

Edamite Thrash and Tamatha's story is
CAPTIVATING THE WITCH

MILLS & BOON®

Why shop at millsandboon.co.uk?

Each year, thousands of romance readers find their perfect read at millsandboon.co.uk. That's because we're passionate about bringing you the very best romantic fiction. Here are some of the advantages of shopping at www.millsandboon.co.uk:

* **Get new books first**—you'll be able to buy your favourite books one month before they hit the shops

* **Get exclusive discounts**—you'll also be able to buy our specially created monthly collections, with up to 50% off the RRP

* **Find your favourite authors**—latest news, interviews and new releases for all your favourite authors and series on our website, plus ideas for what to try next

* **Join in**—once you've bought your favourite books, don't forget to register with us to rate, review and join in the discussions

Visit **www.millsandboon.co.uk**
for all this and more today!

MILLS & BOON®
n o c t u r n e™

AN EXHILARATING UNDERWORLD OF DARK DESIRES

A sneak peek at next month's titles...

In stores from 7th April 2016:

- **Dark Journey** – Susan Krinard
- **Otherworld Renegade** – Jane Godman

MILLS & BOON®

Helen Bianchin v Regency Collection!